EVERYTHING ALL AT ONCE

EVERYTHING ALL AT ONCE

KATRINA LENO

HARPER TEEN
An Imprint of HarperCollinsPublishers

HarperTeen is an imprint of HarperCollins Publishers.

Everything All at Once
Copyright © 2017 by Katrina Leno
All rights reserved. Printed in the United States of America.
No part of this book may be used or reproduced in any manner whatsoever without written permission except in the case of brief quotations embodied in critical articles and reviews. For information address HarperCollins Children's Books, a division of HarperCollins Publishers, 195 Broadway, New York, NY 10007.
www.epicreads.com

ISBN 978-0-06-249309-5

Typography by Alison Klapthor
17 18 19 20 21   PC/LSCH   10 9 8 7 6 5 4 3 2 1

First Edition

To the ones who call me Auntie:

Harper & Alma
Saige & Addison & Whitney
& Locke

You understand that this pain is endless. And that in and of itself is a kind of comfort, because you have found your own eternity.
—from the essay "How to Say Good-bye"
by Abraham Reaves

❖

Keep going, be nice, make friends.
—from *Alvin Hatter and the Overcoat Man*
by Helen Reaves

Prologue

The day we threw Aunt Helen's ashes into the Atlantic Ocean was very windy. I'm assuming you've never seen someone get a mouthful of their dead sister's ashes, but that is exactly what happened to my dad, in slow motion, his mouth opening into an O as he lifted the top off the urn and thrust it forward. We all watched the ashes fly in a perfect arc out of the urn, and then we all watched them change direction in midair as a sudden gust of wind sent them back, back, directly into my father's waiting, horrified mouth.

His emotions cycled quickly from surprise to confusion to disgust to alarm to a kind of panic as he choked and spit and dropped the urn on his foot, where it bounced and rolled over a few times and came to rest near my brother's sneaker. Abe kicked the urn gently, maybe to make sure he wasn't just imagining it, and then Dad sprinted a few yards into the bushes and we listened to him vomit at least eight times.

"Holy shit," my mom said, in her soft, lilting accent. She put her hand over her eyes and tilted her head up as if she were praying. But I knew she wasn't praying. I knew she was trying not to laugh.

"Is this for real?" Abe said softly, kneeling down to pick the urn up from the ground. It was still half full with ashes. Or half empty. I guess it depended on how you looked at it. "I mean . . . did this happen? Lottie?" He looked at me, still kneeling, still holding Aunt Helen's urn. My favorite aunt, my father's younger sister, barely forty years old when she found the lump in her breast that would grow and spread and kill her pretty quickly.

"I think Dad just swallowed Aunt Helen," I said, and although I didn't mean to, I really didn't mean to, I started laughing. A powerful, takes-over-your-body kind of laugh, and then Abe joined me. My mother, trying so hard to be the adult, to be the rational one, snorted so loudly that it turned into a half cough, half wheeze. She bent over and held her belly and gasped for breath.

"Well, this is nice," Dad said, coming back, wiping his mouth with the back of his hand. He grabbed a Thermos of water from our picnic supplies. (The picnic had been one of Aunt Helen's final requests: *spread my ashes, have a picnic.* It was all her favorite foods, listed very specifically, a grocery list for the dead.) Dad washed his mouth out once, twice, spitting noisily on the ground, careful not to wet his shoes.

"Dad," Abe said, struggling to catch his breath, tears streaming down his face. He still clutched the urn, Aunt Helen's earthly remains, a gray mess that was finer than soot, more delicate. "There's more."

"Somebody else do it," Dad said grumpily, trying not to smile. He settled back into one of the chairs we'd dragged up to the cliff face: plastic and yellow and too cheery for the occasion.

"Lottie?" Abe said, offering me the urn.

I took the urn and looked into it and tried to stop giggling. A manic, panicked giggle, a giggle that covered up the deepest of sadnesses, the most painful of losses.

"Say something," Mom said, getting control of herself finally, taking deep breaths of the salty air.

"Like a eulogy?" I asked.

"Just some words," Dad said. He'd found a Tupperware bowl of watermelon and was eating it frantically, one chunk after the other, trying to get the taste of death out of his mouth.

"Like a nice memory," Mom added.

I wished we were all still laughing, but we had remembered that someone we loved was dead and that was it, that was the moment to say good-bye to her. I held the urn against my stomach and put my hand on the side of it. It was cold and smooth.

I thought of everything that had happened since my aunt Helen had died. I thought of everything I had learned about her and the books she had written, about the magic that had slithered its way into her very existence. I thought about the time when I was six years old when she had plopped me, terrified, on a sled at the top of the schoolyard hill and unceremoniously pushed. I thought of the millions of people who had worn black on the day she died. I thought of Alvin and Margo Hatter, their story complete now, their tale finally finished. And I thought about Sam, of course. Mostly I thought about Sam.

And I thought about the letters, twenty-four of them addressed to me and placed into my hands two months ago by the lawyer who read her will.

It hadn't seemed real then. It barely seemed real now.

I hugged the urn closer to my chest and tried to think of something to say. Something important and real.

Something immortal.

Two Months Earlier

Alvin Hatter had always liked his birthday. And he had always liked the number thirteen. So he had naturally always looked forward to his thirteenth birthday; it seemed to him inevitable that the day would mark the start of something great.

If only he'd known how right he was, he might never have gotten out of bed.

—from *Alvin Hatter and the House in the Middle of the Woods*

1

In the weeks leading up to and following her death, I couldn't buy a carton of eggs without my aunt Helen's face surrounding me at the checkout. Every newspaper. Every magazine.

Helen Reaves Cancer Diagnosis

Helen Reaves: Months to Live

The World Gets Ready to Say Good-Bye to Helen Reaves

Her face: so familiar but so much like a stranger.

"My camera face," she'd explained once and demonstrated a fake smile.

We left the TV off for weeks. News reporters sobbed openly on air; producers cut to commercial, not knowing what else to do. They sometimes let the weatherpeople predict the forecast for ten, fifteen minutes, but eventually even the weatherpeople started crying.

The window displays of every bookstore in the world

were crowded with her books. The Alvin Hatter series:

Alvin Hatter and the House in the Middle of the Woods

Alvin Hatter and the Overcoat Man

Alvin Hatter and the Mysterious Disappearance

Alvin Hatter and the Everlife Society

Alvin Hatter and the Wild-Goose Chase

Alvin Hatter and the Return of the Overcoat Man

Everybody loved Alvin and Margo Hatter.

Six books, six movies, six adapted graphic novels. Dolls and LEGO sets and even a surprisingly popular old-fashioned radio series.

My aunt's death affected not just the small circle of our family; it spread out, like an infectious sadness, until eventually the whole world was in mourning.

Or at least, that was what it felt like to me.

And driving to her lawyer's office to hear her last will and testament wasn't helping matters in the least.

Aunt Helen had an apartment in the city she spent most of her time in (until she got sick, and then she said the noise was too much to stomach), but her lawyer's office was right in town, the lawyer himself being a childhood friend of hers and my father's. All of us went at the appointed time. It had been less than a week since Aunt Helen had died, and I kept waiting for someone to call April fool.

The lawyer's office was downtown in a tiny strip mall that held a handful of other boring businesses. He had a receptionist's desk but no receptionist, and truth be told the place looked like a tornado had torn through it only moments before our arrival. Every surface was covered in manila envelopes, beige folders, stacks of crisp white paper, and coffee-stained mugs. It smelled like the inside of an office supply store (not unpleasant, mostly paper with a little after scent of ink). It was exactly like my aunt to entrust her legal businesses to someone who couldn't seem to find a dust rag.

"I think he's actually supposed to be a good lawyer," Dad said when we'd been standing in the waiting room for a full minute with no signs of life from within the office.

"Mediocre at best, but I get by," a voice said from behind us, and we all turned as one to find the lawyer—a middle-aged man in a dull gray suit—standing in the doorway, holding a Box O' Joe and a small tower of paper cups.

"Harry," Dad said. "It's been ages!"

"Sal, Marisol," he said, nodding at my parents. "Are these . . . ? No, they can't be. These can't be your kids. They're grown-ups! They're real people!"

"They're half real," Dad said, smiling, putting his arm around Abe and me and shuffling us forward like display pieces.

"Lottie and Abe. I have heard more about you from your aunt . . . I feel like I already know you. Can I hug you? I kind of want to hug you," Harry said. He juggled the box of coffee and the cups and put his arms around us both at the same time, a weird sort of hug that was also not weird, kind of nice.

"I brought coffee!" Harry said, pulling away. Abe shot me a look that nobody saw except me, a look I could translate perfectly: *too much hugging lately. When will the hugging stop?* "You guys are so punctual. I love it. Helen was never on time. One of her more endearing qualities, I guess, depending on how you look at it. Better late than early, she always said, but I'm not sure that would have held up in court."

Harry set the Box O' Joe and the coffee cups on the receptionist's desk, and then he crossed the room to a minifridge where he pulled out a small container of half-and-half. We helped ourselves to the coffee and filed into Harry's office, which was small and cramped with three extra folding chairs he must have moved in before we arrived. We sat drinking our coffee while he fussed around with folders on his desk, mumbling to himself until he found what he was looking for, holding up a big envelope with a small "aha!"

He straightened up in his chair and put the envelope on the desk in front of him.

"We are here to deliver and fulfill the last will and testament of Helen L. Reaves, one of my most favorite humans on the entire planet," Harry said, pulling a stack of papers out of the envelope. I noticed him share a brief look with my father, a tiny smile that meant something like: *Holy shit, this is hard.*

"There's a whole bunch of legal stuff here, but we can

go over that in more detail later," Harry continued. "Basically, fifty percent of Helen's estate, including all property and physical possessions not including ones specifically listed later on, will be liquidated and donated to various charities and libraries of her choosing. I'll take care of all that, of course. It's a substantial estate, as I'm sure you're aware."

We were aware. Aunt Helen was listed officially in the *Guinness Book of World Records* (that had tickled her to no end; we'd spent about three hours one afternoon taking silly pictures of her holding the book in increasingly weird locations around Connecticut) as the author of the best-selling children's book series of all time.

And she was gone. Sitting in Harry's office made it so official. This was an outside party, a lawyer, hired to assist in the divvying up of my dead aunt's things. It made me feel cheated, tricked, like someone was lying to us—because Aunt Helen couldn't actually be dead. That just wasn't possible.

"Right, then," Harry said. "There are a few people mentioned specifically, all folks I've been able to track down easily enough. And then there's just one name I haven't been able to find. Has anyone heard of a Mr. Williams? There isn't a first name here, which is why I'm having a hard time. She was supposed to get it to me but then . . . well, you know."

"Williams doesn't ring a bell," Dad said.

"Well, hopefully he'll come to me. Sometimes they do."

Harry opened a desk drawer and withdrew a pair of glasses, setting them on his nose and taking a deep breath. "All right. 'I, Helen Louise Reaves, being of sound mind and body, hereby bequeath the following to my dear, dear brother and my sister-in-law: My remaining liquidated estate, after all previously mentioned articles have been properly distributed. To Sal especially I leave the Picasso and the Van Gogh, because I am sick of telling you not to touch them. Now you can touch them all you want, even though you know it will ruin the paint. And you can take whatever else you like, of course. It's always been half yours anyway.

'To Marisol: my 1953 Chevrolet Corvette, because I know you've always liked the red seats, and because out of everyone who ever drove it, you were the fastest. Although I've told you before and I'll tell you again now, for the last time, it's kind of a shit car.

'To my only nephew, Abe, I leave all my books and all my comic books and all my vintage science-fiction magazines, because he is the one who most loved them all. There are a lot of them, Abe, and I know you'll treat them well.

'And to my only niece, my wonderful Lottie, I leave my jewelry, my journals (don't peek until I tell you!), and my laptop. And most important, I leave you these letters.'"

Harry took his glasses off and rubbed the bridge of his nose, exactly like people do in movies when they're trying to think of something to say.

My ears and cheeks were burning. I missed my aunt so much.

Harry reached into a drawer of his desk and pulled out a thick stack of letters. "She was especially particular about you getting these," he said to me, and handed them over. I took them carefully, looking at the top one, which was addressed to me in my aunt's familiar handwriting. They brought a stab of sadness to my chest. I held them hard in my lap, my fingers turning numb.

"Helen also made it clear that the four of you be allowed to take whatever you like from the Connecticut house, preliquidation. There are only a few exceptions, things she has bequeathed to other people, and I have taken care of them already," Harry explained.

I'd been in Aunt Helen's house a million times and no corner of it was off limits to me, but still the idea of rummaging through her things seemed like a massive invasion of privacy.

"The items she left to you specifically have already been removed. I have these for you—" He took four different-colored pads of sticky notes out of his desk drawer and handed them to my father. "Mark anything you want, and I'll have movers deliver them to you. No rush, of course. You'll let me know when you're finished." He smiled broadly, or as broadly as somebody can smile who is still clearly grieving the loss of an old friend. "Are there any questions?" he asked after a minute, when it became clear that none of us were going to break the silence.

"I think we've got everything," Mom said, sniffling. It seemed like we were all just taking turns. One of us would cry and then another would punch in to give them a little break. I wondered when the cycle would end.

"In that case, I just need a few signatures," Harry said. We stood up and formed a crooked line to his desk, signing and initialing everywhere he pointed.

It was a lot of paperwork, dying.

"Thank you so much for this," Dad said when it was his turn. He shook Harry's hand and then hugged him. They patted each other on the back for a long time as the three of us tried to figure out some other place to look.

"Helen meant the world to me," Harry said, pulling away finally, tearing up again. "The absolute world. And you all meant the world to her. So it's nice to be able to help you along in this process. It's the very least I can do."

I watched Abe inching toward the door, probably anticipating more hugs. He held his cup of coffee in front of him, as if it could protect him.

In the parking lot we all stood around the car awkwardly, not wanting to get inside maybe, enjoying the spring air. It was April and dry so far, sunny and bright and clear.

I was still clutching the stack of letters. My family stood around, talking about where to get lunch, but their voices blended into the background, became unintelligible noise.

In addition to my name, the top letter had a carefully printed number one. And underneath that, *Open now!*

"Lottie? Sandwiches?" Dad asked, the sound of my name snapping me out of my concentration.

"Can I have just a minute?" I asked.

"Take however long you need," Mom said. The three of them got in the car, and I walked a few yards away, to a little metal bench.

I sat down and realized I was shaking. The letters were tied together with twine. Thick, creamy stationery. My aunt loved paper, pens, ink. My name was written on each envelope, with a number from one to twenty-four, in all shades of blues and greens and purples and golds. Fountain pens for every day of the month. She wrote the first drafts of her novels by hand.

Shaking still, I opened the first envelope.

> My dearest Lottie,
>
> I hope that wasn't too bad. I told Harry to have coffee for you because I've never seen a family drink so much of it, and I wanted you to be as comfortable as possible. I hope you're happy with everything I've left you. Fifty percent seems like a lot to donate to charity, but let's be honest, I have a LOT a lot. So you're still left with a lot.
>
> This isn't as easy as I'd hoped. I sat down over an hour ago to write this to you, and so far I've

watered all the plants, hung my laundry out to dry, emptied the dishwasher, and rearranged one already perfectly organized bookshelf. And here I am. Two measly paragraphs written, and I haven't said anything important at all.

All right. Here goes.

I think you're the absolute ace, kid. I've watched you and your brother grow up from cute little babies to bright young adults before my eyes, and although I would stay and watch you continue to grow and learn forever, alas: that isn't in the cards for me.

But maybe these letters can serve as a sort of stand-in for me, once I'm gone. It could be any day now, I know. I'm certainly not ready to leave you, and I imagine (if I may be so bold) that you're not ready for me to leave either. So I hope these will ease you into it. You, who I imagine might need a gentle cushion the most. Your mother, your father, Abe: I'm not as worried about them. But I know things come a little harder for you, and that's one of the reasons I hate to leave you the most—because I would have loved to stay and try to help you a little more. Help you overcome those old anxieties, those old nervous tics (that we both share, by the way).

Here's how it will work. Open these letters in order. Do not open a letter until the task presented in the previous letter has been administered to absolute completion. Do not be overwhelmed by sadness. It won't do you any good.

Eventually, I think something interesting will come out of all of these.

And by that I mean:

I've kept a secret for a very, very long time. And now (in death, as it were) it seems like the perfect time to loosen my grip on it a little bit.

For now: be okay. I imagine you've just left Harry's office, you're maybe even sitting outside reading this as you make your family wait in the car (in addition to our anxieties, we also share impatience!), but now you can go home, Lottie. Do something nice. Read a book. Tomorrow's envelope will be a fun one, I promise.

Love, H.

(and p.s. kid, if I had any capacity for thought or emotion from THE GREAT BEYOND, I would miss the shit out of you right now.)

I wasn't crying as I folded the letter up and replaced it carefully into its envelope, but my eyes were burning and my throat felt tight. Her words, always so three-dimensional, always so close to me, made it feel like she had been standing behind the bench, reading over my shoulder the entire time.

(No, Aunt Helen wasn't dead. She couldn't be dead.

This was all some kind of weird joke, like the time she'd decorated her house for Christmas on Halloween.)

I walked back to the car, slid into the backseat next to my brother.

"Well?" Dad said immediately, and Mom nudged him in the ribs.

"Nothing to report," I said quietly, and I watched my parents exchange the subtlest of looks, watched my mom nod pointedly, watched Abe almost imperceptibly sigh. "Maybe later," I clarified. "I just need a little while."

"It's okay, honey. We get it," Dad said.

It wasn't okay, not even close. But I knew what he meant.

The house was empty. Margo could sense it immediately, by the way the door seemed to shut just a little bit heavier, by the way their footsteps echoed with a tiny bit more resonance through the foyer as Alvin threw his bag to the ground and called their parents' names.

"Mom! Dad!"

"They aren't here," Margo said, but he didn't hear her, and he bounded up the stairs as she followed after him, trying to catch her breath, to make him understand. Their parents were gone, and they weren't safe here.

"Mom! Dad!" Alvin shouted, bursting into their parents' bedroom, turning on the light.

The bed was mussed, but their parents were not in it.

A lamp lay broken on the ground.

A picture of the four Hatters had been knocked crooked on the wall.

There was a broken window, and the night breeze billowed in, making the curtains move like silent ghosts.

"Alvin," Margo said again, this time her voice no more than a whisper, "they aren't here."

—from *Alvin Hatter and the Overcoat Man*

2

Lunch was subdued, sullen, each of us in our own worlds, me refusing to let the letters out of my sight for even a moment, terrified that something completely irrational would happen to them: they would blow away in the wind; they would vanish into thin air; they would spontaneously combust. So I waited in the car while my parents went into the deli to pick up the sandwiches, and then we ate at home, me with the letters stacked neatly next to my plate. I knew my parents and Abe were dying to know what they were, what the first one had said, but I knew if I talked about it I would start crying and probably never stop. Like Alice, crying in our kitchen until I was washed away in a river of my own tears.

After lunch I went up to my room and sat down on my bed, spreading the letters out carefully on my bed-spread, getting my copies of the Alvin Hatter books and laying them out in order. I had read these books so much, loved them ever since I was a little girl, I knew every plot twist and denouement by heart. My copies were torn and creased and dirty; Abe's were pristine and unopened (he had a second set for reading) and claimed the top shelf of his bookshelf, the one with the glass cabinets.

I'd heard Abe's friends laughing at him once about keeping children's books displayed in his room, but then I'd heard him tell them how much each one was worth (first edition, first printing, signed by Helen Reaves, naturally). They'd stopped laughing pretty quickly.

I picked up *Alvin Hatter and the Everlife Society*, my personal favorite. The moment I started reading, I was no longer in my bedroom, no longer sad, no longer even myself. I was an unseen friend of Alvin and Margo Hatter's, following along with them as they escaped with the Everlife Society and tried to find out what happened to their missing parents. There was danger in these pages, but there was also a kind of safety, an underlying knowledge that no physical harm could come to our hero and heroine themselves; they'd found the Everlife Formula and drank from it. Alvin and Margo Hatter were immortal.

And I wondered what my aunt would have done if that same potion were real and right in front of her. If it could have saved her life, would she have chosen to live forever?

Hours later, days later, there was a knock on my door,

and my dad pushed it gently open. "Can I come in?" he asked.

I was halfway through the book and had read right through dinner. That was how good they were. Every time was like the first time.

"Yeah, Dad, of course."

He pushed the door open wider and wandered in with half a glass of wine (truly wandered; he looked a little lost). He sat on my bed and sighed.

"You okay?" I asked.

"I'm okay," he said. "We had a little warning. I guess that was nice. But not too much warning, or else we would have had to think about it for too long. You know?"

"I know."

"Are you okay? You've been up here for a while."

"Just reading."

"Ah, Alvin." He picked up the first book, *Alvin Hatter and the House in the Middle of the Woods*. It had been published when my aunt was twenty-four. She was flat broke, living in my father's garage, two years out of college and still refusing to look for a job (much to his chagrin). "I don't need to eat," she'd famously told him once, "I need to write."

"These books, huh, kid?" He paused, had a sip of wine, sighed again. "I'm so happy you kids got a chance to know her so well. Your aunts and uncles in Peru . . . Well, I know your mother wishes they were closer. Family is important, kid."

Uh-oh.

My father was in the red wine danger zone.

Someone hadn't been paying attention, and I could guarantee this was his third glass, exactly the amount needed for him to turn inward and deep and philosophical.

But I guess he deserved it.

And it wouldn't last long.

The end of the third glass would see him sound asleep within fifteen minutes.

It didn't happen often, but when it did, it was like clock-work.

"I know family's important, Dad."

"That's why I'm so happy you and Abe have each other," he continued. "Helen and I were so close growing up. I'm glad you two are the same way."

"Me too."

"Your aunt was a trip." Another sip, this one so minis-cule that the liquid barely touched his lips. He stared out my window (which was covered by a curtain, so I guess he stared at my curtain).

"What do you mean?"

"There was always . . . just something. Something about her."

"What kind of something? Like she's super famous?"

He laughed, crossed his legs. "No, silly. Not like that. I mean there was something I couldn't put my finger on. Like she was keeping something from me. You know?"

"Abe has a locked trunk of comics he's never let me look through," I said. "Like that?"

"Maybe like that. Maybe different. Weird things, you know? Once I caught her with this little bottle. Just this little glass—"

"Sal?" my mom interrupted, poking her head into the room. She was wearing scrubs; she had to leave soon for an overnight at the hospital. She analyzed the current situation: Dad glossy-eyed, holding an almost-empty wineglass, me looking slightly terrified. She moved into the doorway and held three fingers up so my father couldn't see. I nodded, confirming it.

"Hi, honey," Dad said. "Lottie and I were just talking about Helen. She was great, wasn't she? You liked her, right?"

"You know I loved your sister, Sal. Like my own sister."

Mom swooped into the room, moving so quickly she was almost a blur. But before I knew what was happening she was holding Dad's wineglass and he was standing up, stretching, yawning.

"Let's get you to bed," she said, taking his hand.

"To bed!" he agreed.

He stumbled out of the room before her, and she hung back a second, taking stock of the state of my bed, the letters and the book. She took a step toward me and put her hand on my cheek.

"Are you doing all right, my love?"

"Just sad. But all right."

"The sadness will always be there," she said, never one to mince words. "It will never go away. But you will learn to move around it, and then it will fade a little, and then it will be replaced with happiness that you got to be so close to your aunt."

"Thanks, Mom."

"Get some sleep, Lottie."

She kissed the top of my head and left. I read until dawn.

I woke up early the next morning, *Alvin Hatter and the Everlife Society* still open on my chest.

The first thing I thought of was my aunt's letters. I could open the second one now. She had told me to be okay, I had mostly succeeded, and now I could open her second letter.

I pulled myself up to a sitting position and found it, still on the bed. I opened it carefully, blinking sleep away from my eyes, and began to read.

> Dear Lottie,
>
> I told you this letter would be more fun than the first one.
>
> Forgive me for not checking with you (I have the convenient excuse of not actually being around to check with you), but I have taken the liberty of throwing a party. Everything is taken care of. Harry

is a good lawyer and an even better friend; he had his instructions, upon my passing, to send out a stack of invitations, to reserve the space, to contact the caterers and florist, to essentially plan my wake. See, I was never one for formal sadness. It's depressing to everyone who's alive, and the one it's for, the dead one (I'm sorry to be blunt; it's the mood I'm in), can't even appreciate it. So I want you to have some FUN, Lottie, and that's why I want you to have a freaking party! And the invitations have been sent, yes, but really anyone can come. The more the merrier!

The party will be held the first Saturday after I'm gone, at a hotel called the Nautilus. I've given Harry instructions to book all the rooms: first come, first served. I want you guys to have an absolute blast, and I want you to send me off in style. Sneak some champagne and keep your father away from the red wine. I would have traded my Guinness Book for the chance to be there with you, but I guess that would have defeated the purpose just a little.

Who knows—maybe you'll even meet somebody interesting. (I have a lot of interesting friends.)

Love, H.

The first Saturday after she was gone was . . .

Today. That was today. I took the letter and practically ran downstairs, finding Mom at the kitchen table, her head resting on her folded arms. After an overnight she some-times fell asleep in weird places.

"Mom," I said, almost shouting, trying not to scare her.

She stirred awake, raising her head and rubbing at her eyes just like a cartoon of a sleepy person.

"Hi, honey. I made coffee."

"Mom, I have something crazy to tell you."

She shook herself awake. "Are you okay?"

"Here, just read this."

I wasn't planning on letting anyone read the letters, but this one was different. I knew my mom wouldn't believe it until she actually read it in Aunt Helen's handwriting.

As she read, she straightened, visibly becoming more confused, more alert, then smiling widely. "Wow," she said after a minute, lowering the page, "this is exactly like your aunt."

"Saturday is today," I said.

"When we called Harry to set up the will reading, he seemed very insistent we meet before Saturday. I guess this was why," she said.

"So we're going?"

"Going? Of course we're going, silly. Gosh, I have to figure out what to wear." Then, smiling, taking my hand, she said, "This will be fun, Lottie. This is so her."

When my mom was tired, her accent was stronger. She was 100 percent Peruvian; she'd moved to America when she was thirteen. Most of the time, her accent was undetectable unless you knew what to listen for. She said she'd spent a lot of time practicing how to speak "New Englander." Otherwise, the kids at school made fun of her.

She went to hug me and then decided against it. "I'm filthy. A shower and a nap. I'll see you for the party, my love."

The rest of the day passed in a blur. I texted Em, my best friend, to invite her to the party. She'd been there the night Aunt Helen had died; I had texted her a series of frantic messages about the fragility and pointlessness of life, and she'd gotten to the hospital twenty minutes later. When she hugged me she smelled like the cigarettes her mom smoked and her bobbed blue hair brushed against my cheek in a way so familiar that it set me crying again.

Em was short for Emmylou because her mom had a thing for country music.

When I told her about the party, she wrote:

Holy crap that's awesome!! Can I bring Jackie?

Of course you can bring Jackie, dummy. I'll see you tonight.

Are you doing OK?

Yes. ILY.

Em's response was a yellow face with hearts for eyes.

I decided to wear a dress to the party, nothing too fancy, just a light-blue vintage thing that Aunt Helen had bought for me. She loved vintage shopping and often dragged me along, the plus side being that although I hated shopping, she'd buy me whatever I liked (actually, she'd buy me whatever I liked that she also liked, which was the beauty of Aunt Helen, never compromising her preferred aesthetic).

Em and her girlfriend, Jackie, showed up at my house at six, Em wearing vintage tuxedo pants with a crisp white shirt, sleeves rolled to the elbows and a bow tie hanging untied around her neck.

"Do you know how to do this?" she asked my dad, who brought her to a mirror and gave her a lesson.

Jackie had her blond hair in curls and wore a legitimate pink party dress, petticoat and all.

She gave me a hug and said, "Are you doing okay, Lottie?"

"Better," I said. "Every day is better."

Amy, Abe's girlfriend, showed up a few minutes later, wearing a pale-yellow maxi dress. She wore bright-pink eye shadow, which would look insane on me but was practically glowing against her dark skin.

We took two separate cars: Mom, Dad, Em, and Jackie in one and Abe, Amy, and me in the other. Em wasn't super close with her mom, who didn't really approve of her choice in partners and thought tuxedo pants on a girl were an abomination of the most sincere kind. My parents had adopted Em as their own. My mom was the one who helped her pick out what shade of blue to dye her hair.

"Don't tell anyone I did this," she'd said, handing Em a ten-dollar bill. "I don't need any drama from your mama."

Even though my aunt had rented every room in the hotel for the party, none of us were staying overnight. We'd decided to let the other guests have first dibs, and it wasn't that far of a ride—about an hour long, but it went by quickly. Amy put on some new songs her band had recorded (she played lead guitar, and she was basically the coolest person I knew), and we all sang along loudly, glad for the distraction.

When we reached the hotel, I knew exactly why my aunt had picked it. The Nautilus was situated right on the water, with one enormous octagonal ballroom actually built on stilts over the waves. There were flickering candles illuminating the path to the front door, and the whole place was white and romantic and elegant and exactly like Aunt Helen. This was her, as a building. One foot in the sand and one in the water; completely approachable while at the same time being so, so cool.

The guests were already starting to arrive. The party was slated to go from eight to midnight, with a buffet dinner served until ten and desserts available after that. I recognized famous authors from their book jackets, slipping out of black cars and looking out of place in the way most authors do at fancy parties. I saw news reporters and even a few actors; I tried my best not to stare. I never quite got used to it, how famous Aunt Helen was.

"I should have worn a suit. Lottie, why didn't you tell me to wear a suit?" Abe said as he pulled his car in line for the valet.

"You look handsome," Amy said, putting her hand on his leg. He wore seersucker pants and a matching vest, but no coat.

"You look very New England prep," I said. "But in a good way."

"I should have worn a bow tie," he whined, pulling at his navy skinny tie. "Em looks so cool. I'm so lame."

I tuned him out as we waited our turn for the valet. Abe was sixteen, and his birthday present had been this car, a respectable little Corolla my parents had bought from a used dealership in town. It was a little nicer than mine, a Honda that was a few years older. But I didn't really care about cars. I think my mom was bummed she couldn't drive her new Corvette, but it didn't have a backseat. Plus I'd done some research, and although it was worth a lot, my aunt was right: it was supposedly pretty poorly made, as far as fancy cars go. They'd only made three hundred before they went back to the drawing board.

When it was our turn for the valet, Abe took his ticket and we got out of the car to the sweet smell of salt and flowers. I carried a small purse with my wallet, my phone, and Aunt Helen's third envelope inside it, and part of me wanted the party to be over so I could read it. I couldn't wait to find out what came next.

Except I had to wait, because Dad had grabbed me by the arm and was clenching me so hard I thought he might break something. He didn't like parties. He was an anesthesiologist; he most liked being around people who were asleep.

Mom, on the other hand, was looking up at the Nautilus with wide, excited eyes.

"Everybody liked your aunt Helen," she said proudly, looking around at the droves of people arriving and being ushered into the hotel.

I sympathized more with my dad. Neither of us were thrilled by crowds. They made me anxious; they always had. To be fair, a lot of things made me anxious. Aunt Helen's first letter came back to me—*I know things come a little harder for you*—and I hated that she was right, that they did, that I could already feel my anxiety humming somewhere in the back of my throat. I coughed once, trying to dislodge it. But of course it didn't actually work like that.

"It's going to be fun," I said to Dad, but in reality I probably sounded like I meant the exact opposite.

"It's going to be fun," Mom repeated, and she actually made it sound plausible. She slipped in between my dad and me and linked an arm through each of ours, leading the charge into the hotel, following the trail of candles to the ballroom.

It was unreal.

The entire place was lit by candles—they hung from

chandeliers and lined the walls in delicate sconces and crowded every table. They were the only decoration. A hundred million candles and white tablecloths and music from hidden speakers. The buffet tables were set along one wall, and a wide, open balcony surrounded the entire room. All the doors were open to the night, and guests moved from inside to outside, some with plates of food and others with tall skinny glasses of bubbling champagne.

"Holy crap," Mom said. "Look at the food!"

She made a beeline for the buffet table, Dad following behind closely, looking terrified they may get separated. I headed to the balcony, suddenly needing some air.

It was a breezeless, warm night. The balcony too was lit by candles in mason jars, and it was less crowded out here as people moved inside to eat at the tables. I was wondering whether I could successfully sneak a glass of champagne when I felt something brush my arm. I turned to find Em beside me, holding two glasses.

"You're a mind reader," I said. "She told me to drink champagne."

"Apparently I'm a mind reader who looks twenty-one," she responded with a wink. Then, "Wait—who told you to drink champagne?"

Aunt Helen. And I would tell Em about the letters soon, but not right now. Right now I just wanted to try to enjoy myself.

"My mom. You know how she gets at parties," I said.

We toasted and sipped from the glasses—

Which is when I discovered that champagne is disgusting.

"Oh nooo," Em said, looking into the glass.

"Maybe it grows on you?"

"It tastes kind of like vomit? Or that moment right before you vomit."

"Charming."

"I thought it would be like . . . sweeter?"

"We can see if there's something else."

"Let's pour these out for Helen," Em said.

Together, we stretched our arms over the railing and overturned the glasses. The champagne spilled into the water, and I wondered how much of the ocean was made up of other things. Diluted other things, but other things nonetheless.

Em took my glass from me and disappeared inside again.

And because pouring out my champagne made me miss Aunt Helen, I took the third envelope from my purse and opened it before I was supposed to.

Lottie, Lottie. My little impatient cupcake. I want you to have FUN at this party. (And there are actually cupcakes later, from my favorite bakery. Have one for me.)

Yes, I know you're still at the party, and no, I'm not omniscient, just a good guesser (although—what if you're not at the party? That would be awkward).

I'm not going to make this long because I want you to enjoy yourself. Cut loose a little. Did you try the champagne? Cupcakes are better. Remember: I love you, and I also love parties. Enjoy this one enough for the both of us.

Yours, H.

With a huge, uncontainable smile on my face, I refolded the letter and put it back in my purse.

Now . . . how to have fun?

"Who's there?" the old man called gruffly, opening his door just a crack, enough so Alvin and Margo could see the many metal door chains that snaked from door to doorjamb.

"What's he so afraid of?" Margo mumbled. "We're the ones who are running for our lives."

Alvin elbowed her in the ribs to get her to shut up for a minute. He knew their grandfather wasn't the most welcoming person in the world, and he was trying to make a good impression.

"Grandpa Hatter, it's us: Alvin and Margo." He waited a minute and then added hopefully, "Your grandkids."

"I never asked for grandkids," Grandpa Hatter snapped. "And I certainly never asked for grandkids who show up at ungodly hours of the night."

The door slammed shut.

Margo and Alvin looked at each other.

Margo crossed her arms and said, "Any other genius ideas?"

—from *Alvin Hatter and the Mysterious Disappearance*

3

Em found white wine and poured it into emptied soda cans, which I thought was kind of ingenious except it made the wine taste a little bit like cola. I drank mine slowly, moving aimlessly from the inside to the outside, trying some of all the food Aunt Helen had picked out.

I used to ask her if it hurt.

Every day I'd call her or go to see her and watch her shrink away a little bit at a time. It terrified me, but I couldn't stay away. I had to see the cancer's progress. I kept notes in my head: dramatic notes filled with terrible similes: *Day thirty-two. Pale and listless. Like a sailboat with no wind. Spirits seem dampened. Eyes are dull.*

"Lottie," she said one day, a bad day, a day she had no energy and lay on her couch for too long, wrapped in a thick blanket and sipping cold tea. "You can't keep thinking about things like this. You can't dwell on it."

"What, am I supposed to pretend this isn't happening?" I asked.

"No. But you can't obsess over it. You can't let it consume you."

But it was impossible to watch someone you love die and not let it consume you. It was impossible not to go home from the hospital and look into my own face and wonder if my own body held the same secret disease that Aunt Helen's had. There were countless types of cancer. There were countless ways your body could go wrong and turn against you and eat itself up from the inside.

I'd been thinking about that a lot lately.

My brain did that: it found things to obsess over, things to panic about. I'd had my first anxiety attack when I was only eleven, and it was Aunt Helen who knew what it was, who knew I wasn't having a heart attack, who sat me down on her couch and explained to me that she had those feelings as well, those feelings of being overwhelmed, those feelings of being paralyzed.

In her first letter she'd written that she wasn't worried about Abe and my parents, that she knew things came a little harder for me. She'd written *that's one of the reasons I hate to leave you the most—because I would have loved to stay and try to help you a little more. Help you overcome those old anxieties, those old nervous tics (that we both share, by the way).*

They came and went. They had gotten better for a while. But now, right now, I could feel them tugging at the corners of my brain again.

"Are you okay?" someone asked. Abe, I thought, but I couldn't turn around to look at him, I couldn't make my feet work. I held the white wine soda can in one hand and the railing with my other. I didn't know what time it was, but someone had turned the music up, and people were dancing and laughing inside, but out here it was just me and—turning, finally, jerkily—not Abe.

"I'm fine," I said quickly, because we are taught as children that automatic response: *I'm fine*, when we are not. *I'm fine*, when we are anything but. *I'm fine*, when we can't stop thinking about death, about dying, about ceasing to be.

The boy standing next to me was about my age, about my height, and nondescript but somehow familiar. Brown-black hair that fell in waves to just above his shoulders. Brown eyes. A very well-fitting suit (I didn't think I'd ever noticed something like that about someone before, but it did—it fit him particularly well). He held a glass of something sparkling. Water, I thought.

There was something weird about the air around him, like it was darker. A shade of blue that was almost black. I blinked, and it was gone.

The soda wine was going to my head.

"You sure?" he asked. "You look a little shaken."

"Oh, it comes with the territory," I said and gestured to the party, a big sweeping motion that hopefully meant something to him.

"Ah," he said sadly. "Did you know Helen?"

"I'm her niece," I said, and then wondered, should I have said I was her niece? But I didn't stop being her niece just because she wasn't here anymore, did I?

"I'm Sam," he said, and held out his hand. "I knew your aunt. She's mentioned you, but I don't remember . . ."

"Lottie," I said, and we shook.

"You're still a little pale. Do you want some of this? I haven't had any."

He handed me the glass of water, and I took a long sip, then another, then finished it. I handed it back to him, and he laughed.

"Sorry," I said. "How did you know her?"

"I took her class at the university. A while ago."

Did he have an accent? A slight one, maybe. One that was hard to place.

My aunt taught one class a year at the state university. "Something to do," she always said. "Gotta keep the ticker sharp. Stay relevant with the youths, you know." Like she was eighty and not forty. (*Only forty*, the newspapers had said. *Such a tragic ending to a beautifully written story.*)

"You're in college?" I asked. He didn't look like it.

"Not exactly," he said. "I didn't take it for credit. I just audited."

"What does that mean?"

"It means I squatted. I wanted to hear what she had to say. Your aunt was . . . well, you know."

I did know, and it made me happy that my aunt had touched so many people. Sometimes it was weird, sharing her with the public, seeing people who thought they knew her, having strangers confess their love to her, but it was all part of the bigger package. Aunt Helen was mine, but she also belonged to so many others. She could be both.

"I know," I said.

"Can I get you some more water?"

"Sure. Thanks."

"We could go somewhere a little quieter? I'd love to talk with you more."

I was about to answer when Em burst through the nearest door and launched herself at me. Jackie followed her, much more calmly and supremely amused. She caught my eye and mimicked drinking.

"So I'm guessing you like that soda wine, Em?" I asked, detaching her from my hair.

"It tastes like bubbles," she said, giggling. She saw Sam and stuck her hand out, jabbing him in the stomach. "Oops! Sorry!"

"It's okay. I'm Sam."

"I'm Em! Our names are both one syllable, and they both end in *m*. End in *m*! That sounds funny. End in *m*. Jackie, say it."

"I think it will be a little less funny when I say it," Jackie said, stroking Em's hair.

"Wait—does every name end with an *m*? I can't think

of a single name that doesn't end with an *m*," Em said seriously, frowning.

"Lottie. Jackie. Abe. Amy. Helen. Marisol. Sal," I said.

"Crap. I thought I just figured out some big secret." Em looked crestfallen but quickly recovered, turning her attention back to Sam. "Who are you again?"

"I'm Sam."

"No, I know. I mean, *who are you*? Like, in life. Who are you in life?"

Em was a completely hysterical lightweight. I doubt she'd had more than two gross soda can wines, and she was sure to be this entertaining for hours.

"Oh! In life. Well, my name is Sam—"

"You already said that," Em interrupted.

"I'm a senior in high school," he continued.

"Not our school, right?" Jackie asked.

"No, no. I live in Mystic," Sam said.

"Mystic? That's a made-up place." Em laughed.

"We're in Mystic now, Em," I said.

"Wait. Mystic is not a made-up place?"

"Welcome to the Connecticut shore," Sam said, gesturing out at the water.

"But it's called *Mystic*," Em argued.

"Well, actually, it's an interesting little piece of land. We're technically in Stonington, Connecticut," Sam explained.

"Yeah, Stonington. That's a place," Em said.

"But it's also Mystic," Jackie said.

"How can it be two things?"

"It's kind of like Washington, D.C.," Sam said. "It's not a state, you know. It's kind of like . . . just a place."

"I'm very confused," Em admitted.

"That's all right," Sam said, winking at me. It was weird to have a stranger wink at me. Sort of nice; sort of unnerving. It was almost a personal gesture.

"Mystic," Em said, testing the name out. "It's like magic."

"It's derived from a Pequot term. *Missi-tuk*, a river with unsettled waters," Jackie said. Then, when we all looked at her in wonder: "What? I know things."

"This all seems fishy," Em said. "I'm going to the bathroom."

She turned on her heel and left us. Jackie put her arm around me and laughed. "Two drinks, Lottie." I knew it. "I better go make sure she finds the bathroom. Oh, it was nice meeting you. I'm Jackie."

Jackie and Sam shook hands, and I watched her pink dress swish away as she left to find Em.

"They seem interesting," Sam said. "I like the blue."

"It's been almost every color. Blue is the best."

"She looks like she's having fun."

"I'm supposed to be having fun," I said, remembering Aunt Helen's note suddenly, feeling the weight of it in my purse.

"Oh. Well—would you like to dance?"

"I didn't mean . . . You don't have to entertain me or anything."

"Well, what if I just want to dance? Would you also want to dance?"

"Are people even dancing?"

We looked inside, moving closer to the open door to get a look at the small mob of people on the dance floor. I saw Abe doing some complicated moonwalk-type move and Amy doubled over and holding her stomach as she laughed at him.

The answer to my question was: yes, basically everyone was dancing. I watched my mother and father twirling around in circles so quickly it made me dizzy. I saw Em returning from the bathroom, holding Jackie's hand and leading her through the crowd to get a spot near the DJ. The DJ?

"There's a DJ? Since when is there a DJ?" I asked.

"That's DJ Cloud. Very popular, I guess," Sam said.

"You guess?"

"I googled him."

"Are you from England? Or somewhere else? You have this accent . . ."

"Oh, no. Mystic born and raised," he said.

"My aunt loved Mystic. She loved how it was a place within a place. Like a secret."

"I'm sorry," Sam said. "I can tell she meant a lot to you. I can tell this is probably the last place you want to be."

"Dancing sounds nice. I think I'd like to dance. If you still want to."

Sam took the soda can from me and held my hand. We walked back into the ballroom, and he put the empty glass of water and the can on a table as we passed. His hand was warm, almost feverish, but it felt nice in mine. We pushed our way past dancing bodies—I spotted Harry, my aunt's lawyer, dancing with a man in a top hat and coattails—and found ourselves in the thick of it all. It was like prom, only bigger and louder and more frantically fun, like people's lives depended on dancing.

"Like *Hocus Pocus*," I whispered to myself.

"Hmm?" Sam asked.

"Nothing."

That was a good reference; I'd have to tell Abe later.

Everybody seemed like they were having such a good time. Sam held my hand, and at first it was easy and fun, dancing with him. He was a better dancer than I expected; his movements seemed fluid and effortless. And he was cute, sort of serious and unexpected.

"You're really good," I shouted over the music, but even then he couldn't hear me and cupped his free hand over his ear.

And then suddenly, like someone had hit the off switch, it stopped being fun. The laughter and music and talking that surrounded me turned dark and menacing, and I couldn't understand why any of it mattered, why we bothered with anything, why we went through the motions of dancing and making friends and reading books and cleaning our rooms and all these things that wouldn't matter in a hundred years anyway because everyone in this room would be dead, even the youngest ones, even the kids who seemed like they shouldn't be here, like they should be home in bed sleeping instead of jumping around in small blurry groups. They would all be dead like Aunt Helen had died, because nobody lives forever except in books. Nobody lives forever except Alvin and Margo Hatter, and they weren't even real.

You can't think about things like that, my aunt would have said, but my aunt wasn't here anymore, because no matter how good and how known and how loved you were, it wouldn't matter in the end. None of us was eternal. None of us would beat it.

"Is something wrong?" Sam yelled, but I didn't hear him, just read his lips. "You're not dancing anymore."

"It was nice to meet you," I said, leaning closer to him, putting my mouth next to his ear. "But I think we have to leave soon."

I left him on the dance floor, and the people moved closer to swallow him up, so that when I turned around, right before I left the room to go hide in the bathroom until we were all ready to leave, I couldn't even see him.

She went back sometimes, without Alvin.

He would have killed her if he'd known. (Let him try. She was, after all, immortal.)

She let herself in the back door with a key she wore on a long silver chain around her neck. She walked through the rooms silently, her heart aching, remembering when this house didn't feel like such an empty, pathetic shell.

She did not let herself cry, because tears accomplished nothing except turning your eyes red and blurring your vision.

Would they ever be under this roof again, the four of them: Mom, Dad, Alvin, and herself?

Would this deserted and hollow house ever feel like a home once more?

She always remembered to lock up when she left, even though there was nothing valuable left to lose.

—from *Alvin Hatter and the Return of the Overcoat Man*

4

The ride home was quiet. Amy fell asleep with her cheek against the passenger side window, and Abe turned on the radio but left it so low I almost couldn't hear it. I watched the sea disappear behind us and thought of Sam and how many people were at the party, how many people my aunt seemed to know that I had never even met. How even the people closest to us could be so much a mystery.

When we got home, my parents put Amy and Jackie in the guest bedroom, and Em and I crawled into my bed like we had done so many times when we were kids. Em turned on the flashlight on her phone and made shadow puppets on my ceiling: a dog, a rabbit, a goose. Then she made a face and made its mouth move to say, "I saw you dancing with a strange boy."

"Sam, remember? You talked to him."

"I did not remember, admittedly," the mouth said.

"Now I remember. Who is he?"

"One of my aunt's students, I guess."

"He seemed nice. Did you get his number?"

"Why would I get his number?"

"So you can call him and go on barfingly cute little hetero dates, obviously," she said, abandoning the shadow face, letting her hands fall to her sides.

"He lives far away," I said.

"He lives an hour away."

"That's far. That's basically a long-distance relationship."

"You once said Jackie and I have a long-distance relationship because our lockers are in different hallways."

"It just seems like a lot of work."

"Can I ask you something?" Em turned the flashlight off and put her phone on the pillow. She rolled over toward me. I could see her face in the glow of the moonlight coming through the window. "Why were you hiding in the bathroom?"

"I wasn't hiding in the bathroom," I said quickly.

"You were totally hiding in the bathroom. It's, like, your signature move. Whenever I can't find you, I look under the stalls for your shoes."

"I was tired. I didn't feel like dancing anymore."

"How come?"

"I don't know. Leave me alone."

"You seem a little distant, and maybe that's dumb to say because I know how sad you're feeling right now, but I'm also worried that you're going to pull away, or not talk to me about how sad you are, and you should talk to me about how sad you are, because you can't keep that kind of thing bottled up, you know?"

"She left me letters," I said suddenly. It just came out.

"Helen?"

"Yeah. All these letters. Kind of like . . . instructions."

"Instructions for what?"

"So far just for little things, like—be happy, go to the party, eat a cupcake. Shit, I forgot to eat a cupcake."

"Helen left you a letter telling you to eat a cupcake?"

"Don't say it like that."

"I'm sorry! I didn't mean it. . . . I'm just processing. That must be so nice."

"Nice?"

"To have them. It's like she's still here with you, you know?"

"Yeah. Yeah, I guess it is nice."

"Oh! And!"

Em jumped out of bed, surprisingly spry for this late at night, this many white wine colas. She grabbed her overnight bag and fished around in it for a second and then pulled out a wad of napkins. She presented them to me, smiling widely. I carefully peeled back layer after layer until I got to a particularly squashed cupcake.

"You didn't," I said.

"I stole it," she said, shrugging. "But now you can do

what she wanted you to do!"

"You're really amazing, do you know that?"

"I've heard." She climbed back into bed, and I swear she was asleep in three and a half seconds.

I sat down at my desk and ate the cupcake slowly. It was really good, from my aunt's favorite bakery. She always said it was all about the frosting; the frosting could make or break the cake. When I was done, I wiped my hands with the napkins and then threw them in the trash. And then I found the fourth letter from my aunt and opened it, reading it while Em quietly snored in the bed.

Lottie,

I hope the party was a success. God, I love a good party. I love a bad party too, because then you can steal a little bit to drink and go out on the balcony with a friend and make your own kind of fun.

This next task is less fun but still important, I think.

I want you to go and say good-bye to my house.

Say that out loud (I just did, because I'm dying of cancer and can do whatever I want) and it sounds a little silly.

How does one say good-bye to a house?

But oh, I loved that house. I loved that house with you and your brother. Playing croquet (the silliest game) and making brownies and watching movies. I

have secretly loved that my workaholic brother mar-
ried a workaholic woman because it meant that I got
you kids so often, and we really had a chance to just
hang out. What I wouldn't give for another hundred
of those hangouts!

    But soon it will be someone else's house, and that's
okay too. It will have a whole new lifetime of things
happening inside it.

    But a piece of it will always be ours, I think.

    Go say good-bye to that piece for me.

    Love, H.

I put the letter away. I watched Em toss in her sleep. I tried to imagine a new family moving into Aunt Helen's house, and a tiny sliver of my brain reared up in angry protest.

But that wasn't right. Because the alternative was worse. The house staying empty forever—that didn't make any sense at all. I thought of Margo wandering around her house after her parents disappeared, and my heart broke for her and for me and for the losses we'd had to endure.

I wasn't tired at all. I crept quietly across the room to take *Alvin Hatter and the Return of the Overcoat Man* off its shelf. I opened it to a random page and began to read.

Em was gone when I woke up. She always got up at the crack of dawn to go running, no matter how late she'd been up the night before. She was the golden child of our high school track team and was going to college on an almost full scholarship. I'd never seen anyone run as fast as Em. She said it was because there were a lot of closed-minded people in the world she needed to get away from.

My parents and Abe were already up, and when I told them I was going to go over to Aunt Helen's, they asked if they could come with me. I'd forgotten about the other task Harry had given us, the uncomfortable prospect of pawing through my aunt's things, but it was nice to know that I didn't have to be alone.

The four of us got into the car and drove over to her house. I felt a tight ball of nerves growing inside me.

When Aunt Helen and I were in the car together we always counted cars, blues against reds, to see who would find the most of their color first. I found myself counting blue cars now, trying to remember if breast cancer was genetic or random. I couldn't recall what any of my grandparents had died from; it had all been when Abe and I were little. We weren't allowed to go to the funerals, and I don't think anybody even really explained what death meant. I wish I'd never had to find out.

Next to me, Abe played some game on his phone. The screen was a mess of different-colored dots. I had watched him play that game for months, and I still didn't understand what the point was.

"Are you happy about getting her books?" I asked him,

trying to stop the downward spiral of my brain.

"Are you kidding? Of course I'm happy. She probably has thousands of books."

"I don't know where you're going to put them all."

"Guest bedroom," he said immediately. Clearly he'd already thought about it. "All those built-in bookcases just collecting dust. Maybe I'll move into it, switch rooms. Maybe I'll take it as my second bedroom. You know she has first editions of every single Roald Dahl book, right? I can't wait to . . ." He blushed, turned away from me, and cleared his throat.

"Were you about to say *smell them*?" I said.

"Obviously no," he mumbled.

"You know it's mildew, right? That's what you're smell-ing."

"It's not mildew," he said, raising his voice slightly, then lowering it when he realized he was getting defen-sive about books. "It's the chemical breakdown of . . . You know what? It's none of your business."

"You're going to get high off ink."

"I'm not even talking about this with you," he hissed.

I looked out the window instead, alarmed to find that we were already there, already pulling into her driveway. I tried hard not to imagine her on the front porch, waiting for us, with slippered feet and feathery blond hair piled in a bun on top of her head.

I hadn't been here in a while.

Aunt Helen had gone into the hospital and stayed there for the last few weeks of her life. There wasn't enough time to get hospice care or attempt to move her. We made her room as cozy as we could and every day we watched her slip further and further away from us. I kept hoping for a miracle. And then I stopped hoping for a miracle and just hoped, at least, that it would be painless.

When she died, I texted Em over and over, standing in Aunt Helen's hospital room as everyone took their turns saying good-bye.

> What do you think happens when you die?
>
> Do you think it hurts? I mean, do you think every single death is painful?
>
> Do you think about it ever? Like just the fact that we are all definitely, absolutely going to die one day?
>
> Is life even worth living?
>
> What are any of us even doing here? Is there a point to any of this?

"Well, here we are," Mom said after we'd already been there for two or three minutes, none of us talking to each other, the car still idling. She reached over my father's leg and shut the engine off.

"Here we are," he echoed sadly.

Aunt Helen's house was a white Victorian with a wrap-around porch and turrets and gables. Like something out of a haunted house storybook, only not at all frightening.

Or at night maybe a little frightening. Right now: sad and empty.

I got out of the car first and went around back to get the key, which was under a plant on her deck. It was a spare key, just the single one on an old and tarnished brass keychain, a Mickey Mouse head. I unlocked the back door of the house and walked slowly to the front, where my family was waiting. I just wanted a minute by myself.

The house was big and still and slightly stale—although maybe I was only imagining that. But the air tasted off, and I opened a few windows as I went, pulling back curtains and letting the sunlight in. We could live here if we wanted to. Harry had made it clear that we could take whatever we wanted, and I'm sure that included this house. Or any of Aunt Helen's houses. Or any of her things. But I knew we'd never live here, because it was an hour from our own home and because it was too big and we were used to much less. And because any time we woke up, any time we walked around, we'd be pushing through her ghost. A hundred of her ghosts. We'd eat cereal with her and water the flowers with her and read books with her breathing down our necks. No, the house had to move on. The house was meant for someone else.

"Good-bye, house," I whispered tentatively into the front entranceway.

But my words fell flat and didn't hold any meaning.

I opened the front door; Mom and Dad were on the

porch and whispering to each other impatiently, coming up with an attack strategy. Abe was still on his phone, his fingers flying across the touch screen at a speed I'd never managed. Texting Amy, probably.

"We'll start upstairs," Dad said, gesturing to himself and Mom. "Abe, you want to check out the basement? And Lottie, you can wander around down here?"

He meant the first floor, which consisted of a kitchen, dining room, living room, solarium, library, three bathrooms, and probably four or five more rooms I was forgetting.

Dad handed out the sticky notes from Harry. I got blue; Mom got red; Abe got purple; Dad kept green.

"Don't go crazy," Mom said lightly. "We have room but not *this much* room. If there's any furniture or anything big . . . Just run it by us first."

"What, you don't think the grand piano will fit in my room?" I asked. I meant it as a joke, but then I remembered how Aunt Helen had taught Abe to play, patiently running through the different scales and explaining the differences between white and black keys.

"Count them," I'd heard her say once. "If you count the keys yourself, you'll never forget how many there are."

Eighty-eight.

I'd counted them myself because, although I had no interest in learning piano, I didn't want to be left out.

Abe put his phone in his back pocket and blinked a few

times and then smiled weakly at me. "It's okay," he said. "It's fine."

We split up. Occasionally I heard my parents talking or arguing upstairs and at one point there was a particularly loud crash from the basement, but otherwise I felt entirely alone. I started in the library (so empty now that the movers had taken all the books) and made my way through her study and into the solarium, which was at the back of the house and filled with plants she had managed not to kill. I put sticky notes on things that made me miss her or things I didn't want to see sent to auction. A paperweight shaped like Earth—when you looked inside, you saw galaxies. Her collection of fountain pens. A small potted bonsai with a miniature metal table and chairs set in the dirt underneath it, like fairies had come for tea and left just before I'd gotten there. A stack of photo albums. A dozen small, framed cloth canvases that featured the needlepoints she'd done as a teenager: flower scenes and trees and bridges and a sun with many faded orange rays.

Eventually I made my way into the backyard, needing air, hoping for a breeze.

"Do you think I need a croquet set?" Abe asked, coming up behind me. I jumped a mile and shrieked again, and he held his hands up like *whoa, calm down*.

"Geez, Abe," I said.

"I mean, would you play croquet with me?" he asked. He held the croquet set out to me, an enormous vintage suitcase that held the pieces of the game inside it.

"Sure," I said. "Sure, I'll play croquet with you. As long as you don't bury me in the ground."

"Ah, good reference," he said, setting the case on the deck and adorning it with a purple sticky note. "Come on, you look like you could use a glass of water."

We went back inside the house and he got me a glass of water, and then he left to do more looking around. I drank the water at the breakfast bar. I felt emptied out, scooped clean, exhausted from the party last night. In the books, Alvin and his sister are immortal and don't need sleep. They *can* sleep, and they do sometimes, out of habit. Eternally thirteen (Alvin) and eleven (Margo). That didn't sound so bad to me at the current moment.

They didn't have to worry about cancer, about cells inside your body that might already be inside you, so far symptomless and hiding and waiting their turn.

Aunt Helen had gone to a normal gynecologist appointment on a normal Tuesday or Wednesday or Thursday, and her doctor had done a normal breast exam where nothing is ever out of the ordinary. Only something was out of the ordinary, and *it's probably nothing, Helen, but we don't like to take these things lightly.* She had gone the very next day for a mammogram, and then the week after that she was sitting down with all of us and speaking quietly about survival rates because *I just want you guys to know what I know. I don't want there to be any secrets.*

"Ah, my firstborn," Dad said, coming into the kitchen. I looked up sharply, Aunt Helen's words still vibrating around in my head. She'd told us here, in this house, in the living room. She'd invited us over for dinner and waited until we were getting ready to leave.

Dad sat down next to me, pulled my water glass toward him, and took a sip. "Are you doing okay?" he asked.

"Are you doing okay, Dad?"

"Shit," he said quietly. "No idea."

I waited a minute or two, but I couldn't think of anything to say to that, so I slid off the stool and left him alone. I made my way to the living room quietly, and when I walked through the doorway, I swear I could almost see the five of us, huddled around each other, my dad crying and my mom crying and Abe and me just looking at each other with wide eyes and Aunt Helen not really looking at anything, just letting her eyes scan the room, the walls, the ceiling, the chairs, the windows.

"Oh, Helen," my mother had said while my brain struggled to rewrite the course of that evening. It was not supposed to end like that. We were supposed to have ice cream for dessert and go to bed too full.

I sat down on the couch. I felt a tiny thrill of undirected anger (at cancer, at death, at dying, at everything), but I did my best to ignore it.

"Good-bye, house," I whispered for the second time.

It was the best I could do.

The attic was expansive, its space seemed to not even make sense, like surely there was too much here to have actually fit inside the house. Alvin wondered idly of blueprints, of square footage, as he carefully picked his way through the room, navigating countless wooden boxes and scientific paraphernalia: a telescope, a globe (but not Earth, he noted), something that looked like a printing press. Behind him, Margo banged her knee against a suit of armor and cursed. Her voice sounded quiet and muffled, lost among all the clutter of the room.

Alvin made his way carefully deeper into the attic. He let his hand brush against a stack of scientific journals piled waist-high on the floor. He stopped at a towering shelf unit and peeked at any number of unsightly things kept stored in jars and formaldehyde. Everything was covered in a thick layer of dust; no one had been in this house, in this attic, for a very long time.

And then he saw it: a book.

But not just any book.

This was the biggest book he'd ever seen in his entire life, a giant of a book, like seven dictionaries stuck back to back.

He was drawn to it, no longer caring about watching where he was going, knocking over a silver scale and what looked like a miniature black cauldron as he rushed over to it.

The book was bound in rich brown leather, and the title was printed in gold on the front: *The Everlife Grimoire.*
—from *Alvin Hatter and the House in the Middle of the Woods*

5

We got home in the afternoon, and I went straight upstairs to my room to read Aunt Helen's next letter. I had left it on my desk so I wouldn't be tempted to read it while we were still at her house. I wanted to honor whatever last wishes she had, and part of those wishes were my instructions on how and when to open these. So now, bedroom door shut and outside world temporarily on hold, I was ready to see what she had in store for me next.

Lottie,

I spent a sad, lonely sort of afternoon walking through my house, touching everything I've acquired over the years, thinking about the accumulation of stuff, wondering why little trinkets have the ability to make us so silly-happy. Do you remember that time we went vintage shopping and you found that little ceramic deer and fell in love with it? Not two hours later you dropped it and dissolved into hysterics. (You mustn't be too hard on yourself; you were only eight.) I wonder now, thinking back on that, what causes that sort of immediate attachment? What caused our immediate attachment too, the attachment of aunt and niece? Surely we did not have to be as close as we are. I know plenty of aunts who have more distant birthday cards and see-you-at-Christmas types of relationships with their nieces and nephews. Maybe it's best not to read so much into it. Maybe we were just lucky? Luckier, at least, than that poor deer.

It's funny, the things that occur to you after an afternoon like that. I realized, quite out of nowhere, that I'll be gone soon, and that the people I took for granted will no longer have me in their daily lives in the way I was so lucky to have them in my daily life. (That sounds a bit conceited; I think you'll know what I mean.) I would be devastated if it were one of them who left me first. I imagine they will miss me as well.

So I guess what I'd most like to do right now but can't (it is too late, some other day) is go and see one of our old friends, Clarice. The owner of my favorite bookstore: Page & Ink. Bring her a hot tea and a banana muffin from Kester's. Buy yourself some *books, Lottie. They help with everything.*

Books can make you live a thousand lifetimes, a thousand different lives.

Books make you immortal.

Love, H.

She had slipped three twenties into the envelope.

I texted Em immediately.

> **Last hurrah before I have to go back to school tomorrow?**

Em responded in a few minutes:

> **Absolutely. What are we doing?**
>
> **I'll pick you up in 30.**

She texted back a kissy-face emoji, and I went downstairs to see if there was any coffee made. There was—I poured myself some into a mug that said Luke's Diner (my brother's purchase) and went to the back porch. The backyard was currently being croqueted up by Abe. Amy, in a little yellow sundress and an unreal vintage denim vest covered in patches (she really was the coolest person I knew), sat on the steps, watching. I sat down next to her.

"Are you really measuring the distance between the gates right now?" I asked Abe.

"They're *wickets*, dummy," he retorted, rolling his eyes.

"I don't know why he likes weird things this much," Amy said, a little wide-eyed.

"I think he just likes the club."

He sighed loudly. "It's a mallet, Lottie, geez."

"We should play with flamingoes," I suggested.

"Okay, good reference. Now be quiet."

For Abe's sixteenth birthday, Aunt Helen had given him a first edition, first issue of *Alice's Adventures in Wonderland*. I'd walked past his room one night shortly after and saw him holding it with reverence. He wore white gloves, and the book itself was tucked inside a heavy plastic case.

"Really?" I said, stopping at his door.

"Do you know there are only two dozen surviving copies of this edition?" he asked without looking up. "I need a safety deposit box. I need a fireproof box. I need something really secure. It's from 1865, Lottie. This is history."

"Your popularity is history," I said. I thought it was a pretty good comeback, but it prompted Abe to get up and shut his door.

"How long has he been at this?" I asked Amy.

"Oh, ever since I got here. He says there's a really specific way you have to do it or else you're basically playing bocce."

"The poor man's croquet!" Abe shouted from the other end of the lawn, where he was lying belly-down on the grass to check his work.

"Wow," I said.

"You just have to go with it," Amy said and knocked her shoulder against mine. "Are you doing okay, Lottie? It must have been tough to go back to her house."

"I think everything will be tough for a while," I said. "And then, I don't know. Maybe it will get easier. Actually . . ." I lowered my voice, leaned a little closer to her. "Is my brother doing okay? He doesn't really say."

"Yeah, he doesn't really say to me either. I think he was crying the other night, when he came to pick me up, but I knew he was trying to cover it, so I didn't press him. I think I'm just waiting until he seems ready to talk about it. I hope that's soon."

"Abe is excellent at avoiding things he doesn't want to talk about. He still won't even acknowledge when the Doctor leaves Rose in that parallel universe."

"Oh, I know," Amy said. I could tell she was worried about him (the person currently licking his finger and holding it up to test wind direction, with not even the slightest bit of irony).

"He'll open up eventually," I said.

"I'll let you know when he does."

I left them to their afternoon shenanigans and went to pick up Em. I found her outside waiting for me, wearing an *X-Files* shirt I'd bought her off eBay that she'd cut into a crop top (she cut most shirts into crop tops). Her hair was messy, and she was wearing red lipstick and aviators.

"Hiya," she said, getting into the car.

"You look cute."

"You're going to make me blush," she said, fanning herself with her fingers.

"Are you sure you're okay with spending your Sunday afternoon in a bookstore?"

"Oh, is that what we're doing?"

"Page & Ink!"

"Is this . . . one of your aunt's things?" she asked after a second, nervously, like maybe she wasn't sure she was supposed to bring it up.

"Yeah. And it's okay, you don't have to ask like that. I'm the one who told you about them."

"Well, I don't know. I mean, I know it's personal."

"Well, yes, it's one of my aunt's things. She wants me to buy some books."

"That's great. I read stuff."

"When was the last time you read a book?"

"I read that one about the girl!"

"Oh, the one about the girl! That's a good one."

"I hear your tone, and I resent it. Besides, I really like Page & Ink. My mom used to take me there before she decided I was a straight-up abomination."

"Your mom doesn't think you're an abomination. She's just . . . misguided."

Em snorted. "You know what? Your mom's taken me to Page & Ink too. Those are far better memories."

Kester's Coffee was across the street from Page & Ink. There wasn't any traffic, and we pulled into the parking lot twenty minutes later.

"Do you want anything?" I asked Em.

"When I went to Scotland I had a scone with clotted cream. We don't have clotted cream over here, so I can't eat scones anymore," Em said wistfully.

"So do you want . . . a muffin?" I asked.

"Maybe an iced tea?"

"Okay, weirdo. I'll get you an iced tea."

As per Aunt Helen's letter, I got Clarice a small hot tea and a banana muffin. Then I got Em an iced tea and myself another banana muffin because they were the best banana muffins I'd ever had in my life. And then, on second thought, I got Em a banana muffin because she always said she didn't want anything and then she ate half of whatever I got.

We ate our muffins and shared Em's iced tea in the parking lot as I worked up the courage to drive across the street.

I wasn't sure why I felt nervous about seeing Clarice, but I could feel a tight knot in my stomach, a growing uncertainty that didn't seem to go away, no matter how delicious the banana muffins were.

"We should go over," Em said when we'd finished eating. "Her tea's going to get cold."

I started the car and drove to Page & Ink's parking lot. Clarice was outside, sweeping off the front walkway. When she heard the car, Clarice turned around and shielded her eyes with her hand, then waved when she saw it was us. She dropped the broom and headed over to the car.

Clarice had achondroplasia, the most common form

of dwarfism. I knew this because she'd taken the time to explain it to me on one of my first visits. I still remember how happy she was, how she'd told my aunt that children were her favorite questioners, because they were completely honest and devoid of any judgment.

My favorite thing about Page & Ink was that it had one of those old-fashioned ladders you see in all the movies, the kind that rolled on a track along the perimeter of the store. This was mostly for practicality, Clarice said, but it was a bonus that it was really, really cool.

"Lottie!" Clarice said, hugging me the second I got out of the car. "I've been thinking about you all week. I wanted to come to the party last night, but I've never been one for dancing. Your aunt would have understood." She pulled away and held both of my hands in hers, looking into my eyes as her own glossed over with tears. "Oh, your aunt. I've sold more copies of *Alvin* than I can even count this week. Been ordering all of them like crazy. Can't keep 'em on the shelves. I put a picture of the two of us on the register, and people just burst into tears looking at it. Just start bawling." She paused and touched the ends of my hair, pinching a few strands between her fingers. "Oh, Lottie. I miss her so much."

"I miss her too, Clarice."

"But enough sadness. I can't handle any more sadness."

"We have happiness for you! Happiness in the form of tea and banana muffins!" Em said, skipping around the car and handing Clarice her snack.

"Em! With blue hair! I didn't even recognize you, but you look divine. You girls are too sweet for this," Clarice said, beaming as she took the tea and paper bag from Em. "Come on, come in!"

We followed Clarice into the store, and she settled herself into place behind her desk so she could eat. She waved us away to browse and instructed us to yell if we needed anything.

I could stay in a bookstore forever. My mother had never been that big of a reader, but my father and Aunt Helen were never without a book in their hands. Aunt Helen wrote the first Alvin Hatter book when she'd finished every piece of literature in her house and found it was too late in the day to go and buy more.

"It was the best misfortune I ever suffered," she told me once. "Alvin was born out of the deepest boredom and a desperate longing for new words."

Em and I wandered around Page & Ink for hours. I left Em in the fantasy section (as much as she hated reading, I couldn't count how many times she'd flown through *Lord of the Rings*, and she was one of the few people on earth who'd actually finished *The Silmarillion*) and took myself on a tour of the children's section, touching the spines of every book and wondering how many of them my aunt had read. Of course all six of the Alvin Hatters were there, just a few copies left of each. I had all the editions, every new set of covers they came out with, and it still didn't feel like enough. I always found myself wanting more. I knew how weird that was.

Fulfilling Aunt Helen's instructions, I bought seven books. Clarice slid them all into a paper bag, and I could tell she was trying not to cry as she handed it to me. At first she refused to take any money for them, but I explained about Aunt Helen's instructions and she finally relented.

"Just like her, to send you here," she said. "What a woman, huh?"

We hugged good-bye over the counter, and Em and I went out to the car.

We sat there for a long time before I started the engine. Em looked through the books I'd chosen, and when she was done, she asked, "Is it nice? Or is it hard? Having to do all these things she asked you to."

"It's both, I guess," I said. "It kind of feels like she's still here, which is nice. But she's not here. So I'm not sure it's the best idea to keep pretending."

"Maybe she has some point, and it's just too early to see it."

"I'm sure she does. And I think this is better than the alternative. To just have her gone completely."

Em took my hand and squeezed the tips of my fingers one at a time. "She loved you a lot. That's one of those things everyone says to try to help, but it's true, you know? She really cared about you."

"I really care about you."

"That's nice, but the difference is you're never going to die. You can't. Where would I get my hair dye?"

"My mom, probably."

"Well, who would help me put it in? I can't maintain this level of pigmentation without you, Lottie. Promise me you'll live forever."

"I promise," I said.

We pinkie-swore it.

I wished that were enough to make it true.

The wind at the top of the cliff was wicked; Margo struggled to catch her breath against it. She had no idea where Alvin had gone to, and she felt scared, really scared, for maybe the first time in her entire life.

That fear was amplified tenfold as she watched the dark figure emerge from the tree line. He stepped into the moonlight, and she saw, with another stab of terror, that it was not her brother, but the man who'd been chasing them, the dark figure she'd started to refer to as the Overcoat Man.

He was disheveled, and his eyes were wild.

Margo was completely trapped. Behind her: the edge of the cliff, a straight plummet two hundred feet to the forest floor below. In front of her: the Overcoat Man, looking almost smug, almost pleased.

"Nowhere to go, is there?" he asked.

"Who are you?" she cried. "What do you want?"

"You better tell me how you got in that house," he said. "You better tell me, and quick."

"We opened the door! We walked inside! Just like you get into any house! It's not rocket science!" Margo yelled, because they'd already told him that, and he just kept asking and asking. . . .

"That house is magic! There's no opening of doors! There's no walking inside! You better stop lying to me, girl!"

Margo felt suddenly defiant. A rush of courage surged through her body. She crossed her arms over her chest. "I'm not telling you ANYTHING," she screamed.

And then he'd darted at her, his face twisted into an expression of sharp rage.

And then he'd pushed.

For one beautiful, calm moment, Margo was flying.

And then she realized: Oh no. Not flying.

Falling.

—from *Alvin Hatter and the House in the Middle of the Woods*

6

When I walked in the house that night, I found my dad sitting alone at the kitchen table. He had a book open in front of him like he was reading, but upon closer inspection I saw that it was the operating manual for our stove. He was just kind of staring at it, like he had grabbed the first thing he'd found, like it was just a prop to convince the casual viewer that he was doing anything other than sitting, being sad, doing nothing. I wanted to tell him what was in Aunt Helen's letters. I wanted to show him—*look, see, she's not really all gone yet*—but I couldn't bring myself to speak. I didn't want to interrupt him, intrude on whatever thoughts he was lost in. So I went upstairs.

That night, alone in my bedroom, I read the next letter from Aunt Helen.

As usual, the sight of her handwriting made my breath catch in my throat.

Dear Lottie,

Nothing like a good book, huh?

I've been asked a hundred million billion times—where did you get the idea for Alvin Hatter? Is he based on a real person? He seems so real!

I can think of a million characters who have seemed as real to me. Edmund in Narnia—such a little shit but at least so unabashedly true to his every desire. He's the realest one of them because he makes mistakes, he owns up to them, he forges forward even when his brother and sisters hate him for it. Alice in Wonderland—real enough to cry an entire lake's worth of suffering, real enough to make an entire imaginary world seem similarly real. Milo in the Tollbooth land—real enough to admit the hardest thing in the world, that contentment sometimes leads to the sharpest of boredoms, that often our own brains are our very worst enemies.

I could go on and on. But I think that is the best compliment to give a writer—your characters seem so real. That's what makes a book, isn't it? That's why I've read PRIDE AND PREJUDICE a thousand times and STILL can't figure Mr. Darcy out. That's why we return again and again to Middle Earth, to Discworld, to Never-Never Land.

I'm rambling again. It's so easy to ramble in these, you see, because I have an endless supply of blank paper and a love for filling it up with ink. And I don't have to imagine any scenario in which you don't read every word, and happily, because they're my letters and I'll be gone when you read them and then it will be up to you. Does that make any sense? It's late. I guess I'm getting tired.

Is Alvin based on a real person? Oh, of course, and of course not, because everything we can ever write is just a mixture of all the things we already know and all the things we're just guessing at. It's contrariwise, as Alice would say.

But let's suppose for a minute that he is real.

Let's suppose for a minute that the idea of a forever boy wasn't entirely ludicrous.

What would YOU do, Lottie, if you were immortal?

What would you do if you knew you could not be hurt doing it?

I think you should do something a little reckless. Just a little, to see how it feels.

—H.

I went to school Monday wondering what I could possibly do that was reckless enough as to be a little unsafe, not reckless enough as to cause me any real harm. I kept coming up blank.

First period Em and I had history together. We sat in the back, and I passed her a note that said:

I have to do something a little bit reckless. Any ideas?

She read, considered, then wrote:

I know exactly what to do. Your aunt would approve.

What?

Secret.

This is terrifying.

That's a good sign.

When?

After school. We'll have to swing by your place first to pick something up.

Pick what up?

Secret.

Em looked too pleased with herself, which made me nervous.

There were a *lot* of things Em might consider an appropriate amount of reckless. Skydiving. Bungee jumping. Zip-lining.

All things Em would find perfectly acceptable for a Monday after-school event.

Em jabbed me in the side with a pen and handed me another note.

It said:

Relax. I know you.

That was true. Em did know me, and she wouldn't take me skydiving.

She would never take me skydiving.

I scribbled a quick message and threw it back at her:

Is it skydiving??

She read it, rolled her eyes, and didn't look at me for the rest of the class.

When the bell rang I tried to grab her arm, but she was excellent at evading me. It helped that she was so fast. She was out of the room before I'd even packed up my things. I started rushing, shoving my history book and notebook and pen into my bag quickly so I wouldn't be alone for too long. I'd already been approached by four people telling me how sorry they were about my aunt, and I'd only been at school an hour.

It wasn't that I didn't appreciate it.

Because I *did*.

But it also made me a little angry.

I mean—it was bad enough that she was dead. I didn't really need the constant reminders.

The thing we needed from my house was small enough to fit in Em's backpack, which, to be fair, was kind of a big backpack. I had no idea where she was heading, but I'd decided to go with it.

Em drove a black Jetta she'd bought secondhand with her own money (she'd worked at a juicery in town since she was fourteen, "Not because I think juice cleanses work, Lottie, but because everybody else does."). She'd named the car Joan Jetta, something she thought was very clever, and she told anyone who showed even the slightest interest.

"Are we going alone?" I asked when she merged onto the highway.

"Jackie has dance—"

"I can't believe you're actually dating a ballerina."

"And Abe said he's been spending too much time with you as it is. And I've been getting the feeling you need some alone time lately. And yes, I'm dating a ballerina and you're clearly jealous."

"By alone time, do you mean alone time with you?"

"Of course I mean alone time with me. Gross, do you want alone time with, like, just yourself?"

"That's actually what alone time is, you know. Like—alone."

"Whoever invented alone time did not have a best friend as interesting as I am."

Em liked being alone when she was sleeping. Other than that she was either with me or Jackie or with various members of the track team.

She wouldn't tell me where we were going. All I knew is that we were headed toward the ocean. She stopped at a drive-through and bought us fries and salads (I never asked questions when it came to her culinary preferences), and we ate them in turns, passing each between us. I found myself wondering, not for the first time, what the rest of my aunt's instructions would be. And also—why had she written the letters in the first place? Because I couldn't deny that it was nice to have them, but it was also sort of frustrating. Was there something obvious they were doing that I wasn't smart enough to see yet?

But at the same time I found myself wishing they would never stop, because as weird or creepy as it might have been to get messages from beyond the grave, I missed my aunt too much to say good-bye quite yet. And so much of her writing was public and popular. . . . I liked that these were just for me.

"Lottie, seriously? You have such a problem sharing," Em said, grabbing the almost-empty carton of fries from me.

"Sorry," I said. But I wasn't sorry. You should never apologize for fries.

"We're almost there, anyway. Are you excited? Any ideas?"

I looked around the car for a landmark, but all these little seaside towns started to look alike after a while. I hadn't been paying attention; I had no idea what exit we'd gotten off.

"I don't know where we are," I said.

"Seriously? You are so unobservant."

"Are we going to the Nautilus?"

"We are nowhere near the Nautilus," she said, sighing. "I worry about you. If your phone died and you woke up in the middle of nowhere, you would literally never find your way home. You would end up in Tibet."

"Tibet?"

"Yes. I am absolutely certain that you would end up

in Tibet. And then you would ask to borrow a stranger's phone and you would try and call me, but we both know you haven't looked at my phone number since the day you saved it to your phone. That's the problem with all of us."

"That we don't memorize phone numbers anymore?"

"No. Yes. Well—that is *one* of the problems with all of us."

"Someday I'd love to hear your breakdown of all the things that are wrong with people nowadays."

"It's a long list."

"And really, where the hell are we?"

Em didn't answer but pulled her car into a dirt parking lot. She chose a spot in the shade and turned to look at me.

"Do you remember that place your aunt used to take us swimming? We were young, you know, I hadn't even come out yet, but my mom knew, and she was already convinced I was going to the special hell they have for people who like people with the same genitalia as them. Because it's so important, you know? What our genitalia looks like. It's, like, a very big deal to the big guy."

It made me uncomfortable when Em got like this, so down on her mom, but I couldn't really blame her. Her mom really did think like that. It was so sad.

"I remember."

"Well," she said, and swept her arm in front of her.

"You want to go swimming? That's not really that reckless."

"No, I don't want to go swimming," Em said. "Just follow me."

We got out of the car. It was hot and a little muggy, and I thought we were heading down to the beach, but Em led me up a little path that led to the top of a cliff that overlooked the water. We got sweaty and out of breath almost immediately. We passed a few people coming down, but when we finally got up there, we were alone.

Em took a bathing suit out of her backpack and handed it to me.

She smiled her special kind of smile, the one where her face got darker and her eyes got very bright and you were suddenly absolutely terrified of whatever it was she was planning.

Then it dawned on me.

"Absolutely not!" I shrieked, backing away from the cliff's edge, throwing my bathing suit at her.

She caught it with one hand and said, "Get naked, Lottie. We're doing this."

"We are not doing this, Em. If you think I'm jumping off this cliff . . ."

"I *know* you're jumping off this cliff, Lottie. I can see the future, and it very much consists of you and me jumping off this cliff."

"You're insane. We will literally break our entire bodies."

"Oh, relax. I've done it before. Abe did it when he was

twelve. Don't tell your parents that. Nothing is going to happen to you."

"That water is *freezing*. And very, very far away."

"Trust me, Lottie. You will be perfectly fine. All we have to do is jump far enough to clear the rocks that stick out—"

"Nope, nope, nope, nope, nope."

"I wouldn't let anything happen to you."

"Says the lady who's about to push me off a cliff!"

"I would never push you off a cliff. We are going to jump. Together. It's going to be great. And don't you see the parallel here? It's kind of ingenious."

"I don't know what you're talking about."

"You don't know what I'm . . . *Alvin Hatter and the House in the Middle of the Woods!*"

Oh. Right. At the very end of *Alvin Hatter and the House in the Middle of the Woods*, the Overcoat Man catches up to Margo and Alvin. He knows they've found a way to get into the house that holds all the magic of the world, and he wants them to tell him how. In a final life-and-death struggle, the Overcoat Man pushes Margo to her death over the cliff and then flees. But of course she doesn't die, because she's already drank the Everlife Formula, and she's immortal (Alvin drinks it right after this, because he can't deny the appeal of not dying when pushed off cliffs).

"But we're not Margo, Em. We are going to die."

Em kept trying to give me the bathing suit, and I kept

pushing it back at her. Finally she threw it at my feet and took her clothes off. She was wearing her own bathing suit already: black with teal polka dots. She shoved her clothes in her backpack and crossed her arms, staring at me.

"Em . . ."

"Look, Lottie, I get it. I get that you're scared of hurting yourself and you're scared of dying, but you can't go through life that way."

"I can absolutely go through life without ever jumping off a cliff," I argued.

"Yes, you can, but you can't go through life without taking risks. And this is a risk, sure, but it's a relatively small one compared to the risk of getting into an accident every time you get in a car or the risk of losing your luggage when you go on a plane or the risk of getting a paper cut every time you pick up a notebook. Life is a risk, Lottie. Sometimes you have to answer its call."

She had gotten more and more exaggerated throughout the speech, and by the time she finished she had jumped up on a rock and was practically screaming.

"Did you practice that?" I asked.

"Obviously, yes. On Jackie in fourth period."

I stared at her for a minute. She was an inimitable staring-contest contestant; she could go without blinking for hours.

"Okay, fine," I said, already pulling my shirt over my head, kicking my shorts down to my ankles.

"Fine, fine, fine," before I could change my mind.

"Fine, fine, fine," before I could think of the million reasons this was a terrible idea.

Em picked my bathing suit off the ground and held it out for me as I stripped naked. She'd seen me naked a hundred times, but I appreciated that she squeezed her eyes shut (and held her breath, like a dweeb) until I snapped the shoulders of the suit, signaling that I'd gotten it on. She had brought my one piece, a very old suit that was starting to fade. I felt twelve in it, like a kid only playing at the idea of maybe one day being an adult. Em turned around and raised her eyebrows and whistled in appreciation.

"Oh, shut up."

"Can't a friend tell a friend she looks like a super cutie?" Em said. Then she dug around in her backpack for her phone, and we took a photo of the two of us. Okay, we took about ten photos, smiling in some and laughing in some and making weird faces in some. Then Em tucked the phone back in her backpack and took my hand. "No more stalling."

My stomach flipped over as she pulled me closer to the edge.

"What about your bag?"

"There's no one around. We'll come back and get it after we jump."

"What if we die?"

"Then we won't be around to care about the bag. Win-win."

I looked down and my stomach flopped again and my heart started racing like mad. I couldn't do this. If the fall didn't kill me, the heart attack would.

"What about . . . I mean, we're going to be wet. So. We're just going to be really wet."

"There are towels in my trunk. Relax. I've thought this through. You need to *breathe*."

I tried to, but my lungs weren't working right. They'd taken the afternoon off. They'd found something better to do.

"On three," Em said.

I missed my aunt.

"One . . ."

I didn't want to die.

"Two . . ."

I wasn't like Margo.

"THREE!"

I was doing this.

Em gripped my hand tighter and pulled me forward, and I bent my knees and jumped, propelling myself off the cliff with a force that came from somewhere foreign, somewhere new. The air was instantly colder, the wind rushed by my ears in a strange, long howl that mixed with Em's whoop of pure joy, every color of the world blending together before my eyes and mixing into one beautiful blue and green and red and yellow blur until—

We hit the freezing-cold water with an unexpected jolt.

My mouth filled with salt and bubbles, and every inch of my skin was on fire, some strange confusion between freezing and boiling. And Em's hand had slipped from mine, and I didn't know which way was up. When I opened my eyes everything was dark. I paddled frantically toward the surface but it wasn't the surface, so I turned around but that wasn't the right way either. I had survived the fall, but I was going to die anyway; I was going to drown out here. That seemed exactly like something I would do. If only I had Em's fearlessness or my brother's strength or my mom's perseverance or my dad's dumb luck. If only I had something . . .

I almost screamed when I felt something wrap itself around my arm (tentacles? teeth?), but you can't scream underwater, and it came out as a gurgled moan. Then something was pulling me up and up and up, and my head broke the surface of the water and without meaning to I was laughing, laughing, laughing and breathing deep gulps of air and *alive*, really, and so happy I could cry.

Em was laughing too, and throwing her arms around me and kissing my cheek and practically pushing me under the surface again. We swam and kicked our way to the shore and pulled ourselves onto the rocks there, both just happy in that moment to be alive and together.

Is this what you meant? I thought to myself, a question

for someone who would never be able to answer me. *Is this what you wanted me to do?*

Maybe it was and maybe it wasn't, but at any rate, it felt okay.

It was late, and everyone in the house had gone to bed when Alvin crept across the hall to his sister's room and knocked as loudly as he dared. He heard her voice like a sharp whisper inside: "Come in!"

He turned the handle and pushed into the room. He found Margo quite awake, dressed, and busily packing her clothes into her small suitcase.

"What are you doing?" he asked.

"The question is what are THEY doing?" Margo said, turning to face him. "The Everlife Society. What are they doing to find our parents? Not enough, I don't think."

"So you're leaving?"

"Don't play dumb, Alvin. I know you, and I'd bet another swig of eternal life that your bags are packed too."

They were, in fact.

He'd thought he was going to have to convince his sister.

He'd thought he was going to have to drag her out of there.

"I don't think I've ever loved you more," he said.

"Gross. Go get your bags. No time to waste."

—from *Alvin Hatter and the Wild-Goose Chase*

7

My father came into my room at midnight. I was reading *Alvin Hatter and the Wild-Goose Chase*. I hadn't
even showered yet; my hair was a thick mess of sea salt
and wind.

Dad stood in my bedroom doorway and watched me,
half amused and half, I think, concerned.

"Are you doing all right, kid?" he asked.

"I'm okay, Dad. This is much worse than it looks." I
pointed to my hair. He raised his eyes, like: *yeah, it's pretty
bad though*. "Are you okay?" I asked, if only to get him to
stop looking at me.

"I'm doing okay. It comes and goes. You remember and
then you forget for a few minutes and then you remember
again."

"Yeah. I know what you mean."

"I have a favor to ask you, though."

"What is it?"

"You get out early on Tuesdays, right? Would you mind driving down to the Nautilus for me? Your mom and I both have to work."

"The hotel? How come?"

"Because I've been informed I left my suit jacket down there on the night of the party, and I just don't know when I'll have a chance to go and get it. But I really like that suit jacket, so I thought I might give you some gas money and you'd be so kind . . ."

Which is how I ended up driving back to Mystic (the town that wasn't, really) on Tuesday afternoon after school. I asked Em to come with me, but she had plans with Jackie, and Abe had classes all day (I had back-to-back study halls at the end of the day—being a senior was great!). So I went by myself, accepting my dad's offer of gas money and wondering after I'd left if my mom would have let me take the Corvette. I doubted it.

I drove to the Nautilus with the radio low and the windows open. It was both predictable for my father to leave a piece of clothing somewhere and predictable for him to ask me to go retrieve it for him. He had a very small wardrobe and a very big sense of sentimentality.

I pulled into the valet turnaround and told the man working I'd just be there a minute. He took my keys and let me run inside.

It never failed to amaze me how completely different a

place can seem in various circumstances. On the night of my aunt's party, the Nautilus was a fantasyland, a dream, something from another world. Now, just a few days later, the candles were put away and the sunlight was streaming in and it was still beautiful, of course, but it was firmly rooted in reality. I stepped through the double white doors and into the lobby, and everything felt real. Believable. Normal. I asked the concierge where my father's coat was being kept, and he left and returned a few minutes later with it draped over his arm.

"Here you are," he said. "I'm just glad we knew who to call."

"Oh, yeah—how did you know?" It wasn't like my dad sewed his name into the lining of his clothes.

"A young man brought it to us at the end of the night. He said it belonged to the brother of Helen Reaves. We had his number in our contact sheet. The man asked for this to be left with it." The concierge reached into the pocket of the suit jacket and removed a little white envelope stamped with the Nautilus's symbol. A name was written on it.

My name.

My heart gave a little lurch as I took the envelope and the jacket from him. I looped the jacket over my arm and saw my hands starting to shake as I read my name on the envelope again.

Lottie.

In tiny, neat handwriting.

In tiny, neat handwriting that couldn't have been . . .

Hers? Right?

It couldn't have been hers.

I mumbled a thank-you and went outside quickly, almost running back to my car, catching the keys the valet threw in my direction ("Nice one!"). I tossed the jacket and the envelope on the passenger seat and drove away quickly; my entire body was suddenly cold and shivery. I drove for five minutes until I reached a parking lot for a small strip mall. I pulled in and parked and turned the car off and rested my head against the steering wheel.

I had Aunt Helen's next letter with me. I was planning to read it before the drive home.

Could this letter also be from her? But that didn't make any sense. Right? Right.

Because dead people could not slip letters into the pockets of your father's suit jacket, right?

That was not something that could happen.

Or could it? I didn't know. If any person could figure out how to become a ghost and hide letters in suit jackets at fancy hotels, it was definitely my aunt.

And there was only one way to find out.

I picked the envelope up and withdrew the Nautilus letterhead from inside.

I enjoyed talking to you. —Sam

A sudden rush of embarrassment.

Get a grip, Lottie. You're losing it.

Sam had written his phone number underneath his message, and I didn't even think about it, just typed it into my phone and texted him before I could change my mind:

How did you know this was my father's coat?

The reply came a few minutes later. I'd rolled the windows all the way down and reclined my seat. I felt my phone buzz in my lap.

I saw you leaving. I noticed the jacket a few minutes later; he'd left it on a chair. I tried to catch up with you, but there were too many people.

Okay. That was actually a reasonable answer.

What was I expecting? Something unreasonable?

Thanks. It was nice of you to turn it in.

I considered keeping it.

A few seconds later:

Kidding! How are you?

I'm OK.

Are you still in Mystic?

I'm by the bridge.

Can I meet you?

I checked the time. It was still early, just after two, and I didn't have anywhere to be.

Sure.

See you soon.

I didn't know how far away he lived, but Mystic was relatively small. I adjusted my seat and took my aunt's letter out of my purse.

Lottie—

I've slowed down a lot since my diagnosis. I've had a lot of time to think about this thing or the other, about my life as a whole, about all the little pieces that make up that whole. So often we just skip through life and forget to look at what we're passing. I drove once from Connecticut to California and stopped at not a single "biggest pile of hay in the world" or "biggest ball of yarn in the US" (they have a lot of "biggest" things out there between the coasts), and how silly is that? How silly that I wouldn't have taken my time, made the time, FOUND the time. Whenever somebody tells you they don't have time for you, just remember that we make time for the things we want to make time for, and then kick them to the curb. (Or politely ask them to leave, as seems more in line with your style.)

It is easy now, so near to the end of my run (hindsight is twenty/twenty, etc.) to wish I had done more. Seen more. Been more. So many hours spent inside at my desk writing (not complaining; that writing served me well) and not taking care to balance that time with things more fun. The real good stuff, you know, the stuff that you'll remember forever.

Remember when you were a little girl, maybe ten, maybe eleven, we went to the botanical gardens in

Brooklyn to see the bluebells bloom? Oh, your eyes were as wide as two moons in your face; you told me you felt exactly like Alice in the garden. I said—as long as the flowers are nice to you. Flowers can have such an attitude.

I remember that day a lot now, the look on your face, the absolute wonderment so clearly displayed there. It was one of those days when you forget about the peskiness of clocks and schedules. We were an hour late meeting your parents and Abe for dinner because neither one of us once looked at a clock.

I want you to chase that feeling, Lottie. Maybe not every day (that might get tiring), but at least every so often, every once in a while. Lose track of time. Turn off your phone. Don't rush.

—H.

I tucked her note back into its envelope, slid it into my purse. After every letter I read from her, there was this quiet, this calm, that passed over me. And then I remembered that she was gone, and my heart sped up, my palms started to sweat. The old recognizable physical effects of anxiety. And the anger—that she was so young, that we had such little warning.

I rolled up the windows and got out of my car. There was a small public green here and a tiny boardwalk leading to the drawbridge. I found a bench and texted my father.

Coat acquired.

I tried playing the stupid game Abe always played (I'd downloaded it, determined to figure out why he liked it so much), but I kept dying on level one. Finally I put my phone away and tried to do what my aunt wanted me to do. The ocean, the sky, the people kayaking underneath the drawbridge: this seemed like a perfectly acceptable place to lose track of time.

Instead I kept glancing at the time on my phone, a steady buildup of nerves settling into my stomach. I wasn't the best at meeting new people, but Sam had known my aunt, and I didn't want to pass up the chance to talk to him about her.

So I waited, and I counted the seconds that passed (so basically the exact opposite of what Aunt Helen wanted me to do), and he showed up a minute or two later. He smiled and waved when he saw me. He had the faintest hint of a dimple in his left cheek, and his eyes got all crinkly when he smiled. I stood up from the bench and didn't have time to worry about the proper way to greet someone you've only met once (Hug? Handshake? High five? Rain dance?) before Sam hugged me briefly and then pulled away.

"I'm glad you texted me," he said.

"It was the least I could do to thank you for having an excellent memory for apparel."

"It's a gift," he said, laughing. "Are you hungry? I'm starving. Have you ever been to Mystic Pizza?"

"Of course! And I would have to agree that it is *a little slice of heaven.*"

"Familiar with the slogan and everything—I'm glad you take your pizza as seriously as I do. Shall we?"

"Let's do it."

We made our way over the drawbridge and through the little downtown area to the pizza shop made famous by the movie with Julia Roberts. I'd watched it with Aunt Helen and Abe a long time ago, a massive bowl of popcorn between us. It was mostly fun just picking out the different landmarks we recognized.

"Do you live close?" I asked.

"Just down the road. On Mason's Island."

"Did you walk here?"

"I biked."

"I don't remember the last time I was on a bike."

"Really? Wind in your hair? Sun on your face?" He flipped his hair to demonstrate.

"I flipped over on my bike when I was a kid and landed on my head. I think I kind of lost the taste for it after that."

"We'll get you a really strong helmet, and you'll come around."

We got to Mystic Pizza. Sam held the door open for me, and I stepped inside.

"Let's get it to go," he suggested. "We can take it down by the water."

"Fine by me."

We ordered a medium Mediterranean Delight and then crossed the street while we waited for it, to browse through a little bookstore I liked: Bank Square Books.

Aunt Helen always said if you really wanted to get to know someone, take them to a bookstore. You can tell a lot about a person based on how they behave around books. Sam beelined right for historical fiction and picked up a book about pirates. I trailed behind and tried to ignore the children's section, where I could see a table set up for the Hatter books.

But I couldn't ignore it for long—Sam abandoned the pirate book and wandered right over to the children's section. He picked up one of the Hatter books and started looking through it.

"Do you like them?" I asked.

He looked up at me with a smile on his face—but it was a sad smile. I'd been seeing a lot of that particular smile lately. It tended to dwell on the faces of the mourning.

"Of course I like them. Does anyone *not* like them?"

"There's actually a pretty big online presence that call themselves the Anti-Hatters. They burn the books on YouTube and everything. Very dramatic. They say the idea of immortality is a sin against God. I don't think they quite understand the idea of fiction."

"A sin against God, huh?" Sam said, closing the book and carefully setting it back in the pile with the others. That sad smile still lingered on his face, but I could tell he was trying to shake it.

"I'm sorry."

"Sorry?"

"For your loss. Our collective loss. I know you knew my aunt too. She meant a lot to a lot of people."

"Ah," he said, nodding slowly. "She was a huge inspiration to me. She was a really amazing teacher." I waited for him to say more about her, but he didn't. Instead he checked his watch and said, "We should get back; our pizza is probably done."

It was indeed—we split the bill and started walking back to the little green where I'd left my car. There were plenty of benches there, and we sat on one behind a toy store. The sun was hot, but the breeze coming off the water was enough to keep us cool.

We were quiet as we dug into the pizza for a minute, and then Sam said, "You know, you kind of ditched me at the party."

"Oh," I replied, because I couldn't think of anything better to say.

"Dancing one minute, Cinderella the next. If I didn't see you guys leaving a little while later, I probably would have thought you'd turned into a pumpkin."

"Ha! No. I'm sorry. That was pretty lame. I'm just not the best at parties. Big groups. And then you factor in—"

"The fact that some stranger kept asking you to dance?"

"No, that was fine," I said, smiling. "It was a lot of

things. My aunt, you know . . . It hasn't been easy."

"I know," he said. "I mean, I guessed. I'm sorry I called you Cinderella."

"Please don't ever apologize for calling someone Cinderella."

"I know how much it . . ." He took a breath. That sad smile again. "How hard it is. To lose someone you love."

"Oh, I'm sorry."

"It was a long time ago. But I still remember, of course. You don't ever really forget."

I'd had so many people trying to comfort me lately, but it occurred to me that I didn't really know how to comfort someone else. I wondered who Sam had lost, but I didn't think I should ask—if he wanted to tell me, he would. Instead I found myself wanting to share the letters with him, or at least a piece of them, maybe because he'd known Aunt Helen and mourned her too. And because all of that made me feel like I could trust him.

So I said, "There's more. The night of the party—she left me all these letters. Little things I'm supposed to do now that she's gone. And it's been nice, but at the same time . . . I worry that I'm not doing exactly what she wanted me to do. That I'm not doing a good enough job."

"What kinds of things?"

"Well, the next one is . . . I'm supposed to lose track of time."

Sam thought about it for a minute. It felt a little silly to say out loud, but he looked like he was taking it completely seriously. He folded up the empty pizza box and said, "Do you have any ideas?"

"Not really. I think I know what she means, though. I have a tendency to get kind of . . . caught up with everything. Kind of hyperaware of time and place and all that."

"So maybe she's trying to push you out of your comfort zone a little?"

"Yeah. I think it's something like that."

"All right. I know what we'll do," he said, and that is how I ended up, ten minutes later, on the handlebars of Sam's bike. He gave me his helmet (then rapped his knuckles on it to prove its durability) and wouldn't tell me where we were going. Halfway there I had to get down because, although nice in theory, riding on handlebars over the age of seven is not comfortable at all. I walked around the back of the bike and stood on the spokes, hesitating for a second before I put my hands on his shoulders.

"Okay?" he asked.

"Okay!"

We were off again. He pedaled us past the train station and around a bend and down a road I'd never been on before. I saw a small sign that said Mason's Island and remembered this is where he lived.

He kept going, seemingly tireless. The ocean was to our left; it was low tide and it smelled stronger than by the bridge. Like brine, like salt, like sand.

We kept going until we reached a second bridge that connected Mason's Island to another smaller island. Sam brought the bike to a stop at the end of the bridge, and we both hopped off.

"Enders Island," he said, gesturing in front of us. It was small, and I could see just a few tiny buildings arranged in a loose circle in the middle. "I do yard maintenance here. St. Edmund's Retreat."

"St. Edmund's?"

"I'm not religious," he said. "But they're okay here. They're nice. It's quiet."

He left his bike by the side of the road, and we walked over the bridge. There were perfectly manicured lawns, religious statues and shrines, a gazebo, a small reflecting pool, benches, stone buildings, and stone arches . . .

We walked to the very tip of the island, the Atlantic spreading out in front of us like a dark-blue blanket.

"Sometimes I come here to think," Sam said.

I could understand why—it was so peaceful, being almost completely surrounded by water. I could see other small islands dotting the coast and countless sailboats and powerboats. It made me wish I lived closer to the ocean. It made me think of my aunt's big house by the sea, a house I would probably never see again.

Anger again, but just a tiny flare in the pit of my stomach. It was manageable, and I mentally swatted it away and sat next to Sam on the grass.

"What's your nicest memory of her?" he asked.

A hundred things popped into my head at once. Breakfasts on the front lawn, books read in blanket forts, day trips to the city. It was hard to pick one.

And then I remembered her letter, the bluebells in Brooklyn, the late dinner, the timelessness she spoke of.

Aunt Helen was a fan of the many intricacies of time— its inconsistencies, its betrayals (how a perfect day could slip by in the blink of an eye and a terrible one could last forever—like the day she died, stretching out to reach infinity). And she was a fan of the ocean, and of being still, and of getting swept up in a normal afternoon. And she was a fan of changing her mind. . . . Jumping off cliffs one minute and slowing down the next. I think that was exactly what she was trying to show me. All the options of a day.

Sam lay back and rested his arm over his face to shield himself from the sun.

I looked out at the water and tried to imagine a field of bluebells.

I glanced down at Sam; he'd closed his eyes.

It was so rare to find someone you could be quiet with.

I lay back next to him, our arms an inch apart, and suddenly the entire world was sky. Just sky forever, blue and white and bright and never ending.

I don't know how long we stayed like that.

"What's that?" Margo asked, pointing to the old book in Alvin's hands.

"Dad's journal," he responded, not taking his eyes off the page.

Margo stepped closer. The journal was stuffed with newspaper clippings, old photographs, pages and pages of tiny, cramped writing that she recognized immediately as her father's.

"You need to get some sleep," Margo said.

"I just know there's something in here," Alvin said, still not looking at her. "Something about the Overcoat Man, about how to find him. If we find him, we find our parents. It's like the answer's right in front of me, and I just can't put the pieces together."

"Maybe in the morning . . . ," Margo said gently, but she stopped when it became clear that Alvin couldn't even hear her anymore, so deep was his attention to the book in his hands.

She went downstairs to their grandfather's kitchen and made him a cup of tea.

—from *Alvin Hatter and the Wild-Goose Chase*

8

I'd missed most days of school last week, and now that I was back in the swing of things, I couldn't help but notice how many people seemed interested in me. Abe too—when I saw him in the hallways, he was constantly surrounded by a small gathering of people I didn't recognize. I even saw someone handing him an Alvin book, but I turned away before I could figure out what they wanted. I would recognize those covers from miles away, from outer space, and I was mortified to think they might be asking Abe to sign it. Not like he would, of course.

I really, really hoped he wouldn't.

I got to my study period before anyone else and took a seat near the back. I took out *To the Lighthouse*, a book I was supposed to have finished last week (a bereavement absence gave many leniencies for missed assignments). I'd only read a paragraph before my phone buzzed.

The text was from Abe.

Meet me in the bathroom.

A weird text to get from your brother maybe, but I knew he meant the second-floor boys' bathrooms. They were kept locked and supposed to be only for teachers, but Abe was so well liked (and Aunt Helen was so recently deceased), I had a hunch he'd weaseled his way in.

I let the study hall teacher know where I was going, and then I made my way to the second floor. I knocked on the door to the bathrooms and waited—nothing. I knocked again. Then I called his phone and heard the buzzing from within.

"Open up!" I hissed when he answered.

The door opened a minute later, and he pulled me inside, locking the door behind me.

"Well, this is a nice surprise!" he said, leaning up against a sink like this was his private office. "How'd you know where to find me?"

"You literally just told me."

"Can't be too careful, though," he said.

"What do you want?"

"Just to see my sister. Is that a crime now?"

"Have you been to any classes today? You look pretty comfortable in here."

"Relax, I've been to all my classes. We just haven't gotten a chance to talk lately, and Mom possibly let it slip that the letters Harry gave you in his office were some kind of list from Aunt Helen? I was just curious."

"Oh."

I hadn't told my brother, hadn't told my father, had kind of given the Cliff's Notes version to my mom and Em and Sam. They still felt just too private a thing, too close to me.

I had the next one with me now, in my back pocket, waiting for the right moment. A chance to be alone. I'd gotten home late last night and didn't want to rush through it.

"They are, kind of. Lists. More like . . . things to do."

"Things to do."

"Like, going to the party. That was one of them."

"What else?"

"Different things. I think she just wanted to make sure I was okay. You know. When she knew she wouldn't be here."

"Oh," Abe said.

"What do you mean?"

"I just said oh."

"But you said it like it meant something."

"Well, it just makes sense."

"What makes sense?"

"Mom told me, you know, and it just made me wonder. Why she had left something like that to you and not to me."

"And now it makes sense?"

"Because she thought you would have needed it more."

"Oh." A track record of panic attacks and the kind of

anxiety that didn't let you sleep. Obviously people had known, my family had known, Em had known. But to hear it like that from my brother? It was just . . . something. I didn't know what it was.

"It's not a bad thing," Abe said quickly. "I shouldn't have said it like that."

"No, it's totally fine. It's just a thing. It's not a bad thing," I repeated. And it wasn't a secret, I reminded myself. One of the downsides of having such a close family: things weren't secret.

"I'm sorry. But you're doing so much better now, so probably she just wanted to check in with you."

"Yeah, probably," I said, thinking my aunt had probably not written twenty-four letters for the simple purpose of checking in with me.

"What are you supposed to do next?"

"I don't know; I haven't read the next letter yet."

"I'll go!"

"What?"

"This is perfect; nobody ever comes in here, so you'll have privacy. I'll go, and then we can just talk later, okay?"

I could tell Abe felt bad. He was practically tripping over himself to get out of the bathroom (four things he hated the most: hugs, confrontation, hurting people's feelings, and people who dog-eared the pages of books). I barely had time to say good-bye before he disappeared out the door.

Now that I was alone in the bathroom, though, I saw Abe's point. I had privacy, I had time, I had toilets: What else could I really ask for? I pulled myself up to sit on the row of sinks and started reading.

Lottie,

There are many different types of writing. Light-hearted, serious, believable, fantastical, political, romantical . . . I've spent my life writing about a little immortal boy and his sister, Margo, and I've had such a nice time doing it. Writing isn't for everyone. It takes a lot of time and a lot of effort. It takes a little bit of talent, but mostly it takes practice and determination. There's a saying, something about talent and work and the ratio of 10 percent to 90 percent, respectively. I agree with that completely. I've watched hugely talented (more talented than I, certainly) people do nothing at all with their writing, and I've watched people who can't write a proper sentence chug through it and patch together a story and go on to become a best-selling novelist (no names). You can see, then, how perseverance is really the key to any sort of success.

But aside from Alvin Hatter, I've really been writing all my life. You have my journals now (not quite time to read them yet) and my computer, and I really think I've written about a thousand times more words than I've actually seen published. That's a good thing. There's a lot of junk in my brain that needed to come out before the really good stuff could find its way.

So, something easy next:

Write in your journal, Lottie. You used to do it all the time, and I think it might be good for you.

Who knows, maybe you'll even discover your own immortal boy.

Love, H.

My first journal was a gift from Aunt Helen when I was eight years old. I filled it with glittery cat stickers and stick figure drawings and profound musings on the day, like: *Peter Garbo is an idiot* and *Abe eats his own boogers* and *If I could be any animal in the world it would be a cat with wings. Rainbow wings.*

When I had filled it up, I presented it to Aunt Helen proudly, and she pretended to be floored by my observations.

"This is great stuff, Lottie. Someday you'll look back on this and be happy you wrote it all down."

She bought me another one, and I went through two or three a year until I was fifteen and it suddenly felt like all the things I wanted to write about were too heavy for the paper. My anxiety was worse than ever, my brain was a treacherous place to navigate, and I thought those feelings might be better left trapped inside me than free to fill up a page.

So I piled the journals in a box in my closet.

I hadn't looked at them in years, but that night I took the last half-finished journal from the box and went into the attic, which was hot and stuffy but at least afforded the maximum amount of privacy, and I wrote.

Or—I tried to write.

My pen hung an inch or so above the paper, but I couldn't think of anything to do with it. Where there used to be words, there was now only a quiet kind of emptiness. My ears were fuzzy and ringing slightly, like how I imagined it would sound to be buried alive.

I'd been thinking a lot about death lately. About the many different ways a person could die.

I'd been doing so well keeping my anxiety under control, but then Aunt Helen had died, and it was like a flood had washed into my brain.

Now all I could think about was being buried alive and getting cancer and even the most obscure, unlikely deaths, like elevation sickness on Mount Everest and spontaneous human combustion.

I tried to focus on the blank page in front of me but instead of being comforted by that finite expanse of white, I imagined it stretching out to fill up the room, choking me in its blankness, taking over everything.

I closed my eyes and squeezed the pen tighter in my hand, and then I opened my eyes and wrote:

I miss Aunt Helen a lot.

And then:

I feel like I didn't do enough.

But what else could I have done? I wasn't a doctor, and even if I were, they said Aunt Helen's cancer was the type you couldn't cure.

So why did it feel like I was somehow to blame? Why did I find it so hard to forgive myself for something I had no control over?

I'm so sorry.
    I don't know why I'm sorry.
    But I am.
    I jumped off a cliff the other day and I thought it would be terrifying, but for the first time in a long time, all the worries just melted away. It was like I was suspended even as I was hurtling through the air. Like I found some kind of peace even as everything was screaming.
    Maybe that's the point. Maybe when things are fine, that's when I can't handle it. Maybe I mess up all the good things because my brain doesn't know how to process them.

Maybe I can only be truly happy when everything is hanging on by a thread.

I don't know. It's been a while since I've done this, and I'm not sure I'm making any sense. If you were here now I guess I would just try and make it really, really clear that I loved you.

And I don't know why I always feel so afraid.

I don't know how to calm down.

I don't know how to stop thinking about everybody dying, about Abe dying and Em dying and my parents dying and even people I don't know dying, people all over the world. I read that over 150,000 people die every single day, and I don't like that thought, all of those bodies just stopping throughout the day, going limp or dropping to the ground. We are going to run out of places to put them. We are going to need another Earth. We are going to have to figure out how to live on the moon.

I put the pen down again and closed my eyes so tightly that spots of light danced on the insides of my eyelids. Aunt Helen, I knew, wrote every single morning of her life, at her desk with a cup of coffee and her hair in a bun and sometimes still in pajamas. When I was younger I would sit underneath her desk with LEGO bricks or a coloring book, and the sound of her pens scratching across the paper would lull me into a calming trance.

"Are you writing more Alvin?" I'd say. Before I could

even read for myself, Alvin was read to me. The final book, the sixth book, ends unresolved. Alvin and Margo stand in front of their grandfather's burned-down house and absorb the knowledge that they have lost everyone; they are truly alone.

"I'm trying," she would always answer and peek down under the desk, smiling at me. "It's not coming very easily."

"They have to end up happily ever after," I'd say. "On an island."

"An island? Why an island?"

"That's a happy place to end up. Like, they had a really hard time and now they just get to relax."

"That's a nice idea," she'd say and go back to writing.

If only it were that easy. If only we all ended up on islands, our own private islands with nothing but sunshine and sea.

I thought Aunt Helen would have approved of that ending. At least more so than the one she got.

"Are you ready?" Alvin asked his sister. "This will kind of change everything."

They stood together in the foyer of the house in the woods, the house that had become their home, their safe place. Every so often, every few weeks, someone came to knock on its front door: more often than not a member of the Everlife Society. But Alvin and Margo gave no indication that they could even hear the knocking. And since no one could open the magic door except Alvin, eventually their unwanted guests left, discouraged, sometimes after walking around the house and trying various windows even though they must have known it wouldn't do any good. Sometimes their guests shouted things at them, not-nice things. Sometimes Margo threw tomatoes down at them from the second-story windows and the not-nice things turned into VERY not-nice things.

It wasn't much of a life, but it was a life. A safe, quiet life. They played board games and read books about magic, and Margo became very good at braiding her own hair.

And now they were faced with leaving it all.

Now they had decided to leave it all.

Because living safely wasn't the most important thing in the world.

Not when their parents were still out there and still needed their help.

"I'm ready," Margo said, impressive resolve settling on her face.

Alvin put his hand on the enchanted doorknob, the one that would only open for him, and pulled.

—from *Margo Hatter Lives Forever*

9

The things we had picked out from Aunt Helen's were delivered while I was in the attic. I came downstairs to a small mountain of boxes in our foyer.

"My eldest returns!" Dad said, hugging me harder than he needed to. "Where were you anyway, out somewhere? I checked your room."

"I was doing stuff."

"Ah, stuff. The mysterious stuff of youths," he said, winking.

He was in a good mood, probably because he'd taken Aunt Helen's long-lusted-after pool table, and I guessed it was already set up in the basement. It was nice to see him in a good mood anyway. It was nice to see him smile.

My mom was unpacking boxes, unwrapping Aunt Helen's footed teacup collection from layers and layers of tissue paper. I spent the next half hour moving my own boxes to my bedroom. When I was done I sat on my bed and looked at them. Some days it was harder than others, and this day had been like a hundred tiny battles one after another.

I thought of Sam, for some reason. I hadn't talked to him since Mason's Island, our pizza by the water. I texted him now:

I had a really nice time the other day.

His reply came later. I'd opened one box—Aunt Helen's photo albums. I stacked them neatly on the bottom shelf of my bookcase, and then I changed my mind and stacked them neatly back in the box, not yet ready to relive the memories she'd chosen to capture and stick inside them. My phone buzzed on my bureau, and I stretched to get it.

We should get together again sometime. If you want.

I didn't answer right away. It was late, and I changed into pajamas and then washed my face and brushed my teeth. I covered up the boxes with one of the blankets from my bed. It almost looked like a fort, like the kind Abe and I used to build with couch cushions and pillows. I got into bed and opened the next envelope from Aunt Helen.

Lottie,

I've been thinking about writing since I finished my last letter to you.

I always imagined I would write something truly

incredible, something one could appropriately call THE NEXT GREAT AMERICAN NOVEL. It's hard sometimes, writing silly children's stories about immortal children and societies of corrupt magic-keepers. You begin to think you aren't putting anything important into the world. So many times I tried and failed to write something that fulfilled this idea of IMPORTANCE, but then one tiny, brief encounter showed me just how stupid I'd been. I was in the park, just having a stroll, and a young mother came up to me. She had a little boy with her, a darling little boy of six or seven. The mother recognized me from a TV show, some interview, and she brought the boy up and said, "This is the lady who writes the stories about Alvin and Margo." His face just lit up, and he said, so excited, "You're friends with Margo?" His mother told me in a whisper that his first word—his very first word!—had been Margo. It broke my heart and then mended it up again all in one second. I thought to myself: this is important. This is big. This is enough.

So here's your next task, Lottie. On my computer you will find a file called **MARGOT HATTER LIVES FOREVER**. Yes—it is indeed the conclusion to the Alvin Hatter series (I thought Margo, for a change, ought to take center stage). Please deliver this to my agent. She's in New York, and her name is Wendy Brooks. You'll find her online. Yes, you must go in *person. She'll be thrilled to meet you, and I think you might find a little road trip provides a lovely distraction in times of sadness.*

And yes, sometimes those thoughts come back, those nagging thoughts of IMPORTANCE and ACCOMPLISHING SOMETHING BIG and all that.

But I think if even one immortal boy has identified with Alvin's struggles, it will have all been worth it.

Love, H.

Holy shit.

Another Alvin Hatter book? People were going to go crazy. She had said she was done with them, that she didn't have any more Hatter stories in her, and now this. And she wouldn't even be here to see its reception.

I googled Wendy Brooks on my phone and found her easily. Her office was in lower Manhattan, on Broadway.

My aunt's computer was somewhere in these boxes. I took the fort apart and searched until I found it, a skinny laptop in a gray padded sleeve. I took it to my bed and opened it, and there, on the desktop, was a file called *Margo Hatter Lives Forever*.

I opened it up immediately and scrolled past the title page to the dedication.

To S.W. For all those years.

And for all the years I'll never get.

S.W.? I had no idea who that could be. The last six Hatter books had been dedicated to my dad, my grandparents, Abe, Wendy, my mom, and me. Probably it was someone else my aunt had known in the writing world.

A new Hatter book!

It was the best possible news.

I could go to New York this weekend, on Saturday. I could ask Em to go with me—but she had a track meet in the middle of the day at some school an hour away from here. And I knew Abe and Amy were planning on a sort-of-cute/sort-of-nauseating marathon of John Hughes movies.

And there wasn't really anyone else I felt like going with.

Unless . . .

But that was kind of weird.

It was weird to ask a guy you'd just met to go to New York with you, right?

But I guess I was in a weird mood. I picked up my phone and texted Sam:

Do you want to go to New York on Saturday?

Almost immediately:

Yes!

I set the phone on my nightstand. I turned the light off.

And then, in the dark, I stayed up for hours and hours.

For Margo and Alvin's last adventure.

I woke up Saturday before my alarm, filled with excitement about the trip to the city. I saved the Hatter file to a flash drive and put it into my purse and took a shower as the sun was dawning.

It had only been a few days since I'd learned about the last Alvin and Margo book, but I hadn't told anyone yet. It was nice to have it just be my secret—I was the only person in the entire world who had read *Margo Hatter Lives Forever*! It was thrilling, like the biggest, most important kind of secret. But it was finally time to share it.

I found Mom and Dad having coffee in the kitchen, and I placed Aunt Helen's computer on the table between them.

Dad looked at the computer, then at me, confused.

"Who's this?" Dad asked Mom.

"It looks a lot like our daughter," she replied.

"Our daughter, Lottie?"

"We only have one."

"And what time is it?"

"It's eight, Sal."

"And what day is it?"

"It's Saturday, Sal."

"That's what I thought."

"I'm going to New York," I said.

"You're going to New York? For what? With who?" Mom asked.

"This is huge, okay?" I said, sitting down at the table. "I have something huge to tell you."

"Oh no," Mom said.

"What?" I asked.

"I don't know. It seems like nothing good ever follows 'I have something huge to tell you' on a Saturday morning at eight o'clock."

"Well, this is good. This is huge." I put my hand on the laptop. "It's another Alvin Hatter book."

Mom's mouth fell open slightly, and Dad looked like he hadn't heard me.

"No," he said.

"Yeah. She wrote another book, and she wants me to bring it to her agent."

"Holy crap," Mom said.

"And it's good. I read it."

Dad looked dazed, but like he was slowly getting it. I watched as an enormous grin spread across his face. He laughed and said, "I knew it! I knew *Alvin Hatter and the Return of the Overcoat Man* couldn't be the last of the story! This is amazing! This is great! When do we get to read it?"

"It's all here," I said, patting the laptop. "Enjoy."

I got up from the table and kissed them both, then filled a Thermos with coffee and drank it while I drove, the windows down and the music loud and happy and warm.

Sam and I had agreed to meet at the train station in Mystic at nine thirty. That way we could take the train into the city and not have to worry about driving and traffic in Manhattan.

He was already there when I pulled into the parking lot,

sitting on a bench and drinking a coffee. He waved when he saw me and walked over to meet me.

"So what's this all about?" he asked as I stepped out of the car.

"You're not going to believe it," I said. "She wrote another Hatter book! It's going to be published! We're taking it to her agent right now."

Sam leaned against my car. "Wow."

"I know, right?"

"I always knew there had to be something! That ending—standing in front of their grandfather's house, I mean, that couldn't be the end for them. Wait—did you read it? Tell me they find their parents! Tell me they finally defeat the Overcoat Man! You have to tell me!"

Sam was like a little kid, bouncing up and down on the balls of his feet and tugging the bottom of my shirt.

"I will tell you no such thing," I said, pushing past him and heading to the booth to buy my ticket.

"Wait!" he said. I turned around. He was holding two tickets. "I'll give this to you if you tell me what happens."

"I can't tell you what happens. It would be dishonest."

"Did she tell you not to tell anybody?"

"No, but . . . I just know I can't tell you. It has to be a secret. I don't know if I can trust you yet."

He looked legitimately devastated, but he handed me my ticket anyway. "Here," he mumbled.

"You didn't have to buy this! Thank you."

"I'm sad you won't tell me what happens."

"I know. But you'll read it for yourself soon enough."

He seemed resolved to his fate and only pouted a little while we waited on the platform for the 10:04 train to Penn Station. I couldn't remember the last time I'd been on a train; when I'd gone to the city with Aunt Helen, we always drove. I was wide awake with excitement and the coffee I'd drunk in the car. I was almost shaking with the anticipation of delivering the manuscript. And I'd brought Aunt Helen's next letter, because I had a hunch it would have something to do with New York.

The train arrived a few minutes early, and we found seats in the back, across from each other, our knees almost touching.

I thought of the flash drive in my purse and how Aunt Helen hadn't told anyone she'd written another book, hadn't even told us she was working on something. Then I thought about what my dad had said, about how it felt like Aunt Helen was always hiding something.

I knew what he meant.

Sometimes I caught her staring at a window, and I knew she was watching something that wasn't happening in front of her, but on another plane or another planet or another world.

Sometimes I'd ask her questions, easy questions, like, "Do you ever wish you'd done something other than write?" and instead of answering like normal, she'd get very serious and quiet and say something weird like, "There are always things we wish we'd done differently."

Sometimes I would look at her and see a shadow over her face, a shadow caused by nothing, something she had that I could never find on anyone else.

Except Sam.

Sam had the same kind of shadow. It moved when he moved. It disappeared in bright light. It followed him everywhere.

"You're seeing auras," Em said once, when I tried to explain it to her. "You're like a psychic. But not a predict-the-future psychic. More like a gut-feeling-woman's-intuition psychic."

I didn't think it was like that at all.

In front of me, Sam shifted in his seat, and his knee brushed against mine. The train jerked a little, and my brain immediately flew to track fires, derailments.

Getting hit by a train would be a great way to go. Messy, of course, but quick and painless.

Being in a train crash, on the other hand . . . I needed to do more research about that. I didn't know any of the statistics. But it was probably like a car crash, a toss-up of whether you lived or died or got seriously hurt. It could be painful.

"It's all right. It's supposed to do that," Sam said.

"Oh, I know. I was just thinking."

It was three hours to Penn Station, and the first thing we did was buy pretzels from a street vendor. Sam dipped his into mustard and made me try it and then let me finish all of his when I kept looking at it. The day was perfect—breezy and warm and exactly like how a good New York day should feel.

"Let's walk," I said.

"What's the address again?"

"Broadway. By Fulton Street."

"Right, that's about fifty streets away from here."

"I don't want to ride the subway. Look how beautiful it is!"

"We can walk until we get tired," he compromised. "And then we'll get a cab."

But we walked the entire way. Fifty blocks, talking about everything from our favorite books (Sam had read every single book I mentioned and then some. He said he was a fast reader; I said I didn't know how he had done it without decades of free time on his hands) to our favorite bands to our favorite subjects in school to what we wanted to do when we graduated. I felt a strangeness at that, an almost undetectable hesitation on his part. He said he didn't like to think too far in the future.

"What about you?" he asked.

"I'm going to the University of Connecticut. For elementary school education."

"A teacher, huh? Like your aunt."

"She would have liked being referred to as a teacher," I said. "Most people only saw her as a writer."

"I get that. But she was the best college-level teacher I've ever had."

"Wait—how many college teachers have you had?"

"Oh, I audit a lot," Sam said, maybe blushing a little, pretending to be very interested in a nearby skyscraper.

"How do you have the time? Isn't that so much work?"

"I like learning," he replied, then laughed a little. "Was that the nerdiest response ever?"

"Absolutely. What other types of classes have you audited?"

"Oh, just a handful. Like, um . . . English Literature, Irish Literature, Middle Eastern Literature . . . Poetry, Creative Writing, Advanced Mathematics, Woodworking."

"Woodworking?"

"I'll whittle you a flute if you want."

"You are truly a jack-of-all-trades."

"I just like to keep busy."

"Seriously, that's impressive. I suddenly feel embarrassed for all the TV I watch."

"It's not that impressive," he insisted.

"And modest too. Is there anything you can't do?"

He thought for a minute, then said, "I can't write in cursive. I've taken a class and everything. I just can't make all those little loops."

"A true tragedy."

"Tell me about it. My signature looks like a four-year-old's."

We'd reached Wendy Brooks's office building: a sky-scraper close to the Freedom Tower. We told the doorman our names and no, she wasn't expecting us. He phoned up to her, then waved us toward the elevators. I was nervous. Should we have made an appointment? Should I have emailed her? But my aunt told me to just show up. I hoped Wendy didn't mind.

When the elevator doors opened, she was standing in the hallway with her hands clasped tightly and her hair in a lopsided bun. She hugged me before I'd even stepped off the elevator, clutching me tightly before holding me at arm's length to look at me.

"Lottie. I've heard so much about you," she said. "I wanted to meet you at your aunt's party, but there were so many people there, and the food, and the drinks—by the time I remembered to look for you, I think you'd already gone."

"I'm happy we're meeting each other now," I said, taking the flash drive out of my pocket. "I have something for you."

She took a tiny step back as I held it out to her.

"It isn't," she said.

"It is," I said.

"It can't be."

"She asked me to bring it to you."

She reached out to take it but then withdrew her fingers. "I love these books so much. I loved your aunt so much."

"I know. She wouldn't have trusted this with anyone else."

"Have you read it?" she asked. She still hadn't taken it. Her fingers were outstretched and shaking.

"Yeah. It's really good."

"Is it better than *Alvin Hatter and the Mysterious Disappearance*? That was always my favorite one."

"It's better than all of them. Honestly. It's the best one."

"I knew it couldn't be over," she said. She took the flash drive finally. "So many people are going to love this book. Thank you for bringing it to me."

"Don't thank me," I said. "Thank her."

And then we were quiet. Because, more than anything, we wanted to. We wanted to be able to thank her. And we couldn't.

"Here, I made these for you," Grandpa Hatter said, pushing a plate of impeccably decorated pink-and-white frosted cupcakes toward Margo. She stared at them as if not sure whether she would eat them or they would eat her.

"You made these?" she repeated after a moment of silence. "You made these pink cupcakes?"

"You're not a very nice child," he said.

"No, no! They look really good! I just didn't know you baked."

"I bake, I cook, I do whatever I want, okay? You either want them or you don't. I don't care either way. The garbage can is right over there."

He gave the plate another push and busied himself with other things in the kitchen, drying an already-dry glass, wiping an already-clean counter. Margo couldn't help but feel like he was waiting for her to take a bite. So she did.

"Oh, wow," she said.

"Do you like them?" Grandpa Hatter asked, suddenly in front of her again, his face lit up in an expression she could only describe as utmost hopefulness.

"They're REALLY good," she said, her mouth still full.

"Oh, you're just saying that," he said, batting the air, looking about as pleased as she had ever seen him look before.

—from *Alvin Hatter and the Mysterious Disappearance*

10

Wendy's office was crammed with children's books, a floor-to-ceiling library of anything and everything worth reading. She made tea for Sam and me, and she read the first chapter of the new book aloud while we burned our tongues and were quiet and listened to Margo tell us about her brother's deep depression, about their new lives living in the house in the middle of the woods (the safest place for them, as the Overcoat Man could not enter it), about her haphazard plans to make them some money so they could eat.

"Oh, they simply *have* to find their parents," Wendy said, finishing the first chapter and closing her laptop. "It's been such a long journey for them. They need their happy ending."

"She won't tell me," Sam said. "She says I have to wait for the book."

"And she's right! You have to find out for yourself, or

it won't mean anything." Wendy took a sip of her tea and put her hand on her laptop. "I can't thank you enough for bringing this to me. I've been having such a hard time. She was one of my best friends."

"And you've been her agent for all six books, right?" I asked.

"Seven!" Wendy corrected me, the smile on her face so wide that it became infectious in turn. "Going on seventeen years, if you can believe it." She looked somewhere over the tops of our heads, lost in thought, then turned conspiratorial and whispered, "Did you know—I talked her out of calling him the Seersucker Jacket Man."

"No . . . ," Sam said.

"She had a thing with seersucker; I can't explain it," Wendy insisted, laughing now, pulling her laptop toward her as if it held the very reincarnated soul of my aunt.

Which . . . I mean, sort of, kind of, it did.

"Ah, this is going to stir things up. This is going to stir things up very nicely," Wendy said, still patting the laptop, still laughing. "And don't worry," she continued, "they'll want to rush this. It won't be long at all. I'll call the publisher the moment I've finished it."

"How long do you think it will take?"

"Oh, a few months—basically the blink of an eye in the publishing world. And I'll make sure you're the very first one to get a copy. I know that's what your aunt would have wanted."

"Thank you."

"Don't thank me, are you kidding? Thank *you*!" she said, lifting herself out of her chair and coming around the side of the desk to hug me again. "This is the best day I've had since she told me the prognosis. The best day I've had in a very long time."

Sam and I left Wendy to read the rest of the book ("I'll be in touch so soon! I'm a very fast reader!"), and I opened the envelope on the sidewalk outside. Sam pretended to be very interested in a map of the subway that someone had discarded on the sidewalk, allowing me some privacy that I very much appreciated.

> *Lottie,*
>
> *I love that you always loved New York as much as I do. It is a place unlike any other. I have been to many cities in my lifetime, and I have loved all of them for different reasons. But New York—well, it has an energy and a history that buzz together and sweep you up and move you along at a breakneck pace, just excited to be alive and among its streets. And we share a little secret, New York and I, one that I'm slowly preparing myself to share with you.*
>
> *And there is always something new to explore. Here is something we never did together: the Freedom Tower. It is just a short walk from Wendy's office. Go to the top, Lottie. Sometimes it helps to see things*

from a different perspective. (My apologies if you're already back in Connecticut, but I imagine you're barely out of Wendy's office. I hope she's well. I hope you liked the book.)

Love, H.

Another mention of a secret.

(Was this the point of the letters, Aunt Helen? A big reveal?)

I told Sam where we were going. He was excited—he walked a few steps ahead of me, leading the way to the building's entrance, but I hung back a little. I didn't love heights to begin with, and this building stretched too high into the sky, twisting and reaching into the clouds.

Falling off a building—providing it is a very high building—is sure to result in death. The downsides are: very messy, a fair amount of time to consider your imminent landing, and the danger of taking someone else with you, just minding their business on the sidewalk below.

"We'll stay away from the edge," Sam said, taking my hand for just a brief second before we pushed through the revolving doors and into the lobby. "They have barriers anyway," he continued as we waited in line to purchase our elevator tickets.

"I don't even know what you're talking about. I don't even care."

"Right. So you've turned completely pale because . . . you're scared of elevators?"

I actually didn't love elevators either, but I could deal with them. Elevator crashes were rare, but they posed the same risks as falling off a building: if it were a short enough trip, it would hurt a lot.

"I'm not scared of elevators," I muttered.

"Are you scared of ticket lines?"

"I'm not scared of anything," I said as we reached the window. We paid for our tickets and then took our place in the elevator line.

"That's impressive. I'm scared of plenty of things."

"Like what?"

"Like mustard. I really don't like mustard."

"You just ate mustard. With your pretzel."

"Oh, right. Well—I think the best way to get over your fears is to confront them."

"Ah, is that it?"

"Okay. I'll tell you something I'm really afraid of if you tell me something you're afraid of," he said, turning to face me.

"I'll tell you at the top." It would give me enough time to work up the nerve.

We reached the front of the line and stepped into the elevator with a small group of other people. I started counting when the doors clicked shut; I didn't get to forty before we reached the top.

"These are the fastest elevators in the Western Hemisphere," I heard a dad tell his kids, who looked thoroughly

unimpressed with their dad's elevator trivia. "We just traveled two thousand feet a minute!"

"Planes go faster," his son said, shrugging.

"Do cars go faster? Cars probably go faster," his daughter added.

We filed out of the elevator and into a wide-open space
surrounded by massive windows. My stomach flipped as
I saw New York spread out all around me. Every single
person took out their phone or camera or iPad and started
taking pictures of the view. I walked as close to the glass as
I could without starting to feel dizzy.

"See," Sam said, pointing. "Barriers."

I remembered hearing a story about a man who had
thrown himself off the top of the Empire State Building a
few years ago. They didn't have windows there; they had
fences. He had run and jumped and climbed up and over
before anyone could stop him.

I will never, ever understand suicide.

If anything, I would understand the exact opposite.
Locking yourself up in a hermetically sealed bubble for
all eternity. Forsaking friends and family to ensure a life
free of disease and germs and bacteria. Taking every possible measure to preserve what little time we're given on
this planet. I completely understand why Margo Hatter,
only minutes after her and her brother had broken into the
house in the middle of the woods, had picked up a dusty
glass bottle with a little label that said Everlife Formula

and drank it without another thought. Boom. Immortality with only the faintest bit of an aftertaste.

I don't ever want to die.

I saw my aunt die.

I don't know why anyone would want that.

Being so far above the city was beautiful, sure, but more than anything it made me think of all the people down below and all the terrible things that could happen to any one of them. I wished we could pause it all. I wished we could rest; I wished we could relax. But we couldn't ever relax. We had to constantly fight to protect ourselves.

"A really, really long time ago, I made a terrible mistake," Sam said. "That's what I'm most afraid of. That I can't go back and fix it."

It took me a minute to remember what he was talking about.

I looked over at him. His hair was in a low ponytail, and he bit his lower lip and looked faraway and lost, and it made me feel protective of him. I felt protective of everyone sometimes, but with Sam it was almost frantic. I didn't know why. I just did.

"Death," I said. "That's the only thing I'm scared of."

After the Freedom Tower, we walked up to Bleeker Street and stood in line for cupcakes at Magnolia Bakery.

"This is the line for cupcakes?" Sam asked, craning his

neck to see past the line of people and into the small bakery.

"These cupcakes are worth the wait, trust me."

We hadn't talked any more about the things we were afraid of. We walked around the perimeter of the Freedom Tower, and I'd sent a photo to my mom (her response: *looks nice, be safe, can't talk, reading the new book!!!*), and then we rode the elevator back down and it felt too much like falling for my taste. It felt too out of control.

It was good to be back on the ground, back outside, and it even felt good to be waiting in line on one of my favorite streets in the city. That old Simon & Garfunkel song played quietly in my head, and I started humming it without meaning to. Then Sam started humming it, and I tried to remember the lyrics to sing along, but I couldn't think of them.

"I haven't heard that song in a long time," he said.

"It's a sad song," I said. "I remember something about clouds."

"All songs can be happy or sad. It just depends on how you look at them. It depends on how you want to feel when you listen to them."

"Lucky for us, cupcakes can only be happy."

"Are you going to get a happy chocolate cupcake or a happy vanilla cupcake?"

"I'm going to get a happy vanilla cupcake, and then you should get chocolate, and we should cut them in half and sew them back up with their opposites, and then we'll have the best of both worlds."

"That is a truly remarkable cupcake strategy. I can tell you've done this before."

"One or two times."

We ate our doctored cupcakes on the front stoop of a brownstone. I ate mine so that every bite was chocolate and vanilla. Sam ate his chocolate first, then vanilla. He closed his eyes after the first bite.

"I told you," I said.

"Wow."

"They're good cupcakes."

"I mean . . ."

"I know. You don't have to say anything."

It was getting later, but I didn't want to go back to the train. I didn't want to go back to Connecticut. I wanted this day to last forever. I wanted time to behave for just once. I imagined an oversized remote control: a button to pause, a button to stop. A button to rewind, so Sam and I could sit on a stranger's front steps and eat cupcakes forever, and whenever we reached the end we could do it all over again. I would never get bored with this.

"We better get a cab," Sam said. "The last train leaves at seven."

"We could miss it?" I suggested.

Sam laughed. "You're a bad influence, Lottie Reaves."

We hailed a cab on the corner of Bleecker and Eleventh Street, and we rolled the backseat windows down to get as much of the New York air as we could before we had to leave it.

"One day I could move here," I said while we waited for our train.

"Not here, I hope. Grand Central is much nicer."

I laughed. "You know what I mean. I could get an apartment on Bleecker Street. I could eat lunch in Washington Square Park. I could teach at a school on the East River."

"You could do whatever you want," Sam said, and at first it was nice but then it faded into something sad, something darker. "You have your whole life ahead of you."

"Well, so do you," I said.

The dark look got a little darker.

"Is something wrong?" I asked when we'd settled into our seats and the train started barreling back toward home.

"Nothing. I had fun today; I'm glad you invited me."

"Then why do you look so sad?"

He looked out the window for a long time. "Remember when we were talking about the things we're most afraid of? I guess this is one of them. . . . That the good things in life: friendships, trips, trains, the fastest elevators in the Western Hemisphere . . . none of it can last."

"Damn," I said.

"Sorry. I didn't mean to . . ."

"No, it's fine. I want to tell you that you're wrong and that life is a blessing and you're going to have time to do all the things you want to do and then you're going to be ready when it's all over, but you're right. It sucks. It almost makes you wonder why we bother doing anything."

We were sitting across from each other again. Sam took my hand for three seconds and then let go.

"You remind me of someone," he said.

"Who?"

"Someone who was a lot smarter than I am."

"There's always someone smarter than you," I said. "The sooner you accept that, the sooner you stop trying to be right about everything."

"Wise words, Lottie," he said.

I didn't tell him I'd heard them from Aunt Helen, because for some reason I got the feeling he knew.

I got home close to midnight and the only person still awake was Abe, reading a book in his favorite armchair in the living room. I sat on the ottoman across from him and said, "Have you ever had one of those days where you keep repeating in your head: *This is important. Remember this. Remember all of this.*"

He put the book down on his lap and thought about it. "When Dad taught me how to drive. When we snuck onto the track to see the meteor shower. When I met Amy."

"So you know what I mean, then."

"Of course I know what you mean. Why? What happened today? Mom and Dad told me about the last Hatter book. Is that it?"

"It's that, it's everything. It's these letters, it's this guy . . ."

"The guy from the party?"

"You saw him?"

"I saw him from a distance. Very nice hair. Good dancer."

"He went to New York with me."

"Did you have fun?"

"We had fun. But I feel like there's something he's not telling me."

"Like what?"

"I don't know. I don't think it's necessarily a bad thing. There's just . . . something."

"Well, you have good intuition, Lottie, so I bet there *is* something he isn't telling you. It's probably not a big deal. Oh, like maybe he has a third nipple?"

"Like Chandler?"

"Good reference." Abe yawned exaggeratedly and stood up. "I'm exhausted. Mom and Dad were hogging Aunt Helen's computer all day, so I didn't even get to read it. Is it good? Do they find their parents? Do they really live forever?"

"Abe, holy shit. It's so, so good. And I'm not telling you anything."

Abe rolled his eyes and pushed past me. "I'll find out for myself."

"That's the point," I whispered after him.

I got ready for bed and checked my phone once I was under the covers. There was an email from Wendy (I'd given her my contact info before we left her office):

Lottie. Oh my gosh. I just finished the book for the second time. I haven't even left my office all day. What a marvel. WHAT A MARVEL. I'll be in touch soon. This is amazing, and it's all thanks to you.

It wasn't really thanks to me, though. I didn't write it. I had only followed my aunt's instructions. I was just the messenger.

My phone buzzed in my hand. A text from Sam:

I had such a great day. I can't stop smiling.

It had been a week since he'd introduced himself to me at Aunt Helen's party, a few days since we ate pizza by the ocean and lay down together on the grass to watch the clouds, a few hours since we stood at the top of the Freedom Tower and told each other our greatest fears.

I wrote back:

Me too. I hope I see you soon.

Then I picked up the next envelope from my bedside table and tore it open.

Lottie,

How was the view from up high? I hope you are back safe now, in bed or on the couch, tired after a long day but somewhere warm and comfortable. It is one thing to crawl into bed after a normal day, but it is another thing to crawl into bed after an adventure—that's the best kind of sleep, the still-excited, still-buzzing kind of sleep where dreams blur into reality and it's almost like the sleeping and waking worlds blur and become one.

Here is something easy, something that may lead you to an interesting discovery. A long while ago I let someone borrow a book that was very important to me. It was never returned. I'd like you to have it, because I have a feeling it will be important to you too. But you'll have to do some digging. Ask for Leonard at Magic Grooves. It's a very fun store that I think you'll enjoy. I mean—I hope you've enjoyed all of this so far. There is so much more to come.

—H.

I opened the maps app in my phone and searched for Magic Grooves. Only one possible location popped up, in Groton, Connecticut. The description said it was a record store.

I texted Em:

Another errand tmrw?

She wrote back almost immediately:

Yes, yes OK. I'll come over early. <3

I put my phone down on my nightstand. Then I grabbed the nearest Alvin book—*Alvin Hatter and the Mysterious Disappearance*—and started reading it all over again.

"The Overcoat Man didn't die?" Alvin asked quietly.

"What's worse," A. said, "is that you left him alone in the house in the woods. He has access to EVERYTHING. We have no idea what magical secrets he's stolen!"

"A., calm yourself," E. scolded.

"It wasn't OUR fault," Margo spat. "He was trying to kill us, remember? How about a 'congratulations on not ending up dead'?"

"Of course," E. said. "We are all very happy about that." He paused again, looking from Margo to Alvin as if just now noticing how tired they looked, how pronounced the circles under their eyes had become, how pale their skin was. "We are being incredibly insensitive; you both need rest. We'll continue this discussion in the morning."

He and A. left the room presently.

Alvin paced a tight circle on the rug while Margo sat heavily on the bed, arms crossed.

After a minute, and with a smile on his face, Alvin said, "'Congratulations on not ending up dead'? You do know that isn't really an overachievement for us, right?"

"Well, they don't know that," Margo snapped. "Stupid society with their stupid names. Whoever heard of a woman called A.?"

"It's for privacy. They don't trust us yet, obviously."

"Well, I don't trust them either," Margo said.

And even though the Everlife Society might be their best shot at finding their parents, Alvin wasn't sure he trusted them either.

—from *Alvin Hatter and the Everlife Society*

11

"Where are we going this time?" Em asked. We were in my kitchen, dividing a pot of coffee between two Thermoses.

"Back to the shore," I said, dumping cream in each thermos and stirring them with a long spoon.

"I haven't seen the ocean this much since . . . I don't know. I'm not complaining."

"Have you heard of a music store called Magic Grooves?"

"Magic Grooves!" Abe exclaimed, walking into the kitchen, his eyes still puffy with sleep. "Love that place."

"You've been there?"

"I used to go with Aunt Helen. Is there no more coffee?"

"I'll make some more," I said, getting the grinder back down from the cabinet.

"I like music stores," Em said.

"Oh, this is the greatest. Are you guys going? Can I go? They still sell vinyl and cassettes. Like, *cassettes*. When was the last time you saw a tape?"

"Aw, someone made a mixtape for me once. It was sweet but, like, bittersweet. I had no way to play it, and I had to tell him I was a lesbian," Em said.

"Joshy Fredericks?" I asked.

"Joshy Fredericks," she replied. "I wonder how he's doing."

"He went to juvie for attempting to shoplift a five-thousand-dollar necklace from a mall jewelry store," Abe said, his mouth full of toast.

"Hey, that's my breakfast!" I said.

"You drank all the coffee."

"I'm making more," I said, scooping whole beans into the grinder, fitting the cap in place, and turning it on.

"What even makes toast so good?" Em mused, leaning back against the counter. She held a piece in her hand and turned it over. "It's just bread. Hot bread."

"Hot Bread would be an excellent name for a band," Abe pointed out.

"A five-thousand-dollar necklace. I don't buy it. Mall jewelry stores don't stock shit like that," Em said.

I dumped the ground coffee beans into the French press and poured boiling water from the electric kettle over them. "Some of them do. The nicer ones."

"Let me get dressed. I can come, right? Or is this a girl

thing? Whatever, I'm coming."

Abe went back upstairs, and Em and I ate toast standing up, not bothering with butter or jam, even though I'd put both on the counter already.

"So how was New York?" Em asked, trying not to sound that interested but pretty much failing.

"Do you mean 'how was Sam?'"

"Oh, did he . . . I totally forgot. Did he go with you?"

"You're funny. Yes, he went with me, and we had a really good time."

"Like . . . a *really* good time?"

"If you're asking whether we made out at the top of the Freedom Tower, the answer is no."

"Bummer. That would have been romantic."

"Nobody in the world likes making out as much as you do, I swear."

"Well, it's nice. It's not my fault you've taken a vow of celibacy or whatever."

"I haven't taken a vow of anything. There's just nobody at our school I can see myself making out with at the top of a tower. Or anywhere."

"That's fair. We do have some slim pickings."

"I always figured I'd get to college and have more options."

"But now you see a light at the end of the tunnel . . . And the light's name is Sam. . . ."

"I didn't say that either."

"Okay, whatever. But you had fun?"

"I had a lot of fun, yeah. He's easy to be around. It's like you, in guy form, with less snarky comments."

"Huh. And he lives in Mystic, right?"

"Yeah."

"And we're going to a record store in Groton?"

"Yeah."

"Which is right next to Mystic . . ."

"You want to meet him?"

"Of course I want to meet him! I have to check out the guy who's stolen your stone-cold heart."

"He hasn't stolen my . . . Okay. I'll see if he's around," I said, pulling out my phone. I sent him a short text, and he wrote back right away:

Definitely! Text me when you get here.

"What did he say?" Em asked.

"He said, 'Is your drunk friend going to be there?'"

"He did not."

"He did not. He said okay. I guess we're hanging out."

"Wow. And you went to New York with him. Wow. This is huge. You're, like, getting married."

I handed Em another piece of toast because she couldn't talk with food in her mouth.

When Abe was dressed, we took the Thermoses of coffee and the remaining toast and got in my car. We drove with the windows down and the music up, and Abe and Em had a long conversation about the merits of vinyl versus digital and whether there was a point at all to preserving history like that and only when I got off the exit for Groton did I ask Abe if he knew where the store was. He directed me the rest of the way, and we took side streets to get to a little shack-like structure on a little street in the middle of nowhere. The small parking lot was crowded with cars and a faded sign on the building said Magic Grooves.

"This place looks interesting," Em said.

"It looks like Championship Vinyl," I said.

"Excellent reference. This place is famous," Abe declared, getting out of the car. "People come from all around to get their albums here. They even do concerts in the back, record release parties. It's the real deal."

I texted Sam before I got out of the car:

We're in Groton. Magic Grooves.

The inside of the store was dark and dusty and kind of perfect, exactly the sort of place I could imagine spending hours sorting through old musty records. I mean—I would have preferred if they were books. But still.

Abe and Em drifted off to lose themselves in the stacks, and I approached the man behind the counter. He was in his early thirties, with short brown hair that swooped to one side, a flannel shirt (the store was air conditioned significantly), and small, round, wire-framed glasses. He looked approachable and friendly—even doing paperwork, he had a smile on his face. When he saw me he looked up, and it grew even larger.

"Hi!" he said. "Can I help you find something?"

Every movie or book I'd seen or read that featured a record store like this had pretentious, miserable people manning it. I was happy that wasn't the case here.

"You're not Leonard, are you?" I asked.

"That's me! What can I do for you?"

"I think you knew my aunt. Helen Reaves?"

"Oh man," he said, his face darkening instantly. "Professor Reaves. Of course I knew her. She was your aunt? I was so sorry to hear the news."

"You were one of her students?"

"Years ago. Eight years, maybe? Best class I ever took. She was so good at explaining what she wanted you to know. It was like she was just an open book, just blowing all her knowledge over the class. Wow, that's a terrible analogy. She would have flunked me for that," Leonard said, smiling again, pushing his glasses up the bridge of his nose.

"Actually, speaking of books . . . I'm supposed to get one from you. She said she lent you one and she never got it back?"

"What a memory! Eight years later . . . Of course I still have it. It's at my house, though. I can call my girlfriend and have her bring it over. She's home now."

"Oh, she doesn't need to do that. I can wait until you close up, maybe?"

"It's really no problem. She was going to meet me here

anyway. I'll give her a call."

"Thanks, Leonard. I'll wait outside."

"Anything for Professor Reaves," he responded.

I joined Abe and Em in the back of the store. They were silently browsing bins next to each other, serious looks on their faces.

"His girlfriend is bringing the book. I'm going to get some air," I said. Abe grunted in reply. Em shrugged.

I made my way through the store and out the door. Remembering what Abe said about concerts in the back, I walked around the building to see a tiny raised platform and a dozen or so folding chairs spread in a loose semicircle around it. I wondered if Leonard owned the store or only worked here. I wondered whose dream it had been to open a record store in the middle of nowhere, to hold concerts where only a few people could attend.

"I saw Conor Oberst here," a voice said behind me— Sam, sitting on a folding chair, admiring the stage. "It doesn't look like much now, but they turn on all these fairy lights and there are candles and everyone is so happy to be here. It's like you're watching something really special."

"I can't picture it," I said, sitting next to him.

"It's one of those things. You have to see it for yourself. But the shows are never announced more than an hour or two in advance, so there's a little bit of luck to it. You have to be in the right place at the right time."

"It sounds really nice."

"It was one of the best shows I've ever seen. And I've seen a lot."

"There aren't a lot of concert venues near me."

"This one is worth the trip," he said. Then he looked at me like he'd forgotten I was there. "Hi, Lottie."

"Hi, Sam. How have you been?"

"I've been good," he said. "What brings you here? One of your aunt's letters?"

"I have to pick up a book from the guy who works here. I guess she let him borrow it and never got it back."

"What book?"

"I don't know yet. It's at his house; his girlfriend is going to bring it."

"There you are!" Em said before I could respond. She and Abe carried record-shaped blue plastic bags. When she saw Sam, she waved. "Oh, hi. I'm Em. Please pretend this is the first time you've met me."

"I'm Abe. Lottie's brother." They shook hands.

"Em, do you even have a record player?" I asked.

"I think my dad left one somewhere in the basement."

Abe climbed up on the stage and looked around. "Huh," he said.

"What?" I asked.

"It looks totally different during the day." He hopped down and sat down on the edge of the stage. Em joined him, and they started comparing purchases.

Sam found a stick and drew a tic-tac-toe board in the dirt. We drew ten straight matches, and then I saw Leonard walking toward us. He had a book in his hand.

"Told you it wouldn't be long," he said, handing it to me. "Well, I guess it actually has been a long time. Eight years and ten minutes, give or take."

I took the book without looking at it. "Thanks. I know this would have meant a lot to my aunt."

"I'm glad I could help. I just feel bad I never returned it."

Books have a way of making themselves at home, Aunt Helen had once said. I smiled now, at Leonard, and said, "If she had wanted it before, she would have asked for it."

When he walked away, I read the title: *The Search for Eternity: A History of Juan Ponce de León.*

"Who's Ponce de León?" I asked.

Sam leaned over and read the title, and I swear he did the tiniest of double takes, the tiniest of deer-in-the-headlights, caught sort of looks. Then Abe glanced over and said, "You know, the explorer."

"Ponce de who?" Em asked.

"Why would she want me to have a book about an explorer?" I wondered.

"He was famous," Abe said. "You've really never heard of him? He found the Fountain of Youth!"

"Supposedly," Sam said quickly and laughed, and then, as if on second thought, added, "It was probably research. For her books."

"Oh, yeah," I said. "That makes sense."

"Maybe there's something written in it?" Abe asked.

I opened it and fanned through the pages, and sure enough, toward the beginning of the book, she had circled the phrase "Fountain of Youth" and drawn a line to the margins, where she'd written *S.W.* with three exclamation points next to it.

"S.W. Abe, that's who she dedicated her last book to!" I said, pointing.

"Huh. I wonder who it was. Didn't she have a friend named Susan?"

"Or Sarah?" I added. "I have no idea."

Sam had wandered away again, inspecting the stage. After a moment he came back and said, "It's about an explorer, so maybe she's trying to send you a message? To find your own way. To never stop looking for . . . stuff."

"That's deep, Sam," I said.

"Well, I don't know," he said. "What do you guys want to do next?"

"Give me a minute; I'll meet you out front."

I waited until the three of them had gone around the side of the building, and then I pulled the next letter from Aunt Helen out of my purse.

Lottie,

The first concert I ever went to was when I was in high school. The concert was in Boston; the band was Chicago. I went with your father; we snuck out of the house and drove the whole way and then drove back with our ears ringing (this is before they really knew about sound damage; sick now to think that ringing sound was irreparable damage to our eardrums, but you live and you learn and then you get earplugs). The concert itself was memorable, I think, only because it was our first. Because the venue was so massive and swallowed up more people than I had ever before imagined fitting into one place. Because we had done something incredibly devious, my brother and I, by sneaking out of the house, by driving all that way by ourselves, by parking in a parking spot that might possibly have been a tow-away zone (it ended up being fine, but we contemplated the possibility of hitchhiking home that night). The concert itself, the actual music and the words delivered to us, I honestly can't recall. I just remember the overwhelmingness of it all: it was one of those massive moments in my life that you know you are going to remember forever, but not for any of the obvious reasons.

And then, afterward, your father stood up and patted his jeans pocket to check for his keys and realized they weren't there. So in a very funny turn of events we got down on our hands and knees to search for them while the rest of the audience filed out. And then eventually the lights came on and finally the band themselves came out onto the stage and asked us if we needed help. And so imagine us, just kids, with the members of Chicago searching around the seats for the keys to a car that might not even be there, might be impounded or stolen or just vanished into the night. But it WAS there, and we found the keys, and everything ended up being just fine. Better than fine, obviously, because your father and I talked about that night many times over the course of our lives and almost constantly in the weeks that followed (it helped to remember it when we were both grounded for two months afterward).

It's memories and nights like that one that I keep coming back to, over and over again. I think that is normal, to try to insert yourself back into old spaces, to try to trick your body into believing you're actually there again. Except it never quite works the way I want it to—but almost. Some nights when I put the right music on and open the windows and light a candle or two—some nights I can imagine I am in high school again or living in your father's garage or running after an immortal boy. Sometimes I can imagine I am anywhere or anyone I want to be.

It's been a great comfort, these past few months:

*music. I want to share that with you, Lottie. Listen
to music. I mean listen. Really, really listen. And see
where it brings you.*

*My favorite song is called "Time in a Bottle." Jim
Croce. If you haven't left Magic Grooves yet, go ahead
and buy yourself a copy.*

Love, H.

"Time in a Bottle"? I didn't think I'd ever heard it.

I folded up her letter carefully and put it back into my purse. I walked around the side of the building and found the others by the car.

"Give me a second, okay? I think there's something I want to get," I said and headed back into Magic Grooves.

Leonard's girlfriend had brought him lunch, and they were eating it behind the counter. I found the record quickly—*You Don't Mess Around with Jim*—and brought it to the front.

"Your aunt played us this song in class," Leonard said, turning the album over in his hand. Then, when he saw my wallet, "No, no, no, no—this one is on me. Consider it an overdue book fee."

"Really? Thanks! Hey—do you know anywhere I could get a record player?"

"Sure thing! I know a great spot," he said, and wrote out a few directions on the back of a napkin. "Come back soon."

I took the napkin from him and thanked him again. Outside, Sam and Em and Abe were leaning against the car and looking through their purchases.

"Come on," I said, hopping in the driver's seat. "We have another stop to make."

It was a rainy and gloomy sort of day: Margo's favorite kind. She took the long way home from school, not bothering with an umbrella, letting herself get absolutely drenched.

You're going to catch your death of a cold! her mother would have said, if she had seen her daughter's present condition.

But the joke would have been on her. Margo couldn't catch colds anymore.

Not that they'd actually told their parents of their new immortal status. No, it was still a secret that Alvin and Margo shared. That was why Alvin had been able to stay home from school that day; "I don't feel good" was still an excuse that held water with their parents.

But Margo didn't mind being alone.

She had her headphones, her music.

She had the wonderfully chilly rain.

And she had—all of a sudden—the distinct sense that she was being followed.

—from *Alvin Hatter and the Overcoat Man*

12

S am left his bike in the Magic Grooves parking lot and
helped me decipher Leonard's directions as Abe and
Em carried on a loud, heated conversation in the backseat
about what would have happened if John Bonham hadn't
died all those years ago.

"The *entire trajectory* of music history would have been
changed," Abe said.

"You cannot possibly maintain such a high level of
substance abuse and still remain productive," Em argued.
"They would have broken up anyway. Maybe they would
have released one more album, but . . ."

"Even one more album and the *entire trajectory* of music
history would have been changed!" Abe said.

"You just keep saying the same thing over and over,"
Em pointed out.

"It's a pretty good thing. I'm sticking with it for now."

After just a few minutes of driving, Sam motioned me over to the side of the road and I parked. We must have gone closer to the ocean; I could hear the crashing of waves even though I couldn't see the shore. It took me a minute to see the little store, which was nestled against a thin wooded area. A sign out front said Thrift Sto. The last two letters were faded and unreadable. It was one of the tiniest buildings I'd ever seen, and it was completely surrounded by things for sale: picnic tables and washing machines and doghouses and tool chests and road signs and water-damaged dollhouses. We filed out of the car, and I picked my way between a plastic rocking horse and an oversized garden gnome and slipped through the front doors.

The building was almost certainly bigger on the inside.

"TARDIS," Abe whispered, nudging me excitedly in the side. The building stretched on for an impossible amount of space, and it was filled with more junk than I'd ever seen in one place.

"What's a TARDIS?" Em asked.

"The Police Box," I said.

"Oh. Good reference."

She and Abe drifted away, and Sam asked me what I was looking for.

"A record player."

"Another letter?"

"Kind of, yeah."

He seemed to know his way around. He led me to a

display of vintage record players, all with a tiny white price sticker on one corner.

"Have you been here before?" I asked, looking at the different models.

"It's a small town," he said in way of an answer. "I've been to most places."

"Do you know anything about record players?"

He bent down to examine the options, then pointed to a little suitcase player with built-in speakers. He rattled off some specs (that I didn't understand at all, all about something called RPMs and platter weight), the conclusion being: get this, it's a good one.

"Are you kind of a genius?" I asked as he handed it to me.

"What do you mean?"

"All these college courses, all this random knowledge. Like, who knows this much about record players?"

"I guess I read a lot," he said.

"About record players?"

"About lots of stuff."

"Do you ever sleep?"

"Once a week I try to take a little nap," he said, smiling, sliding past me to the checkout. Em was already there, talking to a very bored-looking twentysomething proprietor about the records she'd just bought. The shopkeeper's features were androgynous, and they wore a small pin on their lapel that listed their preferred pronouns "they/them/theirs."

"Do you like vinyl? Did you go to school around here? Do you like working in a thrift store?" Em asked rapid-fire.

"Yes I do," the shopkeeper responded to Em's questions in order. "Yes I do. No I don't."

I put the record player on the counter.

"Forty dollars!" Em said, reading the price. "That's a steal. Seriously. It's like you're stealing from this store, Lottie!"

Abe dragged Em away from the register as I paid. Sam came up beside me; the shopkeeper smiled when they saw him.

"Hi, Sam."

"Hi, Zen."

"Is your name really Zen?" Em called as Abe all but pushed her out of the store.

"Sorry about her. She can get a little enthusiastic," I said.

"Actually, I'm used to it. Thrift stores make people oddly energized," Zen said.

"Zen, this is my friend Lottie," Sam said. "Lottie, Zen."

Zen extended a hand over the counter and smiled at me, and I got the feeling that any friend of Sam's was vouched for.

"It's nice to meet you," I said.

"Likewise. This is a good little machine you picked out," they said, tapping the record player. "Forty even. No tax for Sam's friends." I handed them two twenties. "You guys should go down to the beach. Mikaela built another driftwood sculpture."

"Really? Oh, we definitely have to check it out," Sam said. "Mikaela is Zen's partner, and she's an absolutely amazing artist."

"Great," I said. "Let's go."

"Thanks for this," Sam said.

"Anytime," Zen promised.

"Mr. Popular," I said, nudging Sam with my elbow when we were out of earshot.

"I told you—it's a small town!"

We met Abe and Em in the parking lot.

"This way," Sam said, pointing around the back of the shop. "Bring the record player."

I grabbed the Jim Croce record out of the car, and then we followed Sam around the back of the shop to a skinny trailhead that opened up in the woods that bordered the property.

We went single file because that was the only way we could fit. Sam was first, then me, then Abe, then Em. It wasn't long until the sounds of the ocean grew louder and the path beneath our feet turned sandy and opened up onto a small, secluded beach. We walked toward the water, and I spotted Mikaela's sculpture immediately. It was hard to miss; it looked like a fully formed tree house in the middle of the sand. It was built close to the water and the tide had risen since its completion; the bottom two feet were underwater. And it was functional—there was a girl sitting on its small raised platform. Mikaela, I assumed. She'd made a torch out of driftwood. The fire was burning thin but bright.

"Wow," Em said.

"This is amazing," Abe added.

"You should have seen her last one. A giant hummingbird. I swore I saw its wings move," Sam said. He caught Mikaela's eye and waved to her. She climbed down a rickety ladder to greet him.

"Sam! I was hoping you'd get to see this one. It'll be swallowed up pretty soon. I've already taken my pictures," she said. Mikaela was a few years older than us and pretty. She had long hair she wore in two braids and there was dirt smudged on her face. Her hands were rough and calloused. "And you brought friends! I guess you're not such a loner after all," she said, winking and smiling warmly at us.

"This is Lottie, Em, and Abe. Do you have power?" Sam asked.

"Over there," Mikaela responded, pointing. Sam took the record player from me and plugged it into a long orange extension cord. I couldn't see where it originated.

"This is beautiful," I said. "You made this?"

"Thank you! Yeah, it's just something I do for fun," Mikaela said.

"What do you mean, swallowed up?"

"The tide's coming in, and it will get washed away. Pretty soon, actually. But I don't use anything that didn't come from the ocean to begin with, so it's all just returning."

"Isn't that frustrating?"

"Not really. I don't think everything has to be so permanent. There are plenty of museums. This is just for me, just for now," she said.

"But isn't that like creating something for the sole purpose of seeing it destroyed?" I asked. "Sorry, that sounded a little harsh—no offense."

"None taken!" Mikaela said, laughing. "I like people who ask questions. And I don't think that's the sole purpose here at all. It's just one of the inevitable outcomes of art: eventually, it will all be destroyed. Even the *Mona Lisa* will one day turn to dust; it will just take a little longer than my structure's destruction. But in the grand scheme of things, in the whole bulk of time, they both exist for just tiny little blips."

"Harsh," Sam said.

"Structure's Destruction! Another excellent name for a band," Abe said.

Mikaela laughed and walked back toward the structure as the record started playing.

"Your aunt's favorite song is on this record," Sam said.

"Did she play it for your class too?"

"Yeah," he said softly. "That's where I heard it."

The music carried surprisingly well over the water as we walked over to Mikaela's structure.

"Will it hold us all?" Sam asked, putting his hand on a beam.

"Only one way to find out," Mikaela said.

We left the record player and our shoes and our phones well away from the water and then, one by one, we climbed the ladder to the shelter Mikaela had made. The five of us crowded together and tried to be as light as possible, and though it swayed a little bit as we settled on it, the tower held. The platform was only ten or so feet high, but it felt significant—the breeze was stronger and the salt air was more noticeable and the music floated through the air and swirled around our heads, blending with the breeze.

I thought about what Mikaela had said and wondered whether the permanence of an object affected its worth.

"Lottie, it's your turn," Em said, shoving something into my hand. A small, sharp pocketknife.

"What's this for?" I asked.

"We're carving the wood. Anything you want to write. Something important or something you want to leave behind," Mikaela said. "I wrote *destruction*."

"I wrote *Led Zeppelin*," Abe said. Then, when Em gave him a look: "What? They're very important."

"What did you write?" I asked Sam.

He pointed to a piece of wood, and I leaned closer to read what he'd carved there.

Time.

"It's important, but it's not everything," he said quietly.

I picked my own piece of wood and started carving. It was harder than I thought it would be. My letters came out crooked and hesitant, but each one was better than the last. When I was done, I leaned back and looked at what I'd written.

"Listen," Sam read.

"It's what she wanted me to do," I explained. "But it's hard."

Abe and Em had sucked Mikaela into their John Bonham discussion. I listened as she laid out a very detailed, highly thought-out timeline of what would have happened if he hadn't died.

"In one of her classes, your aunt said they send kids to school to learn math and grammar and history, but they never teach them about their own minds," Sam said, leaning closer to me.

"She told me that too. That we spend so much time on addition and subtraction but no time at all on how to control anxiety, how to manage anger, how to understand our emotions."

"It seems like a pretty big miss, right?"

"Yeah, it does."

I closed my eyes and tried to block out all distractions. But even the act of trying to block out distractions was a distraction, and I found myself irritated and angry.

"Try this," Sam said. "Sometimes it helps me when I'm feeling overwhelmed. Close your eyes and follow the music. Not the words, but the music. Think about the notes in your head and make yourself tune everything else out. Don't try to concentrate so much as let yourself drift into it."

Drift into it. Okay. I closed my eyes again, and this time I thought of the music like a physical thing, like something manifesting inside my head. One song ended, and "Time in a Bottle" began—I hadn't heard the song before, but he said the title early on. I gave the notes a shape and let them move and act of their own accord. And it worked—suddenly my whole universe was Jim Croce singing about time and love and the fleeting nature of both. The sounds of the beach, the sounds of Abe and Em and Mikaela arguing . . . everything faded away until it was just me. Just me and a guitar and a voice.

When the song ended, I opened my eyes. Sam was staring at me so intently, I started laughing.

"What?" he said, self-conscious. "What did I do?"

"Nothing. It worked! It really worked."

We stayed there long after the record had run out, and the water now was four or five feet high around the base of the tower. We would get soaked on our way down; we'd have to swim to shore. But that was okay because I had towels in my car and none of us minded a little water.

Em went first, whooping as she flew through the air,

tucking her legs into her chest in order to create as big a splash as possible. Then Abe went, more gracefully, and Mikaela, the most graceful of all. It was just Sam and me on the platform and the three of them on the narrow sliver of beach, laughing and shaking water from their hair.

"There won't be long for it," Sam said, and he meant the tower but it felt like he also meant something else, and I didn't know what it was. I was about to ask him, but he took my hand and we jumped together. I didn't even bother trying to keep my head above water. I let the ocean rush over me. I took my time standing up, and the salt water ran into my eyes and my mouth, and, completely soaked and shivering, we walked back to my car. I turned the heat up while we stood around and toweled off.

Zen came out of the store and watched us, and Mikaela danced around, refusing a towel, already rattling off plans for what she wanted to make next.

We said good-bye to them and drove Sam back to Magic Grooves to get his bike.

I left the car running and walked Sam to his bike, which was chained up at the side of the building.

"Thanks for meeting us," I said.

"Anytime," he replied. He unlocked his chain and wound it around the middle bar of the bike, then straightened up. "I hope your aunt's letters keep bringing us together."

"I'm sure they will. She loved it down here."

In the car I watched him bike away down the road, and Abe and Em made kissing noises and hummed the old song about love and marriage in trees.

"Lottie loves someone," Em said in a singsongy, incredibly annoying voice.

"I don't love anyone. I've known him for a week," I said.

"Lottie has *a crush* on someone," Abe amended.

But that didn't feel right either. That was too glib a word to describe it. Everything was too complicated to accurately explain. Did I have feelings for Sam? I didn't know. It was all jumbled in my head, like there was too much information to process and not enough room to properly sort it out.

I ignored Em and Abe until they got the hint and left me alone.

That night I hooked the record player up in my room and listened to "Time in a Bottle" on repeat, feeling like it was trying to tell me something I didn't yet have the capability to understand.

"Alvin?" Margo asked, her voice seeming exceptionally small in the darkness.

"Yeah?"

"What do you think you would have wanted to do? If you weren't going to be thirteen forever?"

"Oh," he said. The question made him instantly sad. A month ago, a year ago, if you had asked Alvin Hatter whether he had wanted to live forever, the answer would have come quickly. *Of course! Who wouldn't want to live forever?*

But the reality had sunk in quickly.

Their parents were gone.

Their grandfather was dead.

The only place they were truly safe was a rather drafty and spooky house in the middle of endless, lonely woods.

Everything felt miserable and spoiled.

He would have given anything to give this curse of a gift back. Let the Overcoat Man have it! Let the Everlife Society claim it for their own! Alvin didn't want it at all.

But he couldn't say that to his sister.

He was, after all, the older one.

The eternal thirteen-year-old to the eternal eleven-year-old.

He had to be positive, for her sake.

"Oh, I don't know," he said after a minute, trying hard to make his voice light and airy. "I can still do so much now. And I have more time to do it too. So that's pretty cool."

Margo's reply came much, much later. They had burrowed

deeper into their separate sleeping bags. The moonlight tried its best but couldn't make it through the filthy windows. It was very quiet in the house. It was a breezeless night.

Just one word floated over into the darkness, reaching Alvin at the very edge of sleep. It would follow him into his dreams:

"Liar."

—from *Alvin Hatter and the Return of the Overcoat Man*

13

Monday marked three weeks left of school. It didn't seem possible—both that I was about to graduate and that Aunt Helen wouldn't be there to see me get my diploma. She had always been such a supporter of education, and she was part of the reason I was working as hard as I was to become a teacher. Just a little while longer and I'd be there. The University of Connecticut's program was a five-year combined bachelor's and master's degree. For some reason, after four years of high school and three years of middle school and six years of elementary school, that seemed like nothing.

I opened her next envelope before school.

> Lottie,
> As I sit here writing these, I try to imagine you going through the motions, answering my every

whim. Of course I have no control over anything, just the knowledge that you've always been so reliable. It's almost like a form of immortality, isn't it? That the things I want are being completed even after my time has run out, even past the expiration date my doctors stamped on my extensive medical chart.

I wish I could have made it through another summer. It was always my favorite time of year. To have another healthy summer . . . I wish that wasn't too much to ask. But I guess it is, because you're reading this, and if you're reading this, it means they were right and I'm gone, and all the rest of my summers are gone with me. But you still have so many, Lottie, so many summers in front of you, and that's something I'm so grateful for, so happy for. I know you will make the most of them.

Speaking of summer, my last class at the college is coming up. I let them know that, should I not be around to complete this year, they may find a substitute for the remainder of my classes except the very last one. I would provide a substitute for my last class, and that substitute is you, Lottie. The information is on my calendar on my computer.

You will find no syllabus, no lesson plan. The students will, I'm sure, be absolutely lucky to hear whatever you decide to tell them. You are a marvel, Lottie, like all born teachers are marvels, all

*those who dedicate their days and nights to impart-
ing knowledge on the youths of our society. You will
be one of them one day; here is your first chance to
prove yourself.*

Love, H.

My heart started beating faster at the thought of teaching a class. What was the point? Did she want me to embarrass myself in front of a classroom of students all older than I was? Did she want me to have a heart attack and die?

Death by heart attack didn't seem so bad. It was probably painful, but it only lasted a minute or two, and there were a lot of worse ways to go.

But I was sure Aunt Helen wasn't actually trying to give me a heart attack. She probably looked at this like a nice opportunity, a chance for me to get some practice at the thing I wanted to do. I looked at it as absolutely terrifying.

It was Abe's turn to drive to school that morning; I met him downstairs and ate a bowl of cereal at rapid speed while he started at me curiously.

"What's wrong with you?" he asked.

"Aunt Helen wants me to teach a class," I said, mouth full of food, words completely garbled.

"What?" he said.

I swallowed. "Aunt Helen. She's having me teach her last class of the year."

"Wow. At the university? Wow."

"I know."

"That's a lot of responsibility."

"I *know*."

"You look kind of pale."

"I know."

"Come on, we gotta pick up Amy. We're gonna be late."

We drove in relative silence to Amy's house. Every time Abe tried to say something, I put my head in my hands and groaned. Eventually he got the hint and stopped talking.

Amy was waiting for us at the end of her driveway.

"It is hot," she said, climbing into the backseat. Abe and I were silent, lost in thought. And then, after a minute of silence: "What did I miss?"

"Lottie is going to teach Aunt Helen's last class at the university."

"Wow," Amy said, echoing Abe in a way that made me smile. "Lottie, you're going to do it? Teach a whole class?"

"I think I have to," I said. "She already set the whole thing up."

"I would freak out," she said.

"Your band performs in front of hundreds of people," Abe pointed out.

She reached up and rubbed his shoulders as he drove. "Yes, but this is different. This is so much more inti-mate. When I'm onstage, I can pretend it's just me and the music. You know?"

"Right on, man," Abe said, making the rock and roll sign with his hand.

"Shut up," she said. "Lottie, you're braver than I am."

I didn't think I was very brave. I wanted to teach elementary school kids, not college students. I wanted to teach one plus one is two. I wanted to read early chapter books and have kids dress up as their favorite historical figures. I'd never been interested in teaching at a higher level—it had always been about younger students, still so wide-eyed and receptive to new ideas. That was what drew me to elementary school: the chance to really make a difference in a younger student's life. I had no idea what I could possibly say to a group of college students that wouldn't make them do anything other than fall asleep.

I checked Aunt Helen's computer that night. Her last class was scheduled for Friday, just five days away. Okay. I could make a lesson plan in five days, right? Wait . . . I didn't even know what they were studying. Fiction? Short stories? Classic literature?

Then I remembered Sam. He had taken my aunt's class; he would at least know the basics. I sent him a message before I went to bed.

> Have to teach my aunt's class on Friday. Absolutely terrified. Do you think you could help me?

I brushed my teeth and washed my face while I waited

for his reply. It came just as I was falling asleep, bringing me gently back to consciousness.

> **Of course. I think I have an idea. What time is the class?**
>
> **Four. I get out of school at noon.**

The university was close to Mystic; Sam could probably even ride his bike.

> **Let's meet outside the library at one? Do you need more time to get here?**
>
> **One works. I really appreciate it.**
>
> **I wanted to see you again anyway, so this works out for both of us.**

I put my phone on silent and set my alarm for tomorrow. This was going to be the longest five days in history.

I wasn't wrong. Every hour dragged on painfully, each one holding its own eternity. Teachers were trying to squeeze in as much last-minute learning as possible, but all except a few of the most diligent seniors had tuned out, creating a stark contrast of priorities. On Friday, Em was sent out of history for drawing a picture of a bunny in the margins of her textbook. I found her sitting against my locker, having finished the bunny drawing and now adding little ducklings to go with it.

"Did you make it to the principal?" I asked her, putting my things away and grabbing my car keys from the metal hook inside my locker.

"She didn't actually say to go to the office, though," Em said, not looking up. "She just said to remove myself from her classroom. This seemed like as good a place as any to remove myself to."

"Excellent reasoning. I'll see you this weekend?"

"Is today the day?" she asked, springing to her feet and following me through the halls to the parking lot. Abe and I had taken separate cars so I could leave for the university right from school.

"Today is the day," I confirmed.

"Are you nervous?"

"Yeah? Maybe? A little?"

"Are you nervous to see Sam?"

"Not really. He's just helping me figure out what I'm going to talk about."

"Oh, sure. Totally," Em said.

"Didn't I ask you to let it go?"

"Yes, you did. But when I first started dating Jackie, you covered my entire bedroom in sticky notes that said EM LOVES JACKIE 4EVER so I'm not really motivated to let it go, as it were."

"In my defense, you do love Jackie forever. And I waited until you actually started dating before I sticky-noted your room."

"So when you and Sam start dating I can get a tattoo that says LOTTIE LOVES SAM 4EVER?"

"Maybe think of something a little less permanent."

"Good point. Well, have fun! Text me later."

With a wave and a promise to text her that night, I got into my car and left Em standing in the parking lot, her defaced history textbook in her hands.

I had sat in on a couple of my aunt's classes over the years, but I didn't remember much. She taught about writing for children and the history of children's literature, things I knew a little about but nowhere near as much as she did. I'd brought her computer with me in case there was anything on there that would help me.

I was wholly unprepared.

In her note Aunt Helen had made it seem like I was the obvious choice for a substitute, like she wasn't worried at all about my ability to actually carry this out. I wasn't so sure. Even Abe might have been a better choice—he didn't want to be a teacher, but he had read every single important children's book in the history of the English language, plus most of the unimportant ones, plus he had an eidetic memory for words. He would probably grow up to be the next J. R. R. Tolkien.

Or the next Helen Reaves, I guess.

I got to the library a few minutes later and opened my aunt's laptop on the grass outside. Although I'd already done this days ago, I spent a few minutes browsing through her Word documents and found a folder labeled Lesson Plans, but of course the last one was for weeks ago, before she died. The students would have had three or four classes without her now, being taught by whatever substitute had been assigned to them. And now me. I really didn't want to let them down.

I felt a hand brush against my hair, and then Sam was sitting down across from me, smiling and happy in sunglasses and a blue T-shirt.

"Hi," he said.

"Hi," I said.

"First of all, you look like you're about to throw up. Are you about to throw up?"

"I don't think so. But I'm not a hundred percent sure."

"Okay, I'll keep my distance. What are you working on? Any ideas?"

"Literally zero ideas. I have no ideas at all. At this point, I think I'm just going to read the first chapter of *Margo Hatter Lives Forever* and be done with it."

"Great! I have an idea. Let's go." He shot up and grabbed my hands, pulling me to my feet. I put the laptop in my bag as he led me away from the library.

"Where are we going?"

"Somewhere very cool," he said.

"That's all I get?"

"That's all you get."

It wasn't long before we arrived at the outdoor amphitheater. I'd been here before, with Abe and my parents, watching the drama department's summer Shakespeare series.

"Are we seeing a play? We're supposed to be working on a lesson plan," I said as we approached the ticket booth.

"You have three hours until class. If you haven't planned something yet, you're not going to. You're just going to have to wing it, Lottie," he said. He bought two tickets and grabbed us each a program. He handed me one.

"The Little Prince," I read.

"A stage adaptation by Reaves Players," he said.

"Reaves?"

"Your aunt was their number one supporter. She made this possible. They used to be called the Seaside Players, but they changed their name when . . ."

"That's really nice," I said.

We found our seats, and I read through the program, just two simple pages folded and stapled together. The Little Prince was being played by Mikaela Barns.

"Hey," I said, pointing.

"I know, she's the one who told me about this. She also made the set and helped with the adaptation. Essentially, she's great at everything she does."

The audience was at least half children and not a single one of them spoke or moved during the entire show, which was a testament to how good it was. Mikaela was amazing as the prince and it was obvious that every single actor who came onstage was so happy to be there. When it was over, Sam took my hand and led me out of the theater, because I was so dazed and happy I couldn't even concentrate on moving myself.

"What did you think?" he asked when we were outside.

"That was amazing. That was so good. Thank you for taking me."

"You really liked it?"

"Of course I liked it. And I know exactly what I'm going to talk about now."

"Seriously? I mean—obviously. Of course. That was my plan all along." He puffed out his chest and looked self-righteous.

"Well, I don't believe you for a second, but thank you anyway."

"Do you mind if I sit in?"

"Of course not. I kind of assumed you would."

"Really? Oh, great. I mean, I didn't want to be presumptuous."

"Do we have time to get a coffee?"

Sam looked at his phone and then showed me the screen. Three thirty.

"There's a coffee shop in the building where your aunt's class is," he said.

"Really?"

"This is college. There's basically a coffee shop in every building."

Aunt Helen's class was held in the Turner Building, one of the larger buildings on campus and one that housed the majority of the English Department. It was exactly how I remembered it: slightly run-down with plenty of offices crammed with books and papers and classrooms with high ceilings and wood paneling. It was perfect, and it was a little creepy, like Aunt Helen's ghost still roamed the halls. I even thought it smelled like her, but I'm sure it was just my imagination.

This was the building I was in when I first decided I wanted to be a teacher.

Every so often I'd sit in on one of Aunt Helen's classes, and I spent most of the time not really paying attention to her, instead noting how completely she held the class in her attention. Students sat with notebooks and pens or laptops and listened—the room was completely silent except for my aunt's voice.

I could do this, I reminded myself. No matter how nervous I was, this was what I wanted to do.

The coffee shop was in the basement, which had recently been redone to include a massive study area with both individual cubicles and long, open tables. The coffee shop was called Alvin's—another stab in the heart—and there was a short line of people wearing glasses and holding books, with pens tucked above their ears. The whole thing made me more nervous. My stomach flipped over with every minute that passed, over and over and over until it didn't know which way was up.

"Just breathe," Sam whispered. I bought us two cups of coffee from an impossibly adorable girl in a gray vintage dress and red lipstick, and I handed one to Sam with shaking hands.

"Where's her classroom?" I asked. "I forgot what number her classroom is."

"It's fine. I know where it is. Come here for a minute," Sam said. We put our things down on a free table and sat next to each other. "Have you ever done breathing exercises?"

"I mean, I breathe a lot. I'm breathing right now."

He laughed. "That's not what I mean. Okay, try this. Breathe in through your nose, as much air as you can take. Then let it out through your mouth slowly. As slow as you can. Do that three times, and every time let the air out slower and slower. You can close your eyes too."

"I'm freaking out."

"I know. This will help."

I closed my eyes and did what he said.

I was acutely aware of every part of my body, from my heart that beat a little too heavily to my breathing, which caught in my chest and stuck there like a hard candy.

This was not quite a panic attack, but I knew one was building, biding its time, getting ready to explode.

All you have to do is get through this class. . . .

I let my breath out slowly, so slowly that my lungs ached. I did it three times, and then I opened my eyes and looked at him.

"Wow," I said.

"Did that help?"

"It really did."

"Breathing is important. We don't give it enough credit."

"I don't think I give *you* enough credit."

He laughed and said, "Come on. Room 404. Let's do this."

The elevator was out of service, so we walked from the basement to the fourth floor. I was panting again by the time we got there, but it was a good kind of panting. The panic was still there, still buzzing around inside me, but I wasn't as nervous now. I knew there was no backing out. I had to do this, for Aunt Helen and for myself. So I might as well try to enjoy it.

It was five minutes to four, and the classroom was already full. I guess word had gotten around that they'd be having a special guest today, and when I put my bags down on what used to be Aunt Helen's desk, I felt every pair of eyes in the room turn to look at me. Sam took a seat in the front row. He gave me a thumbs-up and smiled widely and goofily. I took Aunt Helen's laptop out of my bag and heard a gasp from somewhere as one of the students recognized it. That didn't surprise me—the Apple logo on the front had been painted in rainbow colors (by Em, of course, in nail polish), making the computer easily distinguishable. Aunt Helen had loved it.

"A true *artiste*!" she'd said when Em had shown her. "A *visionaire*!"

"Are those real French words?" Em had asked.

"More or less, I think."

A few more students shuffled into the class as I set up, opening the document I needed and spreading one of Aunt Helen's notes on the keyboard. Number ten. An important one, so I'd been keeping it with me.

At four on the dot, I walked around to the front of the desk and leaned back against it. All I wanted in that moment was for my voice to be steady. *Please let my voice be steady.*

"My name is Lottie Reaves. Helen was my aunt. She asked me to teach your last class in the event she couldn't be here herself." Somebody in the back was already crying: low, quiet sobs that floated down through the lecture hall ceiling and threatened to put me over the edge too. "I don't know what all of you want to do with your lives, but I'm guessing at least a few of you want to be writers. I think that's great. But just like anything we want in life, it's going to be really, really hard. Even for someone as established as my aunt, there were times when it was difficult, when the rejection letters piled up and her resolve started wearing down.

"My aunt spoke often of the idea of immortality. This shouldn't be surprising, given the subject matter she chose to write about. The idea of time comes up a lot in our lives. Time—it seems like there's never enough of it, right? I know there wasn't enough of it for my aunt, but I still think about all she was able to accomplish, and it makes me think that it is possible to do the things we want to do.

"Along those lines, I'd like everyone to take a few minutes to write down the answer to this question: What would you attempt to do if you had all the time in the world in which to do it? Just a sentence or two, and when you're done, you can exchange your paper with a neighbor, somebody random, releasing the idea into the world. That's often the first step of doing anything: admitting it to someone else."

I risked a glance at Sam; for some reason he was unmoving, looking not happy for me but . . . a little worried? But then he saw me watching him and a huge smile spread across his face. He leaned over to his neighbor, who tore a strip of paper out of a notebook and gave it to him. He gave me the smallest thumbs-up again and started writing.

But why that initial hesitation?

Was this a stupid idea?

I was completely prepared to show up and read the first chapter of the new Alvin book, which I was sure would make everybody lose their minds, but then I remembered that Aunt Helen had wanted me to figure this out. If she had wanted somebody to simply show up and read a few words she'd written, she could have asked anyone else to do it. No, this was supposed to be my thing. And now that the entire class was writing diligently, I had to stand behind it.

A few minutes passed, and then I saw the first people begin to exchange their papers. I felt a weird sense of pride that they had written this thing, this short assignment, because I had told them to. Then more and more people started passing papers, and passing papers with people who had already passed, until finally everyone's writing was fully jumbled up and with somebody completely new.

"All set?" I said. "Okay. Now your words are out in the world. It may seem like a tiny step, but tiny steps are just as important as big ones, because they still lead you forward. Can I have a volunteer to read?"

A few hands shot into the air, and I pointed to a girl in denim overalls. She cleared her throat and read, "I would figure out how to build colonies on the bottom of the ocean. Overpopulation is real!" A few chuckles from the room, and I laughed appreciatively too.

"Anyone else?" I pointed to a boy wearing a highlighter-yellow sweatshirt.

"I would figure out a way to bring America's over-abundance of food to those who are starving."

I pointed to a girl with a bun on the top of her head. "I would bring vaccines to countries that don't have access to them."

"This is amazing," I said. "Guys, weren't you sort of expecting answers like 'I would become a millionaire' or 'I would watch every episode of TV ever made'? But so far all of these are about bettering humankind. That's so cool! Anyone else?"

A girl in yellow-rimmed glasses: "I would redesign cities to make them more bike-friendly, and thus eco-friendly."

A boy with a bright-pink shirt: "I would dedicate my life to convincing the nonbelievers that global warming is real."

And finally, a quiet boy in the second row who had black-rimmed glasses and a beanie: "I would try to find a way to not be immortal."

A few people laughed at that one. I definitely wasn't expecting a response like that, and it intrigued me. Who wouldn't want to be immortal? I posed this question to the class, and for a minute nobody spoke, thinking.

Then the first girl who'd spoken said, "It's probably a pretty lonely existence."

Someone near the back called out, "Alvin and Margo were left with nothing."

Someone else: "I bet the appeal wears off pretty quickly, as soon as everybody you love starts dying."

The conversation was easy and natural and flowing. The students went around and argued the pros and cons of immortality. I hoped Sam might chime in, but he kept quiet, his eyes trained toward his desk. I tried not to feel self-conscious about that. Maybe that was how he looked when he was in class? Just sort of bored and uninterested, but he was actually paying attention?

Forty-five minutes passed like absolutely nothing. We ended up debating the very existence of time itself, the implications of its existence versus it being a completely man-made concept. We talked about Alvin and Margo, and finally, nearing the end of the class, I decided to let them in on a secret. I thought Aunt Helen would probably be fine with it.

"I want to thank everyone for letting me get up here today. It means a lot to me, and I know it would have meant a lot to Aunt Helen. And speaking of her . . . I'm probably not supposed to tell you this, but there's going to be a new Alvin book. It's called *Margo Hatter Lives Forever*, and it's really, really good."

The entire classroom went absolutely crazy, cheering and clapping and yelling. The doors opened up, and a professor stuck her head inside. People motioned for her to come into the room, and she was followed by another professor and then some random students and then more random students and then more and more people until finally the room was crowded and the doorways were blocked. I could see out in the hall, and there were even more people there, straining to hear, and everyone was talking about the new book and about Aunt Helen and about immortality and time and nobody seemed to want to leave until finally Sam slipped toward the front of the room and we both left, unnoticed, as the celebrations continued.

"You were great," Sam told me outside my car. I had

put my bags in the trunk, and I was standing and shaking as he told me how good the lesson had been. But I couldn't help but remember how completely disinterested he looked as I talked, how he hadn't contributed a single word to the discussion, how he'd almost purposefully avoided making eye contact with me. He had, right? I wasn't just making that up?

"People were crying," Sam continued. "You broke hearts today, Lottie Reaves."

"Then how come you seem so . . ."

"So what?"

"You just seem kind of weird."

"Sad, I guess. A lot of things."

"Okay. But you thought it was okay?"

"More than okay. I'm sorry I'm not being more convincing."

"I'm just glad it's over."

A tiny flutter in my chest. All that energy, all those nerves—they were starting to turn against me.

"Lottie?" he said, touching my hand, holding just the tips of my middle and ring fingers.

"I'm really tired. I think I better go home now."

"Do you want to get dinner first? I know an Indian place. Do you like Indian? Or Mexican? Or anything?"

"It's not that I don't want to, it's just . . . I'm so tired. I'm sorry. Maybe we can do something this weekend?"

I wasn't tired at all, but all the panic I'd pushed away

was rushing back. The tips of my fingers were tingling. I'd tried so hard to ignore the warning signs of a panic attack, but I couldn't hold it off forever, and I definitely didn't want Sam to see me like that.

"I'd like that," he said, but his face was concerned, worried.

"Everything is fine," I said, and then I realized that when you said that, when you said *everything is fine*, it sounded like exactly the opposite. "I'll text you later. Honestly, I'm just exhausted."

I got into my car and drove away before he could say anything else. I could see him in my rearview mirror, not moving, getting smaller and smaller as I drove.

I'm so sorry, I wanted to say to him. I wanted to turn the car around, go back, and try to explain that this wasn't about him. I was just suddenly having trouble breathing. It felt like I was underwater again, and I couldn't figure out which way the surface was.

Alvin knew that his sister did not like to cry, that she viewed that particular bodily function as betraying too much weakness. Instead, Margo Hatter got angry. Her face turned as red as a tomato; her arms crossed over her stomach and held themselves there so tightly that her breath caught in her chest.

Alvin himself, like his father, was much more prone to tears. This had bothered him once upon a time, but his father had told him that first of all, he would probably grow out of it, and second of all, who gave a flying rat's whiskers what other people might think of him if he cried?

"My father never cried a day in his life and look at him!" Mr. Hatter had said. "He's wrinkled up like a raisin! No, I think a little bit of salt water is good for the skin. Everyone's face needs a little watering now and then."

Alvin knew that if his father had been here to see this, he would have cried.

Alvin was crying—big, gushing tears that he couldn't begin to control.

But there was Margo: a statue, unmoving, her face blank and carved out of stone. He could see the flames reflected in her eyes.

The flames of Grandpa Hatter's house.

There was no way the old man could have made it out alive. It was an absolute inferno.

"Margo," Alvin called, his voice choking, catching.

Margo turned to him. Her eyes were very red, but they

were also dry. He imagined flames coming out of her own ears, her mouth, swallowing her up. When she spoke, black smoke billowed out of the house behind her, and Alvin imagined that it billowed also out of her nose, her fingertips, the very pores of her skin.

"We'll make him pay," she said.

And the way she said it, Alvin could almost believe her.

—from *Alvin Hatter and the Return of the Overcoat Man*

14

Joan Jetta was the only car in Em's driveway, so I let myself in the back door without knocking. I had a key to their house that Em had put in a keychain shaped like a skull.

I found her lying on her bed on her stomach, in the middle of what I could only assume was an hours-long *X-Files* marathon. She looked up when I pushed her door open, and she paused the episode immediately.

"What's wrong?" she said, pulling herself to a sitting position. She held her arms out and I took her hand and sat on the edge of the bed.

"I'm okay," I said, the automatic reply. I didn't even have to think about it. *I'm okay. I'm okay. I'm okay.*

"You look really pale, and your hands are clammy," she said. She put the back of her hand on my forehead, then made a face and placed two fingers on the inside of my wrist. She squinted for a minute, then said, "Your pulse is racing. Why is your pulse racing? Were you running?"

"Driving," I said.

"Then why is your pulse racing so hard?" She pulled her phone closer to her and started the stopwatch. She counted as the seconds ticked by. "One hundred and twenty-five."

"One hundred and twenty-five what?"

"Your heart rate. Do you feel okay? Feverish? Nauseous?"

"I'm okay," I said again, and Em hopped off her bed and forced me to a sitting position, never letting go of my wrist. "I'm just . . . It's just a panic attack."

"Oh, Lottie," Em said, looking both relieved and sad at the same time.

"Or it may be a heart attack," I said. "I don't think we can rule that out."

"Don't worry, okay? It's not a heart attack. My mom gets these all the time. It's apparently really stressful being such a homophobe." Her face softened, and she put her hand on my cheek. "Lie back, okay? I'm going to get you some water."

Em stacked a few pillows on top of each other and then helped me lie down on the bed. When she left the room, I tried to focus on her ceiling, where a few glow-in-the-dark stars still clung with all their adhesive gumption. At one point her whole ceiling had been covered and she'd painted the walls dark blue, and it made her bedroom kind of magical. But then they'd fallen off one by one and what was the point of putting them back up? What was the point of anything?

"I thought I said to lie down," Em said, returning with the water. I'd sat up on the bed without realizing it, cross-legged, rocking back and forth a little.

"Thanks," I said, taking the water and drinking half the glass in one sip. "I'm feeling better. I'm feeling pretty good."

Em didn't reply. She took the water glass from me and placed it on the nightstand and sat next to me on the bed. She hugged me sideways for a long time, until I started to cry. It was like she squeezed it out of me.

"I just can't understand why she had to die. Why we all have to die," I said.

"I know, Lottie. Your aunt was too young, okay? But plenty of people have long, happy, fulfilling lives. And it's worth it."

"But there's no way of knowing. I mean, I could die tomorrow and my parents would have spent all this money and time and energy keeping me alive for eighteen years, and it all would have been for nothing."

"All right, yes, we need to talk about this more, but I think right now we have to work on getting you calmed down, okay? We're going to do some image replacement, okay? This really helps my mom relax and remember that she has a gay agenda to rail against."

I laughed despite the aching in my chest, my lungs. "Image replacement?"

"Think of a memory—it could be a happy moment or a calm moment or just a place you like to go, a picture in your head that you can really insert yourself into. Maybe even something recent, so it's really fresh in your memory."

"Mikaela's structure," I said instantly, not even having to think about it.

"That's great. That's a really good one." Em slid off the bed and kneeled in front of me, taking my hands in hers. "Okay, close your eyes. Now—I want you to picture yourself on the structure. Alone or with me or whoever you want. Try to make the picture as complete as possible. The water, the music, as much detail as you can."

I closed my eyes. I conjured up Jim Croce in my head and heard the first few notes of "Time in a Bottle" as if Em had actually put it on her stereo. I pictured the scene as clearly as I could: the tide rising as we lingered on the structure, the feel of the knife in my hand as I carved into the wood.

"The second you feel yourself drifting, just refocus your energy," Em said, and I heard her as if from a distance, like her voice had traveled over the water to meet me.

But I wasn't drifting. I was solidly placed back in that time, in that place. I could even smell salt on the air, the telltale sign of the ocean.

Gradually my breathing slowed. I focused on the music

and I could feel my body relaxing, resting, my heartbeat returning to a normal rhythm. I could hear Em breathing so deeply I thought for a second she'd fallen asleep, but when I opened my eyes she was still kneeling, her back straight and her eyes closed. She looked utterly peaceful.

After a minute, she opened her eyes and put her fingers on my wrist again, taking my pulse. She smiled. "Hi. You look better."

"How do you know how to do that?" I asked, watching her fingers. "And how did you know how to do *that*?"

"The pulse thing helps my mom. It's an easy to way to show her that she's made progress. You're at ninety now. That's better."

"And the other thing? The image replacement?"

"Like I said, she has a lot of panic attacks. I did some research."

"Well, thanks. You really helped."

"Of course. Do you want ice cream? Let's get some ice cream."

We went to Em's kitchen, and she doled out scoops of vanilla in bowls shaped like grapefruit halves. We ate at her kitchen table, which was white with yellow placemats and napkins. The windows had yellow curtains. The tile was white and yellow. Every room in Em's house had a strict color scheme.

"It's like basically a giant rainbow," Em had said once. "It's like the gayest house on the block. But I'm not going to tell her that, or she'll tear the whole thing down and we'd have nowhere to live."

The yellow was cheery, even though I didn't feel so cheery. We ate our ice cream slowly, Em mashing hers until it resembled a white soup. She ate watery spoonfuls, letting the liquid drip onto her tongue.

"How was the class?" she asked cautiously, when we'd both finished our bowls.

"It went well, I think."

"So you didn't throw up on the desk or anything?"

"No."

"And you saw Sam?"

"Yeah. He was there. I don't . . . I don't know if he liked it."

"If he liked what?"

"My lesson plan. Or my plan–less lesson, actually."

"What do you mean he didn't like it?"

"I mean he just didn't seem engaged or something."

"What did you talk about?"

"Time. Eternity. Immortality. Life."

"Oh, so you kept it real light?" Em said, smiling, putting her hand on mine. "I wouldn't read too much into it, Lottie. It freaks a lot of people out to talk about that kind of thing, you know? Especially when they've just lost someone. But don't tell me you got like this just because of Sam?"

"No, not at all. I think it was a lot of things. The

nervousness of teaching a class, of being in front of all those people, of not knowing what the hell I was going to talk about . . . I started feeling panicky before I even went in, but I just tried to get past it."

"This hasn't happened for a while, right? At least that you've told me about."

"Not for a while. There's just a lot going on right now," I said.

"Of course. Have you talked to your parents about it?"

"Not yet."

"But you will, right? If it gets worse? Or if it happens again?"

"I will. I will. Now can we please watch *The Fellowship of the Ring*?"

"We most certainly can, once we finish this episode of *The X-Files*. Come on."

I didn't look at my phone until I got home. It was around eleven, and my parents and Abe and Amy were playing Monopoly at the kitchen table. As usual, Dad had a thick pile of money and property cards and a smug expression on his face.

I snuck past them with just a few *hellos* and *how are yous* exchanged between us.

Upstairs, I read four text messages from Sam.

Did you make it home OK?

I really thought you did a great job today.

I'm sorry I was kind of out of it.

Are you mad at me?

I wrote him back:

Hi. Yes, home. Thank you again. I'm not mad at you at all.

Then you'll see me again?

Of course I'll see you again.

Sunday? I can come to you or you can come here or we can meet somewhere or whatever you want to do?

Whatever you want to do.

Let's do this: meet me here at noon.

He sent me a pin. I opened it and read the address. New Canaan, Connecticut. About an hour and a half from Mystic and an hour and a half from me. I had never been there before, but I knew it was close to New York. A quick internet search didn't pull up anything interesting, so I wrote back:

I'll see you then.

Someone knocked on my door and then pushed it open slowly. Mom. She looked tired, and she'd changed into scrubs. An overnight shift at the hospital.

"There's an open seat for Monopoly, if you want to play," she said, sitting down on my bed and putting her hand on my leg.

"I think I'll just go to bed soon."

"I'm jealous. I wish I could go to bed."

"You look exhausted."

"A lot of overnights lately. They're short staffed, and I'm too nice."

"When is your next day off?"

"Monday sweet Monday. Nobody's ever said that before," she laughed.

I almost told her.

I wanted to tell her, but I couldn't think of the right words to use.

Mom, I think about death a lot.

Mom, I know Aunt Helen is the one who died, but now it kind of feels like I'm next.

Mom, I can't stop thinking about what happens afterward.

"Something on your mind, Lottie-da?" she said, brushing a piece of hair away from my face.

"I'm fine," I said automatically. Like breathing, like blinking. Something you don't even have to think about.

"Where were you all day?"

I hadn't told her about the class. I'd totally forgotten. Would she have wanted to come?

"Another errand for Aunt Helen," I said.

"Hmm," Mom said.

"What?"

"It's just . . . I'm a little worried you're focusing too much on what your aunt wanted and not enough on what you want. It's the last few days of high school; shouldn't you be out with Em? Getting into trouble?

Breaking some minor laws?"

"But I think I can do both," I said. "I mean, just yesterday Em and I robbed a bank at gunpoint."

"Oh, well, in that case," she said, smiling. "How many letters are left?"

"A few."

The stack was still on my nightstand. It was running out, but I hadn't counted yet. I didn't want to know. When it was gone, she was gone.

"She was something, huh?" Mom said.

"Yeah, Mom. She was something." I remembered what my dad had said, and I wondered if she knew anything about it. "Did Dad ever say anything to you? About her?"

"Are you talking about the missing week?" she asked.

"The missing week?"

"This was before my time. But I guess one summer, when she was about your age, I think, she just disappeared. Nobody knew where she went. When she came back, everybody said she seemed different."

"Different how?"

"Your father said . . ." She zoned out for a second, trying to remember. "She told him she had made a decision she couldn't figure out whether or not to regret." She shrugged and kissed me on my forehead. "Whatever that means," she added, getting up and leaving my room, closing my bedroom door behind her. As soon as she was gone I wanted her back. When she was here, I wanted to be

211

alone. I couldn't figure out what I wanted.

What decision could Aunt Helen have made? Where would she have gone for a week? Had something bad happened to her?

I took the next letter from my nightstand and tore it open. Loopy, messy words, like she'd written it in a hurry.

Lottie,

When I found out about my diagnosis, I didn't cry. It's a weird thing, Lottie, to have to hear someone else tell you that you're going to die. I almost didn't believe the doctor at first, even though it is a doctor I know and trust. Everything in my brain was screaming SHE'S LYING, even the rational parts that knew she had no reason to lie to me. I went home that night and had a cup of tea like I always do, read a book like I always do, watched a bit of TV like I sometimes do. Did. Do I have to say did now? I keep forgetting these letters are for after I'm gone. I keep forgetting that's the inevitable shadow I'm crashing toward.

I began to write these after a few months, after the cancer moved into places the doctor's instruments couldn't reach, swiftly and strategically taking up residency in my body, an uninvited stranger with no home of its own. It had to take mine and turn it against me.

I still didn't cry, not even as I numbered these

letters and called Harry and set my things in order.
I didn't cry as I decided how to divide up my belong-
ings, all those foolish possessions I had at one time
so desperately wanted. Do we crowd our rooms with
material things because we're afraid of the empty
space without them? Oh, I don't know, Lottie. But at
the end of it all I only feel sentimental about a few
of them. My books. My pictures. My first fancy car (I
hope your mom is enjoying it now).

When I was younger people told me I would regret
the decisions I had made. You will regret never mar-
rying, Helen! You will regret never having children,
Helen! I suppose I only regret not knowing what it
might have been like but never the choices themselves. Some women aren't meant to do all those
things. Maybe you are and maybe you aren't. You
have to figure that out for yourself.

Do I have any regrets, then? One, perhaps, and it's
a strange, strange one. It is not the obvious regret
that will reveal itself to you soon enough. It's another,
smaller regret. It's an easier one to get a handle on.
I'll tell you now because these letters allow me to tell
you everything, to not keep any secrets from you. You,
one of my favorite humans ever. Tied with Abe, tied
with your dad, tied with your mom.

Here it is. My one regret:

I never cried.

Weird, right? To regret something so small? But I don't know. In my whole entire life I never had a really good cry, one that lasted for hours and hurt like hell and emptied out every piece of my insides so I could start new. Your mom had a cry like that once, and I was there for it. If you ask her, she might tell you.

Here is my wish for you, Lottie. Or your next task, if that's what you're calling these. Whatever you call them: don't be afraid to let yourself cry. Cry often, cry long, cry hard. Cry when you're sad, cry when you're happy. Cry whenever the fuck you want. Cry for me (but then stop). Cry for you. Cry for everyone in the world. In moderation, it can be the best thing for you.

Love, H.

I put the letter on my comforter.

I was already crying.

I didn't stop for hours. I cried in my dreams, and I woke up empty and not the least bit new.

The members of the Everlife Society introduced themselves in initials: A., E., Q., and V.

A. and V. were women. E. and Q. were men. None of them was particularly welcoming, although it felt like E. imagined he was, by the way he set glasses of chocolate milk in front of the siblings. (Did he think they were six? Also, Margo was allergic to chocolate.)

Nobody said anything for a long time. The chocolate milk glasses sweated onto the wood. Margo considered asking for coasters, but hey, it wasn't her coffee table's funeral.

Then, as if bursting, A. leaned forward and asked, "Did you really make it into the house?"

"A.," E. said warningly.

Margo shrugged and said, "Yup," then pointedly pushed her glass away from her.

"Tell me how you did it," A. said.

"There was a door. We opened it," Margo said. She was in a foul mood, woken in the middle of the night and brought to the secret headquarters of some secret group. Alvin didn't blame her, although he did try and be a little nicer.

"We didn't do anything special," he added. "We just walked in."

"Through the front door?" A. pressed.

"Didn't I just say that?" Margo asked.

"Quite a rude little child, isn't she?" A. whispered to Q.

Unfortunately for her, Margo had excellent hearing.

"One shouldn't throw stones in glass houses," Margo said. And for good measure, she added, "And I'm allergic to chocolate."

—from *Alvin Hatter and the Everlife Society*

15

The morning light either reassures you or is much, much too bright. That morning it was the latter, and I stumbled downstairs with eyes red and puffy and blurred. My mother was just getting home from work; her own eyes were so tired that she couldn't see how I was swimming through the air, drowning in it. She kissed my temple and went upstairs to bed. I made a pot of coffee and took a mug outside. I sat on the deck stairs; it was already hot and humid, but the grass was sparkling with dew.

"Make up your mind," I whispered to the backyard.

"That's my girl, talking to herself as usual," Dad said. I hadn't noticed him sitting in one of the deck chairs, on top of a towel so he didn't get wet.

"I was talking to the grass," I corrected him.

"Even better!"

"Why are you up so early on a Saturday?"

"I might ask you the same question."

"Couldn't sleep."

"Same."

"Who won the Monopoly match last night?"

"Are you really asking a question to which you must surely know the answer?" Dad asked, getting up from his chair to join me on the steps. He put his arm around me and stole a sip of my coffee.

"The reigning champion," I said.

"You're looking at him."

"How did you get so good at Monopoly?"

"Helen. She taught me everything she knew. She had a cutthroat business sense. You need one, if you get as successful as she did."

His voice caught only the tiniest bit on her name. The tiniest hiccup in the back of his throat. It made my chest hurt.

"Mom told me about the missing week."

"Yeah," he said, withdrawing his arm, nodding. "She could be a real mystery, your aunt."

"Where do you think she went?"

"I have my theories. None of them are true, I'm sure."

"Maybe she wrote it down. She left me her journals, you know."

"Have you read them?"

"I'm waiting for her to tell me to."

"That's smart," he said. "She always had a plan, you know. She always knew what she was doing."

"I wonder what that's like."

"Don't be too hard on yourself, kid. Just a skip away from the end of high school. College waiting in the distance. You're doing pretty good from where I'm sitting."

"I guess. I mean, I know what I'm doing and what my goals are, but . . . I guess I'm scared that I'm not going to be able to achieve them."

"Whoa, whoa—where is this coming from?"

"It's just . . . nothing is a given, you know? I got into school, yeah, but that doesn't mean I'm going to be able to actually do it."

"If anyone's going to excel at this college thing it's *you*, Lottie. You've been ready for college since your first day of preschool. You wouldn't even let me walk you into the classroom, remember? *I got this, Dad.*"

I didn't remember, admittedly, and that also didn't really sound like me.

When had my anxiety kicked in? Sometime after that? *And why?*

"And if I don't? If I don't excel? What then?"

"Then we make a nice little in-law apartment for you in the basement, and you live the rest of your days as a shut-in."

"Dad! I'm being serious."

"I have no doubt in your ability to kick this college's ass,

Lottie, but on the off chance it doesn't work out, there are a hundred other paths you could take. A college degree isn't the only thing in life. Look at your aunt Helen."

He kissed my cheek, used my shoulder to push himself up. He went inside the house. I dumped the rest of my coffee on the grass and went inside to take a shower.

I tried to read the Ponce de León book later that day. I didn't understand why she had wanted me to have it. I hated history, and I wasn't particularly fond of nonfiction. I slugged through the first paragraph, and in theory it was pretty cool—it was all about an impossible quest and an unreachable dream—but the writing was so long-winded and dry that my eyes unfocused after just a few sentences.

Aunt Helen had owned the most expansive private library of anyone I'd ever heard of (she was featured on the front page of *Libraries International* twelve separate times). (Yes, *Libraries International* was an actual magazine.) So I wasn't quite sure why one of her last wishes had been to have this particular book back.

I put it back on my bookshelf and went to play croquet with Abe.

The next morning was Sunday, my day with Sam. I woke up early and took a shower and found something to wear and then knocked on Abe's door at ten.

"Go away," he yelled.

Abe was sometimes a morning person and sometimes

not. It came and went in waves.

"It's me!" I said.

"Go away, me."

"Abe, I miss you!"

"You live with me."

"It just doesn't feel like that lately, you know?" I leaned against the door and ran my fingernails down the wood over and over, because I knew that drove him crazy.

"FINE," he yelled, so I turned the doorknob and let myself into the room.

Abe's room was kind of a mystery to me. He didn't love intruders and so every time I was let inside, it felt like my first time. Every wall was lined with floor-to-ceiling bookcases, now packed with first editions and rare hard-covers from my aunt. He'd unpacked much quicker than I had. Aunt Helen's boxes were still sitting on my carpet, still covered in a blanket, waiting.

Abe was lying in bed, the comforter pulled up to his chin, his eyes squinted shut, and his face scowling.

"What do you want?" he hissed.

"I just wanted to say hi."

"Next time, text me."

"Have you ever been to New Canaan?"

"No."

"Is there a Canaan? Is there an Old Canaan?"

"I was sleeping, Lottie."

"Do you think people are inherently good or evil?"

"Are we doing this now? Are you really trying to do this now?"

"I don't mean that in a weird way. Like, just off the top of your head."

"You're killing me."

"What do you think happens after you die?"

Abe, who had shut his eyes, now cracked one open. He looked at me in the long, hard way only a sibling is capable of looking at another sibling. Like: *I love you so much, but I also kind of want to kill you.*

"Lottie," he said.

"Abe."

"Do you want to maybe talk about this later?"

"I'm about to leave."

"Where are you going?"

"To New Canaan. With Sam."

"What's in New Canaan?"

"I don't know. I thought you might."

Abe pulled himself up, rubbing at his eyes. "Lottie, are you okay?"

"I'm fine."

"Let's play croquet again. Whenever you get back, we'll play croquet."

"Promise?"

"I promise."

"With flamingoes?"

"If you can train them properly."

He ducked back under the covers and pulled them over his head until I could only see his hair. I ran my fingertips over the spines of all his books. New and old. History and present. Then I let myself out of his room and went down to the car. I texted Sam:

I'm on my way.

He texted back immediately:

I'll see you soon.

I read Aunt Helen's next letter before I started driving.

Lottie,

I did an interview with a magazine once, some foreign magazine I can't remember now. The interviewer I remember, though; she was a petite girl with thick glasses and black, black hair, a bright-yellow shirt and bright-red lipstick and a bright-blue skirt. She was so bright, is what I'm saying, that it kind of hurt my eyes to look at her directly. But she was also very self-assured and not at all threatened by my intimidating artist demeanor (kidding). She looked me straight in the eye, point-blank, and said, in this beautiful accent I cannot now place, "What is the worst thing you have ever done?"

That was her opening question! My gosh, at the time it kind of ruffled my feathers, it annoyed me a bit. I didn't know how to answer her, and I think I even felt embarrassed, a little accosted, like, where does this little imp get off being so bold? I'm sure I must have given her a half-assed answer, a stock answer, something like "Well, if I told you, I'd have to kill you." Now I'm hoping that expression translated to whatever her first language was, otherwise I might have come off as quite the murderer.

Now, many years and many interviews later, she is one of the only interviewers I can actually remember (I also remember Oprah and Ellen, but that's to be expected). And that question stands out as the most interesting question I've ever been asked. So, for fun, I'd like to answer it now. There is no one left to keep it a secret from; I shall soon be gone, and maybe the one good thing about death is you no longer have to worry about maintaining your public image. You no longer, essentially, have to explain yourself.

The worst thing I have ever done is to walk away from a friend at the very moment he needed me the most. That's as specific as I want to be, for now (if there weren't some cliffhangers to these letters, how could I be sure you'd read them all the way through?). As a much younger person, I was faced with a very difficult decision, and I chose to protect myself and only myself, to put myself first in every respect of the phrase. To abandon completely one of my few true friends. I have never forgiven myself for that (nor should I), and it is something I think about often. I was a selfish person, once upon a time. I am thankful to have (mostly) grown out of it.

You, however, are not selfish at all, and I admire that about you so much. I wonder what answer you would give, if someday an interviewer asked you the same question. I'd like you to have something fun to tell them, a secret that hurts no one, and so that is where my next task comes from:

Do something you're not supposed to do.

Do it with relish.

Enjoy the not-supposed-to-be-doingness of it.

Do it proudly. Break some rules. Hurt no one.

Love, H.

I opened the pinned address Sam had sent while I mentally calculated all the rules I was not prepared to break: stealing, vandalizing, murder. Obviously. I could run a stop sign on the way to New Canaan? But that didn't seem like anything special; it just seemed dangerous and irresponsible.

The map routed me to somewhere called the Glass House. I spent the hour-and-a-half ride wondering both what I could do that I wasn't supposed to, and whether it was literally a glass house.

It was literally a glass house.

Well—not at first.

The address Sam sent me took me to Elm Street, and a

little brick building with a sign that said The Glass House. Sam was already there.

"This is a brick house. This isn't a glass house," I said, instead of hello.

"You'll see," he said.

A few minutes later we were herded into vans, and a few minutes after that we pulled over and disembarked, and I followed our small group up a hill.

It emerged out of nowhere, past a skinny stone wall and just in front of a peaceful pond. A literal glass house. Our tour guide stopped the group outside and began to give a short history, but I hardly heard him. I couldn't stop looking at it.

"This is unreal," I whispered to Sam.

All four sides of the rectangular house were pure glass. It was edged on one side by beautiful tall trees and the grass surrounding it was pristine and green. There was a circular column of bricks on the inside, a small room, whereas everything else was open and bright.

"I've just always liked it here," Sam said as we followed the tour inside. "It's so peaceful. So open."

"It's really beautiful."

The house was small and felt cramped with everyone inside, but it was easy to imagine what it would be like without them, what it would be like by yourself or with a few friends. I imagined it in winter, surrounded by snow, and in fall—all the colors of the leaves. I imagined what it would look like in different places—on the top of a mountain or in the desert or on the bottom of the ocean. I couldn't stop spinning in circles. I wondered how often they had to clean all the glass, whether they used newspapers like my mom, and a blue-and-white can of glass cleaner.

There were other buildings on the property, another brick house, and an art gallery built right into the side of a small, grassy hill. The entrance, the tour guide said, was built to resemble Agamemnon's Tomb. There was a Warhol there, a portrait of Philip Johnson, who had designed and built everything and lived here before he died.

The tour was an hour and a half long, and afterward the van was quiet as the tour guide drove us back to the visitors' center. Sam and I wandered idly through the museum store, touching everything, buying only a single postcard each. In the parking lot, Sam searched for a park on his phone, and we found one called Waveny. We left my car at the visitors' center (I guess that could technically be considered something I wasn't supposed to do, but it didn't feel like a big enough deviance) and went and got sandwiches at a deli close by.

We ate them in the park, under the shadow of a giant tree, on a blanket Sam removed from the trunk of his car. Not far from us a group of kids played a very unregulated game of soccer, using jackets to mark goalposts and a half-deflated ball that whistled and flopped when it was kicked.

"How did you find out about this place?" I asked.

"Whenever I meet someone new, I ask them where they live, and then I ask them—what's your favorite place there? And then I go and see for myself."

"You didn't ask me that."

"I usually ask them. Sometimes I'm too busy dancing."

"So you go to all these places, you audit all these classes . . . I still have no idea how you do it all."

"I guess I just have a lot of time on my hands," he said.

"I feel like I never have time for anything except school."

"You're here now."

"Well, school is basically over."

"You'll have plenty of time this summer."

"I guess. Three months, at least."

"That's enough time to see some cool things. Especially here. You can get anywhere in Connecticut within two hours."

"I guess you're right."

"Usually," he said, smiling.

"Remember when we were younger and there were all those field trips with school? Sturbridge Village, the Dr. Seuss Sculpture Garden in Springfield, the Basketball Hall of Fame. We even went to a waterpark once. Why did those stop? We finally got old enough to appreciate them, and all of a sudden they were taken away from us. And recess. We should still have recess."

Sam laughed. "You want recess?"

"Just a break, you know? We're on the same freaking campus as the middle school. We can see the swings from the English hallway."

"Just out of reach," he said dramatically. "So close, and yet . . ."

"Laugh all you want. Why didn't we come and see things like this? History, you know? Our state. Our world. You have to be in chorus or band to go anywhere in my high school, and when people started figuring that out, everyone signed up because they wanted to go to Disney World. So they stopped sending them to Disney World. Now they just go to New York to see a musical. Chorus attendance has dropped dramatically. It's a catch twenty-two. Damned if you do, damned if you don't actually care about Disney and just want to sing. Just to clarify though, I do care about Disney."

"Do you sing, then? Or play anything?"

"I was terrible at the recorder," I said seriously, remembering our very first music classes as elementary-aged kids. The people who could afford new recorders got smooth, cream-colored ones. The people who bought second-hand got a sickly tan. They taught us how to put them together, take them apart. I slept with mine for two weeks, convinced that proximity would lead to a state of musical affluence. I had seen the posters of Garfield lying on a stack of books, bright text above him that said *I'm Learning Through Osmosis.*

"Then Abe snuck into my room once, found the recorder under my pillow, learned to play 'Hot Cross Buns' in ten minutes, and I was over it. That was the first time I realized (but admitted to no one) that I didn't like things I wasn't immediately good at. Which is why I never play my father at Monopoly."

"Can you sing?" he asked.

"I am potentially better at the recorder than I am at singing."

"In the car? In the shower?"

"The shower has excellent acoustics, but no. What about you?"

"I play some guitar. And sing a little. Not well! And I think you're right, you know. About the field trips. Except we're jerks. We can't even shut up during school assemblies. I don't think they trust us not to act like idiots if they brought us somewhere that actually mattered."

"I couldn't imagine you acting like an idiot," I said. Which reminded me. "I read another letter from my aunt."

"Really? What did it say?"

And there it was suddenly, the answer. I didn't need Sam to tell me what to do, and I didn't need to murder anyone. I just needed the sun to go down.

"What can we do in this town to kill a few hours?" I asked him.

Which is how we ended up playing soccer with a bunch of fourth graders.

✳ ✳ ✳

At seven o'clock—early enough that the sun hadn't set yet, late enough to be sure the last tour had ended—we found ourselves back at the Glass House. We snuck up, Sam carrying the blanket and me carrying a flashlight he'd had in his backseat ("Be prepared," he said, handing it to me). Everything was quiet at the house. The lights were off, and we were completely alone. Sam laid the blanket out near the pond, and I skipped rocks and then taught him how to skip rocks. The hardest part is finding the right kind of stone: flat, round, smooth. The next hardest part is wrapping your fingers around it. The next hardest part is how you let go.

The second Alvin Hatter book, *Alvin Hatter and the Overcoat Man*, opens with Margo trying to teach Alvin how to skip rocks. She is a natural at it, getting six or seven or eight skips a rock. Alvin is hopeless, eventually giving up and trying for the biggest splash. That was kind of like Sam.

With Sam, I didn't feel pressured to maintain a steady stream of conversation topics. Being with Em was usually the exact opposite; she interpreted silence as an indicator that something had gone terribly wrong. She pulled words out of me with both hands, her heels dug into the ground for leverage. Even when I was exhausted, even when there was nothing else to say.

I had the feeling that if I didn't say anything to Sam, he wouldn't say anything to me, and we would continue in that cycle of silence until all that was left was the chirping of crickets and the chirping of frogs. The pond had both of those things. For the first time, it felt like summer.

"Tell me about the saddest you've ever been," I said. Because I didn't want that silence to stretch on forever. Finding a balance: that was the key.

"A lot of people I knew have died," he said after a minute. "It never gets any easier."

He didn't offer any specifics. I wondered if that was the sad smile I so often saw on his face. Was Aunt Helen's death reminding him of all the losses he'd already experienced? "I'm sorry," I said.

"It's just life," he said. "A part of life."

I sensed him pulling away, withdrawing into himself, letting that sadness overwhelm him. I took his hand and squeezed. "Tell me the happiest you've ever been," I said.

He leaned back on the blanket, propping himself up with his elbows. "I like meeting new people," he said finally. "I like seeing new things."

"But the *happiest*," I said.

"The driftwood tower. When we jumped. That was happy."

"But that's not the happiest."

"You don't know that. You can't police my happy."

"You need a really good happy memory. Hold on—I'm feeling inspiration hit." I stepped off the blanket and kicked my shoes off into the grass.

Aunt Helen had said to break the rules, and I suddenly didn't think skipping a few rocks into a pond was quite good enough for that.

"Lottie? What are you doing?" Sam asked.

I was wearing shorts and a tank top. Good enough. I pulled my hair into a ponytail and winked at him.

"Chasing some happiness," I said, and then ran full speed at the lake.

It was colder than I expected—an iciness that took my breath away. But I didn't stop; I didn't hesitate. I pushed myself farther, and once I reached waist-deep water I dove forward, shrieking when the water hit my face. I kept swimming underwater, paddling fiercely toward the middle of the lake. Finally I resurfaced and turned around. I could just make out the shadow of Sam standing by the edge of the lake.

"Don't overthink it!" I said.

"We probably wouldn't have been arrested for skipping rocks, but for actually swimming . . . ," he said, trailing off, looking behind him.

"Oh, who's going to arrest us? Do you see many cops around here?"

"Who knew you had this rebellious streak, Lottie Reaves?" Sam said, but I could see him slipping out of his shoes and pulling his shirt over his head.

I watched him take a deep breath and then wade carefully into the water.

"Oh, come on," I said.

He looked up at me and rolled his eyes, then mimicked my dive. He was much more graceful than I; he hardly made a ripple as he disappeared into the water.

He surfaced a few feet from me and shook the water out of his hair.

"This isn't happy," he said. "This is cold."

"It *is* pretty cold, isn't it?"

But it also somehow didn't bother me—even as I shivered I felt happy, exhilarated.

"You definitely have to pay my bail money if we get arrested," Sam said.

"Deal."

"What are we doing out here, anyway?"

"Getting our minds off things! Loosening up a little! All of the above!"

Sam ran his arms through the water and dipped down up to his neck. "Okay," he said. "I'm warming up."

"Great! Okay, what's the maddest you've ever been?"

"Maddest. Hmm. When I had to read *Wuthering Heights* for an English class. That's a terrible book."

"You're not answering any of these truthfully!"

"I'm trying," he said, laughing. He let his feet rise up and performed an admirable dead man's float. "What about you? How come you get to ask all the questions?"

"Because it's my game, and I make the rules. Now— what's the worst thing you've ever done?"

"I can't tell you," he said. "It's too bad."

"Come on. It can't be that bad."

"If I told you—"

"Right, right, you'd have to kill me, whatever. Just tell me."

"The last person I told didn't take it too well," he said seriously and stood up in the water again. In his floating he'd moved around me, and I saw him look past me to the shore, his eyes growing wide. "Oh shit," he whispered.

"What?"

"Shh!" he said and grabbed my hand, spinning me around to look toward shore, to where a flashlight bobbed over the grounds of the Glass House.

"Oh shit," I repeated.

"It doesn't seem like he's coming down by the lake. Just be quiet," Sam said. He took a step toward me and put his arms around my shoulders; we sank into the water so just our heads were above the surface.

It wasn't an excellent time to be wondering what Sam had meant by *the last person I told didn't take it too well*, but still, I couldn't help myself. Had he been joking? It didn't really seem like it.

I couldn't lie, though; this was kind of nice. My heart was beating straight out of my chest, sure, as I watched the security guard and his flashlight make his rounds around the property, but Sam's arms were still resting on my shoulders and it felt . . . really nice.

"We're going to jail," Sam whispered dramatically, and I couldn't help but laugh (he pressed a hand over my mouth and rested his chin on the top of my head). I felt the same rush of adrenaline, the same sense of fear and excitement as when Em and I had jumped off the cliff.

I peeled Sam's fingers away from my mouth. "Look, silly, he's walking away."

I turned around in Sam's arms and became acutely aware of how close we were, how wet Sam's face was, how his hair dripped little beads of water onto his shoulders.

And for one second I thought maybe he was leaning closer—but then no, he had pulled away, he was wading silently back to shore.

I wondered again what he had meant and whether the worst thing he'd ever done was actually bad, like more-than-I-had-expected bad.

I followed him to shore and searched his face for that sad smile again, or for any sort of hint as to what he was thinking. But he was harmless, smiling to himself as he rolled up the blanket and slung his T-shirt over his shoulder. We crept away from the Glass House by moonlight, and I tried to tell myself the chunk of doubt wedging itself into my brain was an unwelcome intruder, unfounded and meaningless. I wouldn't give it any more fuel.

"This is the last time I follow you into a lake," he said, but he was smiling, and he took my hand and didn't let it go until we said good-bye.

Alvin's hand was shaking. It was shaking so much he could hardly make out the words on the paper, words scratched haphazardly, tripping over themselves in their rush to be read:

I HAVE YOUR SISTER.

TELL NO ONE.

But that didn't make sense, Alvin's brain insisted. Margo was safe. Margo had gone to school. Margo would be walking in the back door any minute now. Whoever had written this letter was very confused.

And though nowhere on the letter did it actually say who its author was, somehow Alvin knew.

He knew who had written it.

He knew his sister was not going to walk in that door.

He knew the Overcoat Man had her.

MEET ME AT THE HOUSE IN THE WOODS.

ONCE I'M INSIDE, YOU'LL GET YOUR SISTER BACK.

Alvin wasn't worried for his sister's life. That was safe, protected, not in danger.

But there were still so many ways to hurt someone who couldn't die.

He had to get her back.

—from *Alvin Hatter and the Overcoat Man*

16

In an effort to take my mind off Sam's cryptic answer from the night before, I read Aunt Helen's next letter before I had to leave for school.

> Lottie,
>
> I certainly hope you aren't reading this from a jail cell.
>
> Kidding! (I hope.)
>
> I've been spending so much time alone lately, so much tying-up-loose-ends time, so much letter-writing time, that I think I'm starting to get a little stir-crazy. There is a fine line to walk between too much quiet and just the right amount.
>
> There can be good that comes out of being alone, of course, but I think at this current moment I am doing myself no favors.

I know you also have a tendency to pull away from others when things get hard, and I challenge you now to do the complete opposite. Let others in. Embrace a crowd. Find somewhere where it is impossible to be alone, and see what comes of it.

I think I will do the same.

Love always, H.

I texted my mom as soon as I finished reading the note:

> **Not feeling great. Don't think I'll make it to school.**

I knew she was at the hospital and that she kept her phone on her for emergencies. Her reply came almost instantly:

> **OK? Should I worry? Need IV? Blood transfusion? MRI? I love you?**
>
> **Just a headache. ILYT.**
>
> **OK, honey. Senioritis. It's going around.**
>
> **Feel better. Get some rest.**

I didn't love lying to her (I felt physically fine), but it was a small transgression and, in the scheme of things, another day missed wouldn't really matter. I got dressed and went downstairs, made coffee and took it outside to the porch.

It was muggy outside—it grew muggier every day, a crescendo of humidity that would break only when the first summer thunderstorm hit, and then for a few hours in the dead of night.

Aunt Helen was right about my tendency to hide away when things weren't perfect. My anxiety made it worse, made me feel like something terrible would happen sometimes when I left the house. I generally avoided crowded places, instead preferring to stay at home with a good book. Or to be with Em. It was probably telling that she was really the only good friend I had.

Of course she was my first thought. I considered texting her and asking her to skip school with me (she would no doubt be thrilled), but then I thought that if there was a point to Aunt Helen's letter (to all her letters, really), it definitely wasn't to get me to spend more time with the people I already spent all my time with.

She was trying to nudge me out of my comfort zone. That much was obvious.

It was nice, in a way. Annoying, in a way. Like everything our families make us do.

I was halfway through my cup of coffee before I figured out where I could go. Where I *should* go.

My anxiety started up before I even left the house, but I pretended not to notice it (because that worked so well last time?). I charged through the motions: putting on my shoes, getting into my car, driving, parking, turning the car off. Only then, when I was in the hospital parking lot once again, the hospital where she had died, did I let myself feel fully the emotions that this place held.

How many people had died here? How many people

were here now who wouldn't make it through the end of the week, through the end of the month? Would I die here one day? My parents? Abe?

I put my hands on the steering wheel and felt the rising panic in my chest. Such a familiar feeling, so easy to let it overtake all sense of rationality. I struggled to picture the driftwood structure again, I closed my eyes and assured myself that I was fine, that nobody ever died from a panic attack, that panic attacks were only caused by the fear of the physical sensations of fear itself.

My heart rate slowly returned to normal. I didn't feel perfect, but I felt better. I got out of the car and walked into the hospital, past the reception area to the fifth floor. The cancer ward. And in particular: the children's cancer ward.

I checked in at the front desk.

Abe had done this many times when he'd needed a break from sitting by Aunt Helen's bedside. He'd always ask me to come with him, but I never had the courage to walk into a room full of kids who were that sick, to look them in the eyes, to talk to them and spend time with them.

It had felt too overwhelmingly sad.

But that seemed incredibly selfish now; if I was sad, what must they be feeling?

I recognized the guy at the children's ward reception desk. His name was Jamie, and he'd gone to my high school. He was a few years older than me and practically famous—he'd won the state lottery jackpot a week before he graduated. His payout was twenty-three million dollars. He'd been on all the news shows and in the papers and everything. He was a quiet guy with modest taste in the face of sudden wealth. He'd bought a bowling alley in town and a small house in the middle of cow country with the winnings and kept his job at the hospital.

He looked up when I approached the desk. He was wearing pale-pink scrubs covered in kittens. He had longish, messy hair and a beard. His smile lit up his face.

"Lottie, right?" he said.

"Yeah. Hi."

"I'm sorry about your aunt. I knew her, you know."

"Oh yeah?"

"She would come in here and read to the kids a lot. After her chemo. Parents were always freakin' out, I guess she was famous or something? Honestly, I don't pay much attention to that. Your brother too. I used to see him a lot. He's a rad guy."

"I'll tell him you said so."

"I haven't seen him since she passed away. People drift in and out of here, and that's okay. There's always someone new, someone who is able to give a little bit of their time."

"Like me."

"Oh, is that why you're here? That's awesome."

"I was just thinking I could read something? That's what my brother used to do, right? Read to them?"

"Yeah, and he did all the voices too, he was a big hit. He

always read this story about a brother and a sister. I think they were immortal or something? Always on the run from some guy in a jacket?"

"The Overcoat Man," I said.

"Rad, you know them? The kids love those stories. I can set you up where Abe left off. This is a good time; just before lunch. We'll get 'em good and hungry."

And so Jamie led me into a little room that looked a lot like a classroom, with many bright colors and art supplies and even a little plastic toy box full of musical instruments. He got me a chair and placed *Alvin Hatter and the Wild-Goose Chase* into my hand, saying, "These books are rad because all the kids like 'em, doesn't matter how old they are." And then he left me alone.

But I was only alone for a few minutes.

The kids started coming in one after another. Some of them walked in, some of them were pushed in wheelchairs and accompanied by a parent, some of them had IVs attached to their arms, needles they scratched at vaguely with the tip of a finger. Some looked sick; some looked just a little tired. A few littler ones sat on the floor in front of me. They wore pajama pants and hospital tops, a sea of pale blue. Jamie himself came and took a seat on a folding chair; he let a small boy climb onto his lap. It felt similar to teaching Aunt Helen's class except I was suddenly completely unintimidated. Unanxious. Unworried.

There was a bookmark in the middle of the Alvin book.

I opened to the right page and began to read. I looked up a few minutes later and saw wide eyes, open mouths, anxious expressions. Alvin and Margo were going through their parents' notes, trying to find a clue that would lead them to the Overcoat Man, and in turn lead them to their missing parents, and every single one of my audience members were completely rapt with attention.

I smiled and kept reading.

Afterward, when the children begrudgingly went back to their rooms to eat lunch, I hung back a moment in the room and tried to imagine my aunt and brother reading where I had just read. Were the children the same, or were these all fresh faces, new victims of a terrible disease they would spend so much energy fighting? It didn't seem fair, that someone so young would have to go through so much suffering, but I knew that life didn't play by the playground rules of fairness.

I closed the book and returned it to its bookcase home with the others. When I turned around, Jamie was standing in the doorway, arms crossed, and I almost laughed at the sight of his beard and those pink scrubs.

"This was great," he said. "Really rad. It means so much to the kids. They said you look just like her."

"Really?"

"Yeah. Don't be a stranger, you know? These kids, they just spend so much of their day waiting around for people to come and pay them some attention."

"I definitely won't be. This was really nice."

"Your whole family, I swear. Just a bunch of gems," he said, and with an unexpected hug, we said good-bye.

I drove home slowly, thinking about the last couple of hours, the kids and Jamie, and the day-to-day life of a hospital. I imagined it must take a special kind of person to devote their life to helping sick people find just a little bit of happiness. It made me proud to think that my own mother was a doctor, that my father was the most beloved anesthesiologist in the area (well, as far as he was concerned). I wondered if being a teacher was a similarly noble goal, a way of devoting one's life to the betterment of others. Wasn't that one of the reasons I'd chosen to do it, because my own teachers had meant so much to me growing up? Because I wanted to one day maybe mean something to students of my own?

I took the long way home, driving the back roads, missing my street once, twice. I felt both exhilarated and happy, like I had done something good instead of just letting myself float along aimlessly.

When I finally got home, my father was in the driveway, washing his car.

I knew my father. He didn't wash his car when it was dirty; he washed it when he was feeling sad. He washed it with slow, deliberate movements, making rhythmic circles with his hand and the sponge. I parked and watched him for a few minutes, and he never saw me, just kept scrubbing the same square foot on the hood.

I came up behind him and cleared my throat. He turned around slowly, blinking, as if he were waking up from a dream.

"Hey, kid," he said. "I'll do yours next if you want me to."

"You don't have to."

"It's kind of nice out, don't you think? Aren't you supposed to be in school?"

"Mental health day," I said. "I told Mom."

"Ah. That's okay. I get it."

"Do you want some help?"

"Actually, I think I might like just a little more alone time. Nothing serious. I was just enjoying it out here. It's nice out, isn't it?"

He looked faraway, repeating himself, not really paying attention. I gave him a hug and went into the house.

I watched him from the foyer, my face pressed against the glass pane in the front door. He was methodical in his cleaning. He would have the cleanest car in the neighborhood before the afternoon was over.

When he'd finished with his, he moved on to mine. I made a pitcher of lemonade and brought it out to him. He took a glass without saying a word, a vague smile on his face, the saddest smile I'd seen in a while. It looked just like Sam's. I left him alone after that.

Grandpa Hatter was annoyed.

Granted, Grandpa Hatter's general state was annoyed, but he seemed a little more annoyed than usual to be woken up in the middle of the night by his two sheepish grandchildren who had previously woken him up in the middle of the night only to then disappear without a trace.

"So you're back," he said through the crack in the door.

"We made a mistake," Alvin said.

"Ran off with that good-for-nothing Everlife Society, did you? No brighter than your parents."

He shut the door in their faces, but they heard him unchaining the many chains and undoing the many locks that protected him from who knew what.

Finally, after much fumbling, he opened the door.

"I knew you'd be back," he said.

"The Everlife Society are a bunch of jerks," Margo said, pushing her way into the house. Alvin followed her. They waited as Grandpa Hatter went through the complicated process of locking the door again.

"We didn't know where else to go," Alvin said. "We thought you could help us?"

"I can't even help myself," Grandpa Hatter said sharply, but then he softened, as if noticing how tired and cold his grandchildren were. "Oh, fine. Follow me."

He led them through the massive house, down hallways they'd never seen before, past more closed doors than they could count. Again they had the feeling that this house, like the house in the woods, was somehow bigger on the inside than it had seemed from the outside.

Finally, after what seemed like ten full minutes of wandering, they stopped at the dead end of a hallway. There was a bookshelf here, with a wall sconce on either side. The candles were extinguished.

"Your father forbade me to show you this, but I've never taken kindly to being forbidden to do something. Plus, maybe you'll find something useful here," Grandpa Hatter said.

Then he reached out a hand, grabbed a very specific book by its spine, and pulled.

At once the sconces sprang to life and the entire bookshelf started rotating to reveal a literal, actual, secret passage.

"No way," Margo breathed.

"I'm going back to bed. Don't make too much noise," Grandpa Hatter said, and he left them alone.

—from *Alvin Hatter and the Wild-Goose Chase*

17

Em cornered me at my locker the next day, her face a perfect cartoon picture of concern. She wore what I knew was her most favorite outfit: a Dashboard Confessional T-shirt (worn in irony, she said, but not really) tucked into a pair of denim cutoffs. Her blue hair was wrapped into a bun on the top of her head. The few pieces that weren't long enough fell down around her ears. She wore little LEGO block money stud earrings. A gift from Jackie, maybe *the* gift, the one that made her realize she was in love.

"Lottie!" she said, slamming herself against my locker as soon as I'd gotten it open. It clicked shut again, locked. "I missed you. Please don't ever leave me again!"

"It was just one day."

"That stretched on literally forever. Okay? Literally."

"Would you think it was weird if you asked somebody

what the worst thing they'd ever done was and they just wouldn't tell you? Like at first you thought it was a joke or something, but then they really, actually wouldn't tell you?"

"I'd think they probably murdered someone," Em said thoughtfully.

"Yeah. That's what I figured."

"Who are we talking about here? Sam?"

"Yeah."

"Why would you even ask someone that? That's on you."

"I don't know, it was on my mind, it was something my aunt had written about in one of her letters. I guess it's kind of a personal question."

"Yeah, I mean, I'm sure he just didn't want to tell you because he likes you and he wants you to have this very curated impression of him, you know?"

"So you don't think it's creepy."

"I don't think it's creepy, no. I think you're probably just reading too much into it."

"So he's not actually a murderer?"

"Oh, no, he's definitely a murderer. I thought we already established that."

"Shut up." I threw my arm out to punch her, but she was too fast for me; she danced away, laughing at her own joke.

***

I read Aunt Helen's next letter that afternoon.

Dear Lottie,

It's strange to think that already, in so little time, so much has changed. When you read this, all my things will have been auctioned off to the highest bidder. My houses will be gone, my cars and my books (Abe better be taking good care of them), my flowers and my flowerpots, my clothes and my shoes and my jewelry (I hope you're wearing it, Lottie, because jewelry is meant to be worn). This bothered me at first, knowing that everything I have collected over the course of my lifetime will suddenly be, quite unceremoniously, not mine. I wondered: Am I materialistic? If I am, is it okay to be? Is everyone? Is it a problem, liking our stuff?

I don't think I have a good answer to this.

I think certainly, as privileged citizens of this world, as people who can afford a few material possessions, there is a tendency to then go overboard and fill up our lives with THINGS. And then, maybe even sillier, we become attached to them! Me! A woman lucky enough to have many friends and a beautiful family and a nephew and a niece I adore! I am attached to my THINGS, Lottie, everyTHING from a painting purchased in Spain to a little wire basket picked up at the local Goodwill. There is no rhyme or reason to this madness! $2 or $2,000, I am equally attached!

Anyway, here's a little exercise I made myself do recently, just to break that initial attachment: I took something I thought I could not live without, and I gave it away.

I think you should do the same. You might find it rather freeing, as I did (after I got over myself and stopped hyperventilating).

Give something away. Leave it for someone else. The where, the what: those are up to you.

Many times in our lives we may be forced to part with things we really do not wish to part with (a friend, one's healthy cells, etc.).

Consider this a small practice.

Just pick something, and let it go.

Love, H.

My offering to the universe, or at least to Aunt Helen's ghost (Did I believe in ghosts? Undecided.), turned out to be a thing I'd been thinking about more and more. A thing I had never showed anyone. A thing I had held on to for years, kept it in between my box spring and mattress, not able to throw it away, not able to look at it, not able to do anything except leave it alone.

This seemed like the perfect fate for it. It was something I didn't need anymore. It was something I should have let go of a long time ago.

I pulled it out now and let it rest on my comforter while I stared at it.

It was innocuous enough at first glance: a small notebook with tiny gazelles on the cover. When I picked it up, I imagined it weighed much more than it actually did. Every page was absolutely covered with words written in thick black ink. Words I wrote when I couldn't sleep. Years' worth of restlessness, an attempt to write the negative, worrisome thoughts out of my head. I scanned it now, a heavy feeling growing in the pit of my stomach: scared, body, death, broken, tired, drowning, broken, pieces.

I knew fighting the rising symptoms of anxiety wasn't as easy as throwing a little notebook away, but it couldn't have been good to sleep on this thing, this weight, this darkness, night after night after night. It couldn't have been good to hold on to a thing that was such a distinct reminder of all those thoughts that lingered in the back of my mind, growing and growing as I did my best to pretend not to notice.

For some reason I didn't quite understand, I got a roll of wrapping paper out from under my bed and measured out a square big enough to wrap the notebook up. I didn't yet know where I was going to leave it, but the distinct cover, those gold-foil gazelles, was making me sick.

My dad walked in as I was taping the last flap of the wrapping shut. The notebook was covered in very cheery wrapping paper. I felt hot and uneasy.

"Wait," he said, seeing the package. "Whose birthday is it? Did I forget someone's birthday?"

"It's nobody's birthday. It's just something Aunt Helen wanted me to do. One of her things."

"Hmm," he said, sitting on the bed.

"What do you mean, *hmm*?"

"You know you don't have to do anything you don't want to do, right? It wouldn't be unlike my sister to ask too much of you. She tended not to think of what effect her actions might have on other people. She might have you doing things for her for the rest of your life."

I knew what he meant. Aunt Helen had called herself selfish in one of her letters, had expressed a hope that she'd grown out of it, but it wasn't really that simple to explain. It was more complicated; it wasn't selfishness so much as it was an inability to understand how someone could not be available to her every whim.

Like once she showed up on a Friday night to surprise me with tickets to a musical. But I had a massive essay due on Monday and knew I had to spend all weekend working on it. She wasn't mad, exactly, but she sulked around for ten minutes, kind of whining, letting it be known that my unavailability was really putting a damper on her night.

But that was silly stuff, that was nothing. She was dead, and the least I could do now was read her letters like she wanted me to.

For the rest of your life, my father had said. But hadn't Aunt Helen proved that *for the rest of my life* might not be that long after all?

I said as much and watched his eyes darken.

"I don't like that," he said. "I don't like that at all."

"I didn't mean it."

"I hope not."

"I didn't."

"Because it's not a very nice thing to think about. You're not thinking about it, are you?"

"No, Dad—it was a joke. A stupid joke."

"Okay. I don't like things like that. You're going to live forever. I'm going to live for just under forever."

"I'm sorry. I didn't mean anything."

"Okay, Lottie-da."

"Okay, Dad."

He left the room as a growing knot of unease bloomed in my stomach. You didn't make dying jokes to someone who'd just lost their sister. I tried—and immediately couldn't—think of what my life might be like if Abe died before me. I didn't care if it was next week or eighty years from now, it could never happen. He needed to outlast me by at least two years, fair was fair.

I touched the package, tried hard to get my breathing to return to normal.

Now that it was done, there was only the question of where to leave it. But I knew that too. I'd known it even before I'd started boxing everything up. I was going back to Aunt Helen's house.

I made the drive on Friday after school. It took me longer than usual to get to the house. It was almost summer now, and people were leaving early to get to beach homes and weekend getaways. When I finally arrived, I parked on the street, because I didn't want to pull my car into the driveway. I doubted anybody had moved in that quickly, but I still felt like I should keep my distance. Even though I was about to trespass, as it were.

I kept to the edge of the property, shaded by the trees that offered the house a respectable amount of privacy. I had the package in a tote that I carried on my shoulder. I'd made a card with leftover scraps of wrapping paper. *Burn this*, it said.

I crossed the backyard and approached the small shed, painted the same white as the house and used, when I was younger, as a playhouse. Aunt Helen had decked it out with a play kitchen and a tiny table and chairs, an old chest filled with crayons and paper and markers and modeling clay. Anything Abe and I might want to disappear with for hours while the adults had cocktail parties or played bocce on the giant lawn.

All those things were gone now. The crayons, the bocce set. The playhouse was unlocked, and I let myself inside. It was empty, but still smelled like Play-Doh and salt and, somehow, chocolate. The floor of the playhouse was slatted wood. I knelt down in the far corner and worked at one of the slats until it came up in my hand. Abe had discovered this, because it was Abe who felt the need to pick at everything, to know everything, to discover everything. I would have been content baking fake cookies in a fake oven forever, but he was over here exploring everything until he found something cool.

The hidden space was small, and its purpose had shifted greatly from when we were kids. We'd hidden everything from Matchbox cars to small bottles of whiskey in here. Now it was empty, and I slipped the brown package inside and closed everything up again the way it was. I stepped back and surveyed; if you didn't know where to look, you wouldn't guess anything was out of the ordinary.

I texted Sam from my car, still parked outside Aunt Helen's house. It looked different already, empty and imposing. The flowerpots were gone from the front steps. There was a For Sale sign on the front lawn that I hadn't noticed before. So it wasn't sold quite yet.

Part of me wanted to go inside. I'd kept the key from the last time we were here, slipping it into my wallet for no reason other than I could, and I wanted to. I could go and open the back door and wander through an empty house and see if the movers had left anything behind. But I didn't see what good that would do.

"How stupid," Margo said, examining her unbroken body, her skin that had stitched itself back up again, her perfectly unharmed bones and organs and muscles. She looked high above her, where the Overcoat Man had pushed her off the cliff. It had felt like flying, for a beautiful, brief moment. And then it had hurt. A lot. "It's the stupidest thing I've ever done."

"You're . . . okay!" Alvin said and hugged her, just happy she was still alive.

"Yeah, but I should be dead," Margo said.

"It's a miracle!"

"It's not a miracle, it's the Everlife Formula. What else did I expect?"

"Right, but, Margo, it saved your life! You're immortal!"

"Sure, okay, but NOW what?" Margo argued. "I'm all alone now!"

"What are you talking about? I'm right here!"

"But you'll be gone eventually, and so will Mom and Dad, and so will Grandpa, and so will everyone I've ever met! How am I supposed to do this by myself? How am I supposed to be alone?"

—from *Alvin Hatter and the House in the Middle of the Woods*

18

I got home from Aunt Helen's house in time to intercept the mailman holding a package on our front porch. I signed for the delivery and took the box from him. It was addressed to Abe and the return address was *Angeles Magazine*. I shifted the box in my arms and opened the front door, finding Abe and Amy watching *The Nightmare Before Christmas* in the living room.

"Hi," I said from the doorway.

"It's almost Halloween," Amy answered.

"It's May."

"Almost Halloween," Abe echoed.

"Okay," I said, grabbing the remote off the coffee table and pausing the movie.

"Hey!" they said in unison.

I flicked the light switch on, and they both covered their eyes in mock pain. It was easy to see how they fit together, how they'd already been together for years. It was easy to see them as eighty-seven-year-old weirdos with matching rocking chairs, Abe on his four hundredth reread of *The Fellowship of the Ring*, and Amy with oversized headphones, trying to figure out how to turn on whatever new contraption we'll have to listen to music.

I held up the box. "You got a package, dweeb."

"Who's it from?"

"Angeles Magazine."

"Really?" he asked, looking up for the first time.

"Yeah. Why, what is it?"

"It's a literary magazine," he said, standing up and taking the box from me. He put it down on the coffee table and used my keys to open it. He removed four thick literary magazines from the box and put them on the couch. The covers said *Angeles*. There was a picture of a palm-tree-lined road on the front and a girl lying in the middle of it, reading a book.

There was an envelope clipped to the top magazine.

It said *Abe*—in handwriting I recognized instantly.

"Abe . . . what are those?" I asked.

"No way," he said. He took the envelope off the magazine but didn't open it right away; instead he picked up one of the copies and turned to the table of contents. Amy stood up to read over his shoulder and started squealing almost immediately, bouncing up and down on the balls of her feet.

"What! What! What! What!" she said, a "what" for every bounce.

"What?" Abe asked, quieter, softer.

"What! What?" I said, grabbing another copy of the magazine from the couch. I opened it and found my brother's name immediately, in the table of contents, under a section titled "New Voices."

"I didn't know you submitted it!" Amy said, still squealing, her voice a high-pitched shriek of pure joy.

"I didn't," Abe said. He finally tore his eyes off the page and looked at me. "Did you do this?"

"No," I said. "I don't even know what this is!"

"An essay!" Amy explained. "He wrote an essay, and it's published!"

"Aunt Helen," Abe said, picking up the envelope with her handwriting on it. "Wow."

"Wow! Wow! Wow! Wow!" Amy echoed, her bounces calming down and fading into little shakes. She leaned into Abe and closed her eyes, her entire body vibrating. "I'm so happy for you! Abe! Holy crap! Holiest of crap!"

Next to my brother's name was the title of his essay: "How to Say Good-bye." Page 53. I turned the pages until I got to his name in big block letters. *Abraham Reaves.*

"Abe, wow," I said.

"She must have . . . I don't know. She must have made them publish it."

"Made them? Don't be ridiculous," Amy said. "I told

you how good this essay was. Abe, I told you. Read her letter; I'm sure she didn't make them do anything."

Abe sank back into the couch and looked at the magazine, turning it over in his head like he expected it to dissolve or burst into flames or disappear in front of his eyes. Then he opened Aunt Helen's letter while I read the first few lines of the essay.

First, how not to:
Do not tell them not to go, this will only piss them off.
They usually don't have a choice.
Do not offer to sit with them while they sleep. Just sit with them.

"I had no idea you could write like this," I said.

"Thanks," he said, turning almost pink.

"I have to go somewhere quiet and read the rest," I said. "I'm claiming this copy for myself, and I want you to sign it later."

"I want you to sign mine too!" Amy exclaimed.

Abe looked so happy; I wanted to take a picture, but I knew it would never capture the moment as perfectly as I wanted it to.

I left him and Amy alone and went upstairs to read the rest of his essay. I was in tears by the end of it.

I realized more than I ever had before that Abe was a secret, that everyone was a secret, and for every single thing you learned about someone, there were a hundred other things you might never know.

I read Aunt Helen's next letter with tears making everything blurry.

>Lottie,
>
>Things are winding down now. I've written so many letters over the course of the past couple of weeks, and I guess I should stop writing them soon. There's only so much I can get down, only so much more I can wish for you. You'll have to start wishing for yourself. But I have just a few more things to give you, things to tell you. There are just a few more secrets left for you to discover.
>
>I left you these letters and not Abe or your father or your mother because I thought you might be the one who needed the most guidance after I'm gone. I hope that doesn't insult you; I don't think there's anything wrong with needing guidance. We are cut from the same cloth, Lottie, the same emotionally complicated, anxiety-ridden cloth.
>
>But that's not to say I'm not thinking about everyone else. I worry about your father, about how he's taking all of this. I always thought of us a little like Margo and Alvin. You can't really have one without the other. The books are named after Alvin, but Margo is just as much a part of them, just as much

a presence (which is why I flipped it around and named the last book after her, because I do what I want and so does she).

If things were reversed, if I knew I would have to live the rest of my life without your father, without my Alvin, I would be devastated. My older brother, the greatest guy I've ever met. Nope, that would be too cruel to imagine.

So I worry about him now and after I'm gone.

I wish you would spend a little time with him, just the two of you. I'm sure a few weeks must have passed by now. See if he's okay, Lottie. Get him talking. Don't let him wash his car four times a day.

Be there for him when I can't.

I hope he is happy. I hope Abe is happy. I hope you are happy. I hope all the people I left behind are happy. I know it's probably too much to ask for, but I hope everybody is happy. I hope all of you are happy, and I hope you stay that way forever.

Love, H.

I didn't sleep well that night. I had dreams about dying. Over and over again, in a dozen different ways.

When I was younger, my mother's youngest sibling, my uncle Gabriel, was visiting from Peru. I don't remember any of this, but it's on video: my uncle picking me up, me laughing, a tiny fumbling toddler, him throwing me into the air, my scalp coming just inches from the spinning ceiling fan. Everyone in the room went absolutely silent. Uncle Gabriel held me to his chest as I squirmed and tried to get away from him, clueless, unaware that I had almost been decapitated. (In hindsight, probably I wouldn't have been decapitated. But maybe. I was just a baby, and the fan was going fast.)

People laughed about it now. Uncle Gabriel always asks me if I need a haircut, and everyone laughs.

Except my mother. She has never laughed about it.

One of the things about death that has always bothered me is that people can die in the most unexpected, terrible ways. People can die while completely minding their own business, while being safe and wearing seat belts and helmets and not doing mind-boggling things like skydiving or bungee jumping. People go swimming in ponds and get brain-eating amoebas that kill them days later. Or people are standing in line to order a cup of coffee in a little coffee shop and an eighty-six-year-old who can't even see over his steering wheel crashes through the doors and runs over everybody inside. Or you get Listeria from a bowl of ice cream. Or, or, or.

The possibilities were endless, and it didn't matter if you played it safe or not. Here one minute, gone the next.

I pulled the blankets over my head, blocking out the morning sun, attempting to block out the thoughts that were making my heart speed up, my breathing skip.

"Get it together, Lottie," I whispered into the darkness of my sheets. "You haven't even gotten out of bed yet."

It was nine o'clock. Abe was still sleeping, and Mom and Dad were gardening, with matching sunhats and gloves and two glasses of lemonade. I joined them in the backyard with a glass of iced coffee.

"There's my girl!" Dad said.

"Do you want some blueberries, honey?" Mom asked.

"We're up to our eyeballs in blueberries!" Dad said, tossing one into the air and catching it on his tongue. He looked very proud of himself.

"Any raspberries?" I asked.

"We are not as up to the eyeballs in raspberries, so you can have just a couple," Dad said, pointing toward a cereal bowl almost half full of the berries. I sat cross-legged in the grass and ate one at a time, examining each for spiders first. A very disturbing encounter with a spider in a raspberry had scarred me for life. Raspberries were Dad's favorite; he watched me out of the corner of his eye as I ate.

"Hey, Dad, what are you doing today?"

"Do you mean besides harvesting food to feed my beloved *familia*?"

"Yes, besides that."

"I was going to see if anything new had been added to Netflix. I haven't checked in a while."

"Do you want to go thrifting with me?"

Dad's faves: raspberries, Netflix (he had recently figured out how to use it, and he was now an unstoppable
force to be reckoned with), and thrift stores.

"I think I could arrange a thrifting break," he said.
"What's the occasion?"

"I need some more ironic T-shirts."

"I could use—"

"If you buy another used pocket square, Sal, I swear,"
Mom said, interrupting him.

"Vintage," Dad whispered, winking at me. "Give me
an hour?"

"I'll go get ready."

We left right on time. I drove; our preferred thrift store
was about thirty minutes away, just over the Massachusetts
border. It was big, and the housewares section was enormous, rows and rows lined with shelves filled with glasses
and plates and pots and pans and knickknacks and things
I didn't need and wouldn't buy but loved to sift through.
Dad was in charge of the radio, and he refused to settle on
a station for more than a few minutes at a time. He'd be
singing along one minute then changing halfway through
a song, suddenly bored, looking for something specific that
he never articulated.

"Have you read anything interesting lately?" I asked,
fishing, wondering if Abe showed them *Angeles* yet.

"Fascinating little article about the likelihood of a dev-
astating seismic event on the West Coast."

So, no. Abe was probably waiting until today to show them.

"How about you, Lottie-da? How are you doing lately?"

Good. Fine. Terrible. Sometimes I woke up in the middle of the night, convinced the normal darkness of my room was a coffin. Sometimes I read the obituaries in the morning paper and googled things like most unusual deaths and weirdest deaths and worst ways to die and accidental deaths. I'd come across a Rilo Kiley song that way, something upbeat and positive but really dark and uncomfortable, and I'd listened to it twelve times in a row one night, falling asleep with the words still crawling across my ceiling.

"I'm fine," I said. "Are you okay?"

Aunt Helen had written that she and my father were like Margo and Alvin, and that had ripped out all my insides, leaving me empty and sadder than I thought was possible. There was Abe and me, and it was easy to see us as brother and sister, but somehow it was harder with parents. Aunt Helen was my aunt, but it wasn't easy to really understand that she was my father's sister first. They had been close for years and years before I even existed.

I felt terrible that I needed Aunt Helen to spell it out for me, that I hadn't thought to do it myself. I'd driven across the state to get my father's suit jacket, but I hadn't sat across a table from him and looked into his eyes to see how far the sadness had traveled. Whether it was receding or multiplying, diminishing or growing. I had watched him wash his car and brought him lemonade, but it had seemed too impossible, too heavy, to really ask him how he was, to really make sure he told me the truth.

"Oh, some days are harder than others," he said.

"Today?"

"Today? Today had raspberries and my favorite thrift store with my favorite daughter. And it isn't even noon yet. Today is doing fine so far."

We got to the thrift store a few minutes later. I found a parking spot in the shade. I turned the car off and looked at my father, really looked at him, studying his face to the point where he noticed and touched his chin.

"Do I have something . . . ?"

"No. No, you're fine."

"Are you ready for this?"

"Ready."

We went inside and grabbed a cart, which we would inevitably fill with things we didn't actually want and wouldn't actually buy. It was all about the hunt for us and not about the purchase. That was why I liked going to thrift stores with my father, because he took just as much time as I did. We sat in chairs and tried on shoes and opened the cabinets of curios and peeked inside and made up stories from stuffed animals and put on coats like we were going to Narnia.

We pushed our cart up and down every single aisle,

sometimes putting things in it only to take them out a few minutes later. I found a pair of tea light lanterns. A nightlight shaped like a lipsticked mouth. An eight ball keychain. My father popped around a corner with a chest-high flamingo, intricately woven with different scraps of pink metal.

"Do we need this?" he asked.

"How much?"

"Seven."

"Yeah, we need that," I said.

Into the cart it went.

I found an ice bucket shaped like a pineapple, and my dad added a light-up antique globe to the pile.

We made our way to the book section, and of course there they were, a dozen copies of Alvin, hardcovers and paperbacks with cracked spines and dog-eared pages (Abe would have died). My dad picked up a copy of *Alvin Hatter and the Return of the Overcoat Man* and turned it over in his hands.

When he looked up, his eyes were bright, and I felt a momentarily jolt of panic. *Dads can't cry, dads can't cry.* But then he blinked and he was okay again, still sad but holding it together.

"Shit," he said. "It just sneaks up on you."

"I know. It sneaks up on me too."

"You never think . . . ," he said. And even though he didn't finish his sentence, I heard it in my head: it will happen to someone you know. He tossed the book up in the air and caught it and then replaced it on the shelf, cover facing out so it was easily recognizable. Then he put his hands on the handle of the cart and said, "How's about we put this stuff back and go get some ice cream. I'm in the mood for ice cream. Are you?"

"Always, Dad. Duh. I'm always in the mood for ice cream."

He walked around the side of the cart and hugged me tightly, kissing the top of my head. Then he grabbed the flamingo and shuffled away with it, and I picked up the book again, flipping open to the dedication page.

To my brother. For everything, everything, everything.

I followed my dad down the aisles, and we set free all of our finds.

Alvin burst into the house in the middle of the woods, the door slamming loudly against the wall as he stormed into the foyer and saw the place the Overcoat Man had lain, dying, just a short hour ago.

"No," he said.

"He's gone," Margo said, entering the house, careful to close the door behind her so no one could follow them. "Alvin, he's gone."

"I see that, Margo," he said, snapping, so unlike him. He began to pace in the foyer, a grand circle that kicked up the dust on the floor, a minitornado of dirt. "He was right here. I gave him that potion. 'Terrible Pain & Suffering'! What's the use of a potion called Terrible Pain & Suffering if it doesn't even kill you!"

His voice grew louder and louder, echoing through the house. Margo had never seen her brother like this; for the first time in her memory, she was frightened of him. He had saved her from the Overcoat Man, but now he was really, truly losing it. Their parents were gone and the Overcoat Man was gone and Alvin was losing it, throwing over lamps and ripping pictures off the wall, slamming them against the floor.

"Alvin!" Margo screamed, backing away until she was pressed against the door.

He continued to rage, screaming nonsense into the foyer,

crying, breaking everything he could get his hands on.

Finally he stopped. He was shaking. He saw Margo as if he just remembered she was there.

"Alvin, you saved me," she reminded him.

"Yes," he said, "but I lost them."

—from *Alvin Hatter and the Mysterious Disappearance*

19

In the way that people can look completely wrong and different in settings you aren't used to seeing them in (teachers in coffee shops, doctors in grocery stores), I hardly recognized Sam when I opened my front door. I had texted him, asked him to meet me here, given him my address, and still when I heard the doorbell ring I had no idea who it would be.

I had read Aunt Helen's next letter that morning and texted Sam shortly after, to help me carry out her next wish.

> Dear Lottie,
>
> The stages of dying are obnoxious and worse than they tell you. Denial, bargaining, acceptance, a hundred more they don't put on the chart. I have to say, I never bargained. That seems important sometimes,

but not important just now, when I wrote it. Who cares if I had bargained? It's my life, isn't it? That seems like a pretty important thing to bargain for. I've bargained for lesser things in my life: persimmons at the farmers' market or a vintage vanity at a flea market. Why not bargain for my life? Why didn't I try that?

Anyway, I've been stuck at anger for a while. This is a tough one to get past because it's sticky. It traps you in and hugs you tight and confuses you. It's nice to be passionate about something, and it's easy to be passionate about anger, you see? It's a nice and easy thing to get worked up about.

I will tell you the lowest of the low, the angriest of the angry: I smashed a priceless, beautiful family heirloom against my bedroom wall and regretted it immediately, regretted it before it even left my hand, at the exact millisecond it was too late to change my mind if I had wanted to. And I DID want to. But I couldn't. A little ceramic devil my father had painted for his mother: I threw it against the wall, and it shattered into a hundred pieces, and I cried for every single one of them.

But here is the worst part of it: it felt good.

In a dark and evil way, it felt good.

I hated myself for being such an evil person (doubly evil: the devil was supposed to have gone to your father when our father died, but I lied and said I lost it because I wanted it for myself) but I couldn't deny the feeling of power (over breaking a freaking tchotchke, gimme a break).

I'm still in that anger stage, Lottie. It creeps over me when I least expect it. I take it to bed with me and tuck it in tight. I eat it for breakfast and stir it into my coffee and let it out at night when I don't think anyone in the neighborhood will see it.

Oh, more and more these letters I've left you digress and become a place for me to write all the things I don't think I'll be brave enough to say until after I've died. That's one good thing about all of this, maybe: death is so freeing. All your secrets spilled to the world; all your wounds open and bleeding. Maybe I should have mailed these into the ground, stamped them in dirt, buried them, and left them to flower into the saddest plants the world has ever seen. Maybe I shouldn't be giving you these things at all. I don't know, Lottie. There's a lot I don't know, and the right answer to this question is one of them.

Find some little anger inside you. Break it; destroy it. Sweep up the pieces and throw them into the trash. I love you forever.

—H.

I considered Sam in my living room now. This was an entirely different version of Sam than Sam in a bookstore or Sam in a driftwood fort on a beach. Every single person had infinite versions of themselves, and they doled them out as needed. He even looked completely different. I shut the door and shrugged.

"So this is my house."

"That explains why you're inside it."

"You might be wondering why I invited you here."

"I just thought you missed me," he said easily, swinging past me into the kitchen, walking around and touching things with one finger.

I followed him, sometimes touching what he had touched, sometimes not. He had his hair down today, and it was wavy and messy and it looked like he had dunked it in the ocean and let it dry while riding a motorcycle along some coastal road.

I hadn't gotten much sleep the night before.

Now my thoughts were confused, scrambling together, and I had texted him from bed, after I'd read the letter, before I'd even looked to see what time it was.

Are you busy today?

What did you have in mind?

Want to come over?

My parents were at a ball game in Boston, something my father pretended to like because my mother's father had been in the minor leagues for six years and she'd grown up with dugout dirt in her hair, baseline chalk underneath her fingernails.

"Do you want something to eat?" I asked. "I could make you an omelet."

"What kind of omelet?"

"We have vegetables and stuff. Whatever you want."

"Are you going to have one?"

"I'll have one, sure."

"I'll have whatever you have."

I made us toast and matching omelets with mushrooms and spinach, bell peppers and tomatoes from our garden, with shredded cheese. We ate on the deck, and I pulled a ceramic figurine of a boy and girl out of my pocket and told him about my plans to destroy it.

"Destroy it!" he said, taking the figurine from me. "Is this a stand-in for Alvin and Margo? Kind of morbid, no?"

I could think of twenty things more morbid off the top of my head, but I didn't say that. Instead I said, "It's not really a stand-in for them. More like an offering."

He thought about it, taking a bite of omelet and then picking up his toast thoughtfully, turning it around in his hand. "Where'd you get it?"

"At a tag sale. A long time ago. Because it reminded me of them, yes."

"An offering," he said. "I get that. I like that."

"I think it makes sense. It's weird to imagine my aunt being so violent."

"Is it?"

"She wasn't exactly the confrontational type."

"Not all violence is about confrontation."

"I guess."

"This is a really good omelet, by the way."

"Thanks."

"So where do you want to sacrifice these poor souls?"

"I have somewhere in mind. Are you done?"

We cleaned up the plates, rinsing them and stacking them in the dishwasher, then I put my shoes on and grabbed a baseball bat from the garage, and we got into my car.

It wasn't a far drive to the sacrificial destination, barely fifteen minutes, and we listened to music and Sam held the little ceramic figurine in his lap, making sure the boy and girl were comfortable in their last hours on earth. Then he rolled the window down and made them surf the wind and said, "Isn't it funny how the air gets thicker the faster you go? That's how planes fly, you know."

"You'd better not drop that," I answered. "No premature sacrificing."

"Don't worry; I have them."

Airplanes were the safest form of travel; wasn't that what everybody said? But still they were terrifying. Nobody was scared of cars, and they killed thousands of people every year (or every day? I made a mental note to look it up later), but lots of people were scared to fly. My mom. Me. There was something about the takeoff that was enough to take my breath away.

My favorite part was coming down, seeing all the houses and cars and fields below get bigger and bigger, trying to pick the exact moment when we were close enough to the ground so we probably wouldn't die if we crashed (there was no scientific basis for this, it was all based on feeling), closing my eyes and opening them the moment the wheels touched the tarmac, breathing a deep, deep sigh of relief.

"Hey," Sam said.

"What?"

"You do this thing sometimes. When you're thinking about something. Your entire face goes blank, like you're in another galaxy."

"Maybe I *am* in another galaxy," I said, shrugging.

"Or another universe," he said.

"There's only one universe."

"Says you. I say maybe there's more."

I pulled into the entrance to the park and started driving up and up and up. We had arrived at the tallest mountain in our town (a smidge over one thousand feet).

"Like that theory where for every decision you make, another universe splits off where you've actually made the exact opposite decision? I like that," I said.

"The multiverse," Sam said.

"Yeah. If that's true, it would mean there's always a part of you that's alive somewhere."

"It would mean we're all eternal," Sam said, looking out

the window. His voice broke on the word "eternal," like how my voice sometimes broke into forty million pieces when I tried to talk about something other than dying, but dying was the only thing I could focus on.

"Exactly."

"Is that something you would want?" he asked, looking at me quickly, looking back out the window, looking at me, looking at his hands.

"Of course. Wouldn't everybody? Wouldn't you?"

"I'm not sure."

"You definitely would. Anybody would. That's why people like vampires so much. We'd all jump at the chance to suck some blood and stay alive forever."

I pulled into a parking spot and shut the car off. Sam held the figurine in his lap, twirled it once or twice.

"I don't know about that," he said. "Maybe."

I swiped the figurine and put it in my pocket. "Nobody would say no," I said. "A vampire comes to you and offers you eternity, nobody would say no."

I got the baseball bat from the backseat of the car, and Sam followed me to the observatory tower. It was five or six flights of stairs to the top, and we were both panting when we finished. It was breezy up there; I wished I'd brought a sweatshirt.

"Some kids tried to burn it down once."

"This thing?" Sam asked, stomping his foot on the wood platform.

"There was this little string of arsons a few years ago. An abandoned warehouse, a church. They made a pyre at the base of the tower, but they couldn't get it to catch."

Every inch of wood up here was covered in graffiti or etched into with dull pocketknives. I ran my fingers along *Don't jump!* and let them settle on *Fly instead.*

"Ready?" Sam said, suddenly in front of me, just a little too close, enough to make me lose my balance. He reached out and put a hand on my arm to steady me. It felt like . . . how when you walked down stairs in the middle of the night and missed a step and everything in your stomach turned over and flipped upside down before you caught yourself and knew you were safe again. It felt like that.

I took the figurine out of my pocket and held it to out to him again. "Ready."

"This feels wrong," he said, taking the boy and girl, tossing them gently once, twice.

He took a few steps back, and I brought the bat up, settling it on my shoulder, holding it like my mom had shown me. Abe hated sports (besides croquet). I had always humored her.

"Hey, batter, batter," Sam said, but his mouth had settled into something like a frown. I watched his gaze drift over toward the view; it was a perfectly cloudless day, and I could see practically forever. And just the way his face looked, the way his gaze went on but never settled on anything, the way he carried around this enormous invisible weight I couldn't pinpoint, how he'd found me at my aunt's party, how his eyes grew so dark every time I said her name.

"It's you, isn't it?" I said suddenly, and I didn't know what made me say it, I didn't even know where it had come from except here I was, getting ready to go through with another one of Aunt Helen's weird requests, my knuckles turning white from gripping the bat so hard, my heart beating a jackhammer's rhythm against my rib cage as it occurred to me that yes, obviously, of course—it was him.

"What?" he said, freezing, pausing, a moment in time.

"What's your last name? You never told me your last name," I said, but I already knew it, as clearly as he was standing in front of me I knew that his name was Sam Williams, Mr. Williams, and that my aunt had left something to him in her will and even dedicated her last book to him: S.W.

He came unfrozen gradually, in slow motion, thawing out, his cheeks flushing pink. He held the figurine in his hands, cupping it carefully. His thumb was on the boy's head. Alvin. "Williams," he said, in the softest possible voice.

"You knew her," I said.

"I told you, I took her class."

"No," I clarified. "You *knew* her."

"I can explain."

"She dedicated the book to you."

"We were friends," he said.

"She left you something in her will."

"She . . . did?"

"Mr. Williams," I said.

"I didn't know," he said.

"And you were friends."

"We were friends. I've known your aunt for a long time."

"How could you have known her for 'a long time'? You only audited her class. That's one semester."

"It's complicated, Lottie."

"I'm so tired of this cryptic thing with you," I said, and my words came out harder than I'd meant them to, but once they were out I realized that my pulse was racing and my entire body felt hot and itchy with anger. "I'm so tired of it. With you, with Aunt Helen . . . These letters, these secrets. Why won't anybody just be honest with me?"

"I can't. . . . You have to trust me," Sam said.

"I don't have to do anything. I've only known you for a couple weeks; I don't have to trust you. You have to *earn* someone's trust. If you had known my aunt, you should have told me."

"I tried, I swear—it's just not that easy."

"So tell me now. Go on. I'm all ears."

I wanted to scream; I wanted to explode; I wanted to know whatever it was that Sam wasn't telling me.

But he didn't say anything. He squeezed the figurine

hard in his hands; his knuckles turned white and his face was unreadable, completely devoid of emotion.

"I'm sorry," he said.

"Pretty sick of hearing people tell me they're sorry. That won't bring Aunt Helen back, and it won't excuse you for lying. Now throw it."

I raised the bat back up and squeezed my hands around it, lining my knuckles up like my mother had shown me.

"What?" he said.

"THROW IT," I yelled, not even looking at him, my eyes trained on the figurine in his hand, my single desire in that moment being to hit the absolute shit out of something.

He threw it; the figurine left his fingers in a slow arc. I followed it with my eyes and the bat flew and blurred and connected with a loud *smash*, and the brother and sister exploded to smithereens and went everywhere, pieces everywhere, sailing through the air like they had momentarily figured out how to defy gravity.

I dropped the bat and looked down at the wood floor of the observation tower, expecting it to be covered in ceramic dust, but it was clean. Then I was running down the stairs and Sam was following so closely behind me I could feel the wind his body made, and we were looking all around the tower for pieces of the boy and the girl, for a single piece, for just some proof that it had existed at all, but we couldn't find any. There was nothing left. Poof.

I whirled around to face Sam.

"Who are you?" I said.

But he didn't answer me. He wouldn't even look at me.

E. sat down with Margo and Alvin the next day. He was alone, having neglected to bring any of the other initials with him to their meeting. Alvin appreciated this. Margo was still prickly. She didn't trust E. as far as she could throw him.

"I hope you'll forgive my associate's behavior last night," E. began. "We're all just a little bit on edge, you see. The house in the woods has not been breached for many, many years."

"How come?" Alvin asked, cutting Margo off before she could say something rude.

"The house is under an enchantment. It will not open to just anyone. I believe it was waiting for you to reach the age of thirteen, at which point it made itself known to you, and you were able to open the door."

Next to him, Margo huffed. Alvin knew it was a sore spot for her that she couldn't open the door.

"That house contains great secrets. Many years of magical study. I wonder . . . if you were able to do a bit of looking around?" E. asked.

Alvin shot a sideways look at his sister.

The look did not escape E.

"In particular," he continued, "perhaps you came across a small bottle. It would have had a label on it—Everlife Formula. A little thing, really. Of no great importance."

"If it's of no great importance, why are you asking about it?" Margo said.

"It has a certain sentimental value," E. explained.

"Our parents have a pretty big sentimental value to us.

Maybe we could concentrate on finding them," Margo spat.

"Of course, of course. But if you'd only be so kind as to tell me whether you'd found anything like that?"

Margo shrugged, and through a great effort made her face look less volatile, less combative. She smiled her sweetest smile, the one that only looked fake to Alvin because he knew her so well, and said, "Nope."

So that was that. They weren't going to tell him. And Alvin thought it was just as well.

—from *Alvin Hatter and the Everlife Society*

20

Em came over late that night, and we made a fort in my room between my bed and my desk, like we had done when we were kids and we didn't have to worry about things like ceramic figurines vanishing into thin air. We turned our phone flashlights on and pointed them up at the blanket-ceiling of our new world, and I couldn't help but think of the poor me in some poor alternate reality that had never met Em and was not, at this moment, sharing a bowl of popcorn with her and thinking up the weirdest possible scenarios for how Sam had known my aunt and why he hadn't told me.

"He could be a sort of boy genius? Like maybe he edited all her books, but they had to keep it a secret because his parents don't want him to be famous?" she said, chewing. I couldn't tell if she was serious. I couldn't tell if any of this was serious.

"You don't think they were like . . ."

"*Oh god*, Lottie. No, I do not think that," she said, covering her eyes with the palm of her hand. "I truly don't think that."

"Good. Me neither."

"I think it's probably something really simple. Like, he said he took her class, right? They probably just got close that way, in a mentor-student type of way."

"But why wouldn't he have told me that?"

"Maybe he didn't want you to think he only wanted to be your love interest because of her?"

"Please never call him my love interest again."

"Fine. Maybe he didn't want you to think he only wanted to be your kissy-face partner because—"

"We haven't kissed. You know that, right?"

Oh no. Was there a universe where we had kissed? I didn't know if I wanted that universe to exist. I hadn't made up my mind about that universe yet, and I didn't want some version of me to have figured it out before this version of me.

"I think that's probably it," Em said. "It's weird, you know, how famous she was. Some people don't know how to deal with that. Remember when Mae Bryant started crying because you knew what was going to happen to Alvin and Margo before she did?"

"I do remember that, yes."

"It was even weird for me sometimes, and I've known

your aunt since I was a toddler. She was practically *my* aunt, but there were still some days I didn't know how to act around her."

"I guess so."

I wasn't convinced. Well, part of me was convinced, but the other part of me wondered whether that first part of me was only convinced because it really, really wanted to find an explanation for all of this. Like, really.

"I'm sure he'll tell you," Em said. "If he was friends with your aunt, he's probably grieving too."

I shoved another small mountain of popcorn into my mouth and lay back on the carpet. I was still angry at Sam and not really interested in giving him an out, so I changed the subject. *"One week,"* I said when I swallowed. "Can you freaking believe it?"

"I've been waiting for this moment since I was six years old and my mom first told me I had to spend nine months out of the year in a jail cell," Em said. "So yes, I can believe it, because it has been the sole goal of my life thus far. Surviving high school."

"That has a ring to it. Maybe you should write a book?"

"I should! Young, queer, raised by a country-music-obsessed mother who mostly hated who I became with every ounce of blood in her body."

"Stop," I said.

"It's true. I can't believe I'm almost out of here. I don't

even have to visit if I don't want! There are no laws that say I have to visit."

"That's true. Do you think you'll miss it?"

"Absolutely not. The things I'll miss will stay with me. You. Jackie. Lunch period."

"I'll miss how easy it is," I said. "I mean—I think I will. How I never had to think about anything. You just know what you have to do. You wake up, you go to school, you do your homework. There aren't any choices."

"You like not having any choices?"

"I'm just saying that pretty soon people are going to consider us grown-ups. Do you know how to do your taxes? How to relight a pilot light if it goes out? How to change the oil in your car?"

"Okay, first of all: Jiffy Lube. Second of all: you are freaking me out. Can't you let us just enjoy this small sliver of freedom between the end of high school and the beginning of college? Can't you just give me these next three months before you make me take a class on how to light a pilot light?"

"Sorry."

"It's okay, and I love you, but you're stressing me out."

Em flapped the edge of our blanket house to get the air circulating. It was getting stuffy, but I didn't want to leave. I wondered if there could be some version of us, some Em and Lottie in a galaxy far away, who stayed hidden in a blanket fort forever.

* * *

I woke up on the floor the next morning, my neck stiff, the ceiling of our fort tucked around me, a blanket again. My phone was chiming its daily wake-up call and I realized this was the last Monday I would ever spend in high school. That both freaked me out and made me unbelievably excited.

I read Aunt Helen's next letter from the floor.

Lottie,

I hope that felt good. I hope you are enjoying at least some part of these little notes, because I have enjoyed writing them, and I'm sad there are only a few left, because we have to stop somewhere and because twenty-four is the age I was when I first started writing the Alvin books, so that seems as good a place to stop as any.

I left you my journals, and the time has come to read them. If I know you, you might feel more than a little strange at the idea of snooping through my life, but please, I implore you: snoop away. There are things in there that I want you to know, things I never told a single soul and things I've saved for you. Because you're me, really. If I could be your age again we would be best, best friends, the sisters we both never had. We are so similar, and that is why I always knew you'd be the one I told.

Start with the red one.
I think you'll find it the most interesting.
—H.

I'd read the letter twice more, once standing at the bathroom sink brushing my teeth and once digging in my closet for the sandals I wanted to wear.

I had to hand it to Aunt Helen; it was pretty suspenseful. Wondering what I'd find in the red journal erased all my curiosity at where Em had gone. (Had she left in the middle of the night? Early in the morning? Into thin air?) I was so flustered by the time I got to school that I tried to open the wrong locker for three minutes.

Everything looked different. Everything had a ticking clock over it, counting down the minutes left of high school, of this long and important stretch of time that every single adult in the world assured me was the absolute best years of your life. It didn't feel like that to me. Maybe it felt that way to a select group of people, the kids who roamed the halls acting like they owned a part of this, the kids who stuck together in packs and wore glossy lip stuff that looked like it would glue their mouths shut.

"Is this really the best it will ever be?" I'd asked Aunt Helen once.

"What, high school? Oh God, no. High school is shit, Lottie. You'll like college a little bit more. You'll like your twenties a little bit more. And then you'll settle in to the life you want, and you'll like that even more. Hell, if you're lucky, you might even love it."

I was late to first period, English with Mrs. Nguyen, a classroom with two doors. I tried to sneak in the back, hoping her back was toward me (she really liked writing on the whiteboard), but I didn't have any such luck. She was front and center, reading aloud from a paperback copy of *To the Lighthouse*, a book I still hadn't read and, let's be honest, probably would never actually pick up.

Mrs. Nguyen paused just a moment, and I slipped into my seat and slid down, trying to make myself as small as possible.

She kept reading:

"'What is the meaning of life? That was all—a simple question; one that tended to close in on one with years. The great revelation had never come. The great revelation perhaps never did come. Instead there were little daily miracles, illuminations, matches struck unexpectedly in the dark; here was one.'"

She closed the book and held it against her chest, and I wondered how many times she had read that exact copy, because its covers were worn soft and its pages were dog-eared and smudged and she held it not like an ordinary book but like something that had saved her once from drowning, a floating ring thrown into a sea she couldn't navigate.

"Well?" she said. "You're about to start your lives, leave

high school behind. Some of you will leave town, make new friends, see new places. Certainly you'll do things now that you've never done before. So: what is the meaning of life?"

According to Alvin and Margo's mother, the meaning of life was simple but one that evaded the large majority of people, because they were looking for something complicated and deep and heavy. But the meaning of life wasn't any of those things, she had told her children, right at the very end of *Alvin Hatter and the Overcoat Man*, right before she and her husband disappeared. The meaning of life was something simple: *keep going, be nice, make friends.*

Sometimes I thought that was too neat a package, too simplistic, something easy for people to understand but lacking true meaning. Then other times it made perfect sense and it came into the utmost clarity: sharp and focused and so, so obvious.

Near the front, Evan Andrews raised his hand. I had forgotten we were supposed to be answering a question.

"Yes, Evan?" Mrs. Nguyen said.

"I think the meaning of life is to try to be happy," he said. A few kids nodded; one kid snorted.

Mrs. Nguyen pointed at the snorter. "Do you disagree, Lilah?"

"The meaning of life is family," she said, but you could tell she didn't really believe it. Lilah was an aforementioned lip-gloss girl. I'd never seen her have a kind word for anyone.

"Family is important," Mrs. Nguyen agreed. "And so is happiness, Evan."

"So is money," someone shouted from behind me. I didn't turn around to see who.

"Money is certainly a factor," Mrs. Nguyen agreed. "Anyone else?"

She looked at me for a fraction of a second, just long enough for me to know what she wanted from me. She wanted Alvin's mother's answer, the six-word phrase printed and reprinted a million times on everything from T-shirts to tote bags to coffee mugs, the neat package, the bow tied into a ribbon on top of perfect wrapping paper. More than anything she wanted that answer to be the right answer, like I could confirm that for her, like I could possibly tell her what was the right answer and what was the wrong answer, like I had any say over that. In reality there were a hundred meanings to life, and they were all true for different people, they were all valid for their own confusing reasons.

Next to me, Mae Bryant raised her hand. I hoped she would say it so I didn't have to, because I knew everyone in the class would swivel to look at me, to see if I agreed or started to cry or ran screaming out of the room, I don't know.

"Yes, Mae?" Mrs. Nguyen said.

"'Keep going, be nice, make friends,'" Mae said, in a voice that sung and twisted her words into the air, spilling each like little gems.

And yes, every single person in the class turned around to look at me, and I looked only at the top of my desk, pretending to be fascinated by what I found there, pretending that my folded hands were a very recent discovery, not wanting to give them the satisfaction of seeing my face and its current state of pinkness.

"Very good," Mrs. Nguyen said, her own voice shaky and uncertain now, because sometimes when we get what we thought we wanted, we realize that it's actually so different than how we imagined it would be. "Can anyone tell me what Mae is quoting from?"

"Duh," Lilah said, because she was the exactly the type of person you might imagine saying *duh*, and not ironically.

"I'd prefer a title," Mrs. Nguyen said, losing her patience.

"Alvin Hatter," Evan said. "The second one."

"And do you think that quotation has a point?" Mrs. Nguyen asked the class.

He muttered his assent, and I tried not to feel annoyed: of course Mrs. Hatter had a point. If she didn't have a point, one of the only things she said in the entire series (before she and her husband were spirited away by the Overcoat Man) wouldn't have resonated with as many people as it did. People with tattoos. People with permanent ink needled into their skin.

Keep going.

Be nice.

Make friends.

Really, what else was there?

I somehow got through the week. The last week.

The red journal sat open on the bed, and I sat on the bed in front of it, my legs tucked under me and the last day of school behind me and just the weekend left before the graduation ceremony on Monday night.

I hadn't read it yet.

I'd picked it up a dozen times, and every time I'd been too scared of what I would find in its pages.

It felt like—

Here it was.

Here were all the answers to all the questions I'd been asking myself.

But I could only put it off for so long.

I opened to the first page and saw the date; she would have been almost my age, just a teenager. It was written in the summer, and the very first line was this:

Finally school's out, and I can relax. Every year seems to be longer, is this normal? I hate math and I hate history and I hate chemistry, so basically there's nothing I like. I like eating. Maybe I'll be a professional eater.

It made me laugh, trying to picture Aunt Helen strapped to a table, a hundred hot dogs in front of her, tucking a napkin into the collar of her shirt.

It made me laugh and then it made me stop laughing, because I kept reading and the next part of the entry said this:

I've been spending a lot of time with that new kid, the one who moved here not too long ago. He's okay. He also hates math and loves eating. He has a pet turtle too. Sam says if he goes away on vacation, I can watch him.

I stared at the journal, still open, its pages worn and wrinkled and yellowed and I was too scared to move or get off the bed because almost twenty-five years ago, when my aunt was a teenager, she had written in her journal about a boy named Sam.

Sam.

Sam.

Sam.

And then, just for good measure, just so I couldn't try to explain it away, just so my brain couldn't hatch any sort of explanation for how the hell a boy I knew now, a boy I'd met and hung out with and knew now was mentioned in my aunt's twenty-five-year-old journal, there was a picture.

She'd taped a picture into the journal.

Her. Him. Sam.

Sam.

Her, my age.

Sam, his age.

Somehow.

Somehow his age. Then and now.

For a hundred million reasons, and not one of them one that I understood, I pushed the journal off the bed and crawled under my covers and burrowed down until every inch of my body was covered.

And then I unburrowed myself and I grabbed the journal again, carefully peeling the picture away from the page it was stuck to. I brought it as close to my face as I could, until it went all blurry, and then I held it at arm's length. And then I smelled it. And then I licked a corner, I don't know, because what else was I supposed to do?

This was Sam—my Sam! This was the Sam I had been going out with, spending time with, the Sam who had let me ride on the handlebars of his bike, who had split a pizza with me, who had taken me to see *The Little Prince* and the Glass House. That was Sam.

But this also was Sam. This photograph was Sam. There was 100 percent no way of denying that this photograph, this twenty-five-year-old Polaroid, showed two people with their arms around each other, laughing as they were frozen forever in faded sepia: Aunt Helen and Sam.

It did not feel immediately different, being immortal.

Alvin found that when he wanted to sleep, he could sleep. If he would rather stay up throughout the night reading, he could choose to do that too. Similarly, he ate because he liked to eat, but his stomach never rumbled with hunger, nor did his eyes ever close with fatigue.

He settled into a state of general contentment. He did not get sick. He did not feel out of sorts. Everything was very even, like a boat plunked in the middle of a calm, windless sea. Floating gently along, but with no sudden lurches to either side.

He had drunk the potion without a second thought, because Margo was so scared to be alone, to be the only one. He had drunk from a little bottle labeled Everlife Formula, and he had felt nothing at all, not even a chill as the liquid traveled down into his stomach and settled there.

"Is it supposed to do something?" he'd asked Margo, who was watching him, still dirty and blood-covered from her fall off the cliff.

"It's already done it," she said and shrugged, and then they'd gone home together and found that they could either sleep or stay awake. They'd chosen to sleep.

Now, after a little bit of time, Alvin wondered if he hadn't made the stupidest decision of his relatively young life.

But how could he have done any differently?

He hadn't had a choice, really.

He'd only been trying to be a good older brother.

—from *Alvin Hatter and the Overcoat Man*

21

I stayed up all night, without changing my clothes or brushing my teeth or washing my face.

I hadn't been able to read anything else in the red journal, but I had read the others, pored over them with an intensity that did not wane, not even at three in the morning, not even at four.

Sam's name wasn't mentioned in any of them. And they were filled with pictures, but he wasn't in any of those either.

They were fascinating, despite that. My aunt grew up in front of my eyes. My aunt got the first sparks of inspiration for the Alvin books. My aunt wrote about Margo's hair color, eye color.

But she hadn't mentioned Sam at all.

Which was nice. I'd almost managed to convince myself that I'd made the entire thing up.

But then eventually there was nothing left to read except the red journal. It was lying innocently on the floor, just a few feet away from me.

Something in there would explain everything. It had to.

Something in there would tell me what I needed to know, would reassure me of the impossibility of a boy who didn't age, not a single day in twenty-five years.

I opened the journal on my lap, holding my breath, holding my guts inside me even though they were trying their best to wiggle free of their tethers.

My father and Aunt Helen, teenagers, friends. They looked so similar and at the same time like completely foreign strangers. Would I be friends with these people if they walked into my life now? Aunt Helen said yes, but I wasn't so sure. My father's face had a smugness that wasn't there anymore; Aunt Helen looked perpetually bored and entitled, qualities I had never once seen on her grown-up face. There were pages after pages of the two of them, in swimsuits at a backyard pool I didn't recognize, surrounded by friends I'd never known, watching a movie on a floral couch, playing catch in the middle of an empty, twilight street. They looked like pages from a magazine, a story on what it was like to grow up on another planet, in another time.

I flipped page after page, and then: him.

Sam and Aunt Helen eating Popsicles on a wooden bench. Sam and Aunt Helen holding a small turtle. Sam and Aunt Helen sharing a milk shake, one tall glass and two straws, exactly like in a movie.

It was much, much too early, but I took the journal and crept across the hallway to Abe's room and tapped on his door with just my index finger while I called him over and over, hearing his phone buzz on the nightstand within, worrying it would vibrate right off the edge and onto the carpet without him waking up.

I didn't want to just go in because my brother was known to sometimes sleep naked, and with everything else I was dealing with now, I certainly didn't want to deal with getting that particular image out of my head. It would be stuck there for all eternity, right alongside the time I saw my parents half undressed in their bedroom (I didn't know they were home; they didn't know I was home) and the time I accidentally found naked photos of Jackie on Em's phone (she told me to look up a number for her, forgetting that she'd left the screen on photos of her girlfriend's most naked bits).

So I kept calling, and the phone kept buzzing, and I kept knocking as loudly as I dared to, hoping more than anything that I wouldn't wake my parents and have to answer their many questions, including *Why aren't you in bed?* and *Why are you holding that photo album like you're scared it's going to come to life?* and *Why are you trying to wake your brother up? You know how he gets in the morning.*

In a perfect world I would have been able to wake up

Abe, but this was not a perfect world, and I'd forgotten that my mother was working yet another overnight, and so when I fell backward in the hallway, landing on my butt and cradling the journal like a misbehaving baby, she was there, standing over me, dressed in scrubs and crossing her arms over her chest like she wasn't quite sure what she was seeing.

"Lottie?" she asked, and I nodded slowly in the dim light (I hadn't even noticed she'd turned it on) as she leaned against a wall and studied me. "I'm sensing a crisis. Do you want to come downstairs?"

I followed her without saying anything, making my way down the stairs with both hands gripping the banister, the journal tucked under one of my arms in a complicated death grip. We went into the kitchen, and she wordlessly dished out two bowls of ice cream, putting one in front of me as she sat next to me at the kitchen table. She took a bite of hers first, made a comically funny *ahhh* face, then leaned back in her chair.

"Okay. What's going on, my love?"

I think Sam is immortal?

I think I'm losing my mind?

I get so anxious at night, all the thoughts of death piling one on top of the other, that sometimes I can't sleep, and I'm exhausted until I try closing my eyes and then I am one hundred percent resolutely awake, drowning under the certainty that I will one day be brutally murdered in the midst of some random home invasion.

"I think something really weird is happening," I said, because I couldn't think of anything else to say. Ninety-nine percent of my words had left me, and here I was with only the vaguest of answers.

"Weird how?" she asked. Then, "Just to get the Mom stuff out the way: Are you in trouble? Are you hurt? Is someone you know in trouble?"

"No. No. I don't think so. I don't know."

"Tell me what's going on."

I put the journal on the table and pushed it toward her. She opened it, and her expression softened immediately as she recognized my father and Aunt Helen as teens. She flipped through page after page until she reached the end, and then she looked up at me, confused. "I don't understand," she said.

"You don't see anything weird?"

"This was before I knew your father," she said. "Weird how?"

I reached across the table and started flipping pages until I found one filled with Sam. It sent a tingle down my spine, a warning signal: *this isn't right.*

"This kid," I said, pointing. "I know him."

She leaned closer to the photos, squinted, then shrugged. "Is he one of your aunt's friends? I don't think I've ever met him."

"I've met him," I said.

"Okay. I'm not following."

"I mean I've met him, and he's still this age. He's my age. Like, I've met him, and he's the same age."

My mom looked at the picture and then looked at me and then took what I thought was the most obnoxious bite of ice cream in the history of the human race, as her expression changed very clearly to one of: *I have no idea how to tell my daughter I think she's full of shit.*

"A lot of people look alike," she said after a minute, after she'd taken her bite and swallowed and thought about how to answer me in the most diplomatic way.

"Identical," I said. "And I have her journals. She wrote about a Sam in her journals, and his name is Sam, and the lawyer even said she left something in her will for Mr. Williams, do you remember? Sam's last name is Williams. And also she dedicated the last Alvin book to S.W., Sam Williams, and Sam said yes, that was him, and yes, they were friends, and this Sam is that Sam," I said, pointing at the picture again, pointing so hard the tip of my finger turned white.

"Honey, I'm sorry," Mom said. "I don't think I understand any of this."

"This person," I said, jabbing the photo with every syllable, "is still alive and still a teenager."

"Okay," she said. "Okay. I believe you think that, honey, but sometimes children look exactly like their parents. Sometimes they're even named after them. There is another explanation for this. And I will help you find it after I've had some sleep. I promise."

She finished her ice cream as I dealt with the hole in my stomach, the growing black spot that was eating up all my organs. I hadn't taken a bite of ice cream yet, so she left the bowl in front of me as she went to the sink and rinsed out hers. When she turned around, she sighed and said, "Will you please stop looking at me like I betrayed you?"

But I couldn't help it. It felt like she had.

And I didn't know what else to do. If I couldn't make my mom believe me, what made me think Abe would believe me, or Em, or anyone? The only person who would believe me was dead, was—

Aunt Helen.

I abandoned the bowl of ice cream and sprinted upstairs, tearing the next letter out of the envelope.

> *Lottie,*
>
> *Don't tell anybody. If you've told someone already, that's fine, because they probably don't believe you, but don't tell anybody else.*
>
> *I'm sorry, Lottie. This is a secret I've kept for so long that the act of keeping it became effortless. My lips learned to button themselves up, and my heart learned to forget the fact that I lost one of my very best friends in the world when I told him I wouldn't do what he wanted me to do. All of it will make sense very soon.*

I hadn't seen Sam for almost twenty-five years. He left Mystic when I was still in high school and spent the time between then and now doing God knows what. Traveling, probably. Seeing as much of the world as he could get his hands on. I got postcards every now and then, unsigned postcards with little messages about how he was fine and Paris was beautiful and he wished things could have been different. Always: I wish things could have been different. So you see, unsigned as they were, I always knew who'd sent them.

He came back when I was diagnosed. The news leaked so quickly to the internet (it's impossible to keep anything a secret nowadays, isn't it?), and then suddenly he was on my doorstep one day, his face at once changed and yet completely the same. He was the same. Of course I always knew he would be, but it was still a bit of a shock. He rang my doorbell, and I somehow knew who it would be even before I opened the door. Of course I knew it would be him because I had been waiting for him.

You were supposed to come over; you had texted to say you were on your way, so I didn't let him stay. I watched him disappear into the woods (he's very good at disappearing, but there's nothing mystical about that, just a lot of practice) and then I watched your car pull up, not ten seconds later. So of course the *next time I saw him he asked me who you were. He'd been watching, I guess.*

At first I wouldn't tell him, but then I did, because I knew he'd figure it out anyway.

Here's the thing, Lottie. I never believed him. Not when we were younger, not when he'd shown me proof, not even when he begged me to, when he swore up and down on our very best friendship that he would never, ever lie to me. I thought I believed him, but I didn't, not even when the postcards kept coming, not even when he stuck to his story for twenty-five whole years.

Only when I saw it for my own eyes. Only just a few weeks ago when he resurfaced, and for once, I couldn't explain it away. Only then.

Trust me, Lottie. Believe what you want from him (because I know he's found you, I knew he'd find you the second he watched you pull into my driveway), but trust me. I would never lie to you. (Omit, yes. I've omitted a lot. But I've never lied.)

—H.

I put the letter down and picked up the photograph that I'd peeled out of her journal. I thought about what my mom had said—that sometimes family members looked alike, that maybe this was Sam's dad—but I knew that wasn't possible. I knew because Sam had told me himself, he had known my aunt for a long time. I knew because Aunt Helen had told me herself: *this is a secret I've kept for so long.*

I knew because my aunt had asked me to do one thing. Believe her.

And I did.

The Overcoat Man was not there.

They'd come all this way, found his lair, broken in, and he'd managed to slip through their fingers once again.

Margo sat on the very edge of a chair, her eyes blank and glassy.

Alvin overturned a small table covered in papers and immediately wished he hadn't. They should really look through these; they might find something useful.

He knelt down and began gathering the papers into a neat pile.

And that was when he saw it.

A glint of silver underneath the desk.

He reached for it, somehow knowing what it would be before his fingers even wrapped around it. He picked it up gently, cupping it in his hands, standing slowly to see it in better light.

"What do you have?" Margo asked.

"She was here," Alvin said. "She was here, and we missed her."

He held the little charm bracelet up so Margo could see. It was their mother's. They had been so close to saving her—

How close? Days? Hours? Alvin couldn't bear to think about it.

Slowly, Margo stood up. She crossed the room. She took the charm bracelet and looked at it for a minute before slipping it into her pocket.

"We'll find her," she said.

And she was so sure, so steady, so confident that Alvin almost believed her.

—from *Alvin Hatter and the Wild-Goose Chase*

22

When my family started filtering into the kitchen in the morning, I was already sitting there, a confusing perfect storm of emotions. Except George Clooney was nowhere to be found.

"Good reference," Abe said. I turned to find him on the stairs, arms folded, looking at me suspiciously.

"Oh, great," I said. My internal monologue had momentarily escaped me.

"I always thought they should have sent Diane Lane out with the ship. She's a legitimate badass. Diane Lane does not get lost at sea."

"How much did I say?"

"Hmm? Oh, no. I was reading your mind." Abe made squiggles in the air with his fingers. My phone buzzed. A message from Sam.

> Want to get together this weekend? I have
> a few ideas.

Do you? Do you have a few ideas, Sam? Was one of those ideas explaining to me how you came about your apparent eternal youth?

"You're doing it again, but you're whispering this time, so I can't hear you," Abe said. "If you're going to narrate your subconscious, you might be kind enough to do it a little louder."

"Did you want something?" I asked, spinning around, dropping my phone dramatically in the process. I watched it skid across the kitchen floor, heard that massive shattering and splintering sound as it clearly broke into a thousand pieces. "Shit!"

"I have twenty-seven missed calls from you," Abe said, crossing the kitchen to pick up the broken bits of my life. "Ouch." He held it out to me. The entire screen was shattered. It felt like some metaphor I couldn't quite put into words.

"I couldn't sleep."

"You couldn't sleep so you called me twenty-seven times at five in the morning?"

I took the phone from him and pressed the home button. The screen turned on feebly, but the touch screen was broken. I tossed it onto the counter.

"Perfect," I said.

"Do you want to tell me what's going on?"

"What's the point?" I thought. Or I guess I said it. Things were getting muddy; words were forming without me seeming to have much say over them.

"The point is, I'm your brother, and I care about you a lot, and you can tell me things. I thought we had established that three years ago when you were getting bullied by that guy, that Jeremy guy, and I confronted him, and then he was like, 'I just have crazy feelings for her, man!' and I was like, 'At no age—but especially not at your age—is it acceptable to show a girl you have feelings for her by bullying her. That contributes to a patriarchal society and reinforces archaic gender roles that nobody has time for anymore.' And then he was like, 'What does patriarchal mean?' and I realized I had overestimated my audience. But remember how I had your back then? And I have your back now. So what the hell is going on?"

Two voices battled for position in my brain.

Tell him! yelled one.

Don't tell him! whispered the other.

The other had a point. My mom hadn't believed me, so why did I think Abe would be any different? Did I really want to go through the whole thing again, the whole explanation, only to be shot down with *Maybe he just looks a lot like his dad*? I knew the difference between two people looking like each other and two people actually being the same person who never aged.

I mean, didn't I?

"Wow," Abe said.

"What?"

"It's just that when you think so hard, I can actually see the smoke coming out of your ears."

"Shut up."

"Seriously. Like an actual cartoon. With the train noises and everything."

"Whatever."

"Do you want to tell me what's going on?"

"Okay, fine." Deep breath. Another deep breath. And one more, for good measure. "I think Sam is immortal."

Abe's expression didn't change in the slightest. He took a tiny sidestep to his left and leaned his elbow on the counter, but other than that he didn't even act like he'd heard me. Now I could see his brain working, something spinning behind his eyes.

"Huh," he said. "Is that why Aunt Helen wanted you to have that book?" he said finally.

I almost didn't remember what he was talking about, but then something clicked in my brain, and I bolted past him for the stairs. I ran into my room, breathless, and grabbed the weird history book my aunt had sent me to pick up from Leonard at Magic Grooves.

The Search for Eternity: A History of Juan Ponce de León.

I opened it, flipping through the pages until I found what she'd written, which hadn't even really registered with me until now—

The words *Fountain of Youth* were circled, with a line leading to where she'd written *S.W.!!!*

This whole time her letters had been spelling it out for me. I'd missed every single hint.

I heard Abe walk into my room behind me. I held the book out to him, and he took it and read what Aunt Helen had written.

"What's Sam's last name?" he asked.

"Williams. Sam Williams."

"And you think he's . . . I mean, Aunt Helen told you he was immortal?"

"Yeah," I said to Abe. "She did. Yeah. Wait—do you believe me, then? Or do you believe that he is . . . you know."

"Do I believe that the Fountain of Youth actually exists and that your boyfriend drank from it and is now immortal?"

"He's not my boyfriend. But yeah to all the other stuff."

"Well, not really, no," Abe said. "But I guess it wouldn't be the weirdest thing in the world. Have you ever googled a blobfish?"

"No."

"Well, you should. Just not before bed."

"You don't seem that freaked out."

"Because I don't really believe it. What's your proof? Besides Aunt Helen leaving you a book about Ponce de León, I mean. Because that doesn't mean anything. Aunt Helen did weird stuff all the time."

"What's my proof?" I said, grabbing the book back from

him, poking the circled word with my forefinger. I took the red journal from my bed and opened it and thrust it into Abe's hand, showing him picture after picture of Aunt Helen and Sam, turning the pages and jabbing at each one.

And the letters.

All the letters were stacked on my desk; I picked them up and started going through them, reading any relevant passages I found:

"I've kept a secret for a very, very long time. And now (in death, as it were) it seems like the perfect time to loosen my grip on it a little bit."

"But I think if even one immortal boy could identify with Alvin's struggles, it will have all been worth it."

"Is Alvin based on a real person? Oh, of course . . ."

"Some nights I can imagine I am in high school again or living in your father's garage or running after an immortal boy."

"AN IMMORTAL BOY, Abe!" I said, breathing too hard, fully understanding now the secret my aunt had been leading me toward. "And she left him something in her will!"

"What was it? Did he tell you?" Abe asked, still holding the journal, still flipping slowly through the pages, studying every picture.

"No," I said. "I don't think he's even gone to get it yet."

"Really? So that means Harry still has it?"

"Yeah, I guess."

"Interesting."

"You don't think I should—"

"Why not? If you're really going down this path, don't you want to know what it is?"

I didn't waste any time.

I got Harry's cell phone number from Aunt Helen's computer and called him from Abe's phone. He answered on the second ring and sounded genuinely pleased to hear from me.

"Lottie Reaves! To what do I owe the pleasure?"

"I figured out who Mr. Williams is, the person from my aunt's will. I know him."

"Really? That's wonderful. Do you have his contact information?"

Yeah, sitting useless in my shattered cell phone.

"He's kind of hard to reach," I said, improvising. "Off the grid, you know? I thought I could bring it to him? If it's small enough to fit in my car, I guess?"

Had Aunt Helen left Sam a piano? A boat? I didn't know.

"No, it's quite small enough, but . . . Well, I don't love that idea, to be honest," Harry said. "There's paperwork, you know."

"I could take that too, and then bring it back to you?"

"If it was anyone else, I'd have to say no. But since it's you, and I knew your aunt so well . . . I'm inclined to make an exception."

"Great! I can come by now? If that's okay with you. I can meet you at your office or I can come to your house, whatever you'd like."

"I guess we'd better meet at the office then, that's where the last of your aunt's things are. I can be there in a half hour or so; I have some work to do anyway. Thanks for calling, Lottie."

"Thank you." I hung up the phone and handed it back to Abe, who'd been listening so close to me that our cheeks were almost touching. He pulled back, thoughtful.

"You don't think it's . . ." He trailed off, shaking his head slightly.

"I'll keep you posted."

"Please do. Especially if you find what Ponce never could." He winked and left the room.

I went upstairs and opened my computer, finding my synced contact list and copying important numbers down on a piece of paper: Sam, Mom, Dad, Abe, Em.

I could text from my computer too, so I sent a message to Sam:

Later today? I'll keep you posted.

The anxiety from the night before was gone. Now I had a clear sense of what I needed to do. I needed to talk to Sam.

I got to Harry's office an hour or so later, after stopping at the store and paying an absurd insurance deductible for a new phone. It was currently wrapped in one of the most expensive cases I could find. The salesperson had personally thrown his phone (same case) against the wall as hard as he could to demonstrate its durability.

Worked for me.

Harry gave me a folder of paperwork ("Have him sign here and here, initial here, and thank you so much, Lottie, you're the best.") and a small wooden box, about the size of a hardcover book. I brought everything out to my car and opened it, sitting in the parking lot, after looking around me like a truly paranoid creature to make sure nobody was watching.

I opened the box slowly. If my life were a movie, there would be very dramatic music playing in the background, a slow buildup to a swelling of instruments as the wooden case creaked open (it didn't creak in real life, and there was regrettably no music playing).

The inside of the box was a mess of tissue paper, and resting on top was a piece of paper. I recognized my aunt's handwriting like it was my own.

S.—
I wish things could have been different.
But not in the way you might expect.
—H.

I set my aunt's note on the passenger seat carefully, my heart speeding up as I reached into the box and pulled out tissue paper after tissue paper, unearthing a small crystal bottle with a cork stopper in it.

I imagined it said—on a brown-colored tag tied to it with twine—*Everlife Formula.*

But it didn't. It was just the glass vial, small and clear and plain in my hands. I held it up to the light and looked at the liquid within. It was completely unremarkable. Like water.

Because it was water, if I believed what my aunt was trying to tell me.

It was a very special kind of water, but it was just water.

A very, very special kind of water, something said in the back of my head. A tiny kind of voice reserved only for the darkest of nights, the loneliest of sleeplessness. The voice you hear right before you fall asleep, the one that whispers suggestions into your ear: *Did you leave the door unlocked? Are your car lights on? Did you remember to turn off the stove? What if everyone you love dies? What if YOU die? What if there's someone under your bed right now? Should you get up and check the closet again?*

Years writing down all the anxious thoughts in my head and all the ways I didn't want to die in a notebook now buried in a floorboard in my aunt's shed, and here I was, holding something that could (if I suspended all disbelief) take care of all of that.

This could be what we've been waiting for, the voice said. It sounded like my voice, a lot like my voice, but twisted and wrong. Just a shadow of who I really was, what I really sounded like. Not me at all. Or—a version of me. One I didn't like.

I put the bottle back in the box and opened another letter from my aunt. This one was addressed to me, slipped into my purse before I'd left the house.

Dear Lottie,

A long, long time ago, I ran away from home.

I don't know how much you know. I can't know, can I, because I didn't drink it. I didn't choose the life Sam chose.

Sam and I met when I was a teenager, and he was both considerably older than that and also, at the same time, just a year older than I. We became friends instantly. There's something about him, isn't there, like he's riding on a wave that's slightly different from all the rest. Like he exists on a plane just a little bit tilted from ours.

We spent one perfect, magical year together. (Wait, let me be clear: not TOGETHER. Never anything more than friends.)

Then he offered me the water. He made me take it even when I refused to drink it. He wanted me to have it in case I changed my mind.

I thought about it.

I packed a bag and hopped on a train and took myself to New York. I spent one week wandering around the city (it was my first time!), imagining what it would be like to pause, to stop, to remain consistent forever. I wondered if I could live alone forever, never see my family again (because I would have to leave them, you know, and so this was like a trial run).

But in the end, I returned to my family.

I wasn't particularly kind to Sam when I told him my decision. The whole thing had thrown me for a loop, I guess (but I was also younger, more cruel, a little terrified).

We fought; Sam left. He wrote me many postcards over the years. I never attempted to find him.

I thought about him often after that, of course, especially in the past few weeks I've found it weighing heavier and heavier on my mind.

But then I figured out what was so different about him, about Sam, and it wasn't a good thing anymore. It is something dark and sad and eternal.

We aren't living some make-believe fantasy about immortality, are we? We're just trying to live our lives and do the best we can in the time we're given.

Anyway, that's what I tried to do.

If I know anything, it's that he wouldn't have gone to Harry's office and you would have.

And if that's true . . . then please, Lottie, give it back to him.

Whatever the little voice is currently telling you . . .

Don't drink it.

—H.

I put my letter back in my purse just as my new phone buzzed. A message from Sam:

Whenever you want! Let me know.

It would be the first thing my aunt asked me to do that I didn't do blindly.

I wrote him back:

Can you really live forever?

His response took a long time. But when it came, I started the car and drove.

Margo did not know why she did it.

Alvin was just a few feet away from her, exploring an oversized, dusty book, not paying her any attention. She poked around the attic for a few minutes but grew quickly bored, uninterested by the grime and the dirt that time had settled over this place. There was a faint unease growing in her stomach; they weren't supposed to be here. Why had the door opened for Alvin but not for her? What did the door have against girls? She'd strained against it with all her might, but Alvin had turned the handle easily and let them inside.

And what was this house even doing in the middle of the woods? It hadn't been here before, right? Alvin and Margo had explored these woods a hundred times, a thousand times; surely they couldn't have missed a house this big, sitting in the middle of a great clearing, looking a little like someone had just set it down out of nowhere.

No, there was something weird about this house, and there was something weird about this attic, and she was tired of exploring, tired of this particular adventure. She wanted to go home, to have something to eat, to know why she was suddenly holding this glass vial in her hands.

Why she was suddenly . . . What?

Where had this come from?

Margo brought the vial up to the light. It had liquid inside, clear, like water. The glass was dusty; she wiped it off against her shirt. There was a little tag around the neck of the bottle. It said: *Everlife Formula*. The bottle was corked.

Margo didn't like that at all. She put the bottle back on the shelf.

Or . . . No, she didn't. She had uncorked it.

But when had she done that?

She had told herself, very plainly, to put the bottle back on the shelf. But now she was holding it and it was open.

She sniffed it. It smelled like nothing.

She should dump it out on the floor. Nothing good ever came from drinking things of unknown origin.

But then . . .

It was already open.

She brought the bottle to her mouth—

And drank.

—from *Alvin Hatter and the House in the Middle of the Woods*

23

I told Sam to meet me on Enders Island. I drove there slowly, letting myself process, letting my brain catch up to what had happened in the short time since Aunt Helen's death.

I didn't know how I felt about her.

For the first time in my life, my feelings for Aunt Helen were in question, tottering on the edge of a cliff as high as the one Em and I had jumped from. I remembered how the wind had blown through my hair, how the colors had blurred together as we fell. I remembered the day Aunt Helen had told us she had cancer and then later, so soon afterward, the day she told us she was dying. I remembered being on Facebook and seeing the trending topics: *Helen Reaves Diagnosed with Terminal Cancer.*

I remembered how it felt like for the first time, her fame was working against her. People showed up at the hospital with stuffed bears and bouquets of cheap, grocery store flowers. They meant well, but we had to hire a security detail to stand outside her door. People took pictures of her with IVs in her arms, her legs sticking out like two pieces of straw from underneath a hospital robe.

"As long as they don't get a picture of my butt," she said once, as my mother turned bright red and yelled at every single person she could find who might have something to do with why people with Alvin books and Sharpies kept ending up in Aunt Helen's hallway.

"People think you should have to exchange privacy for success," she told me once, weak, coughing into a tissue, her cheeks pale and cold. "I don't know when we started being okay with that. I guess whatever sells the most magazines, right?"

When I reached Enders Island, I put Aunt Helen's letter for Sam back into the wooden box, and I held it away from my body when I walked to meet him. He was as close to the water as he could get. He held a tote bag in his hand.

"Hi," I said when I got close enough.

He turned around and smiled, then he saw the box and frowned. "Oh," he said.

"I take it you've seen this before?"

"I don't want it," he said, turning back to the water.

"Well, throw it away then. You can do whatever you want with it. She told me to give it back to you."

"Some things you can't just throw away."

"Like paint thinners," I said. "Turpentine. I know. You have to take them to special recycling centers. But there's always a way. Sometimes it's more inconvenient, but there's a way."

Sam reached into the bag and withdrew two masks. He tried to hand me one, but I took a step back.

"Do you trust me?" he asked. Then: "I guess that's a stupid question now."

I opened my mouth to argue but then stopped myself. I mean—he was right. He'd done nothing but lie to me since I'd met him.

"Everything you told me," I said. "Everything . . ."

"I know. I'm sorry. I wanted to tell you."

"If you had wanted to tell me, you would have told me. That's how it works. That's how friendships work."

His face fell two shades darker, a shadow caused by something invisible, something I couldn't see.

"I haven't had one of those in a really long time," he said.

He lowered the hand holding the mask.

Did I trust him?

Nope.

Did I trust my aunt?

Yeah. I had to. She had meant everything to me.

"Give it," I said, holding my hand out.

He looked surprised but didn't question me. He handed me the mask and took off his shirt. Then he looked at me like I should be stripping.

"Really?" I said.

"I won't look."

He turned around. I scanned the grounds of St. Edmund's but didn't see a soul in sight, so I stripped down to my bra and undies, tucked my clothes and purse and phone and the wooden box into the tote Sam had brought, and jumped into the water before he could get a look at me.

It was cold.

Freezing, actually, because even in summer the water in New England was frigid and angry.

"What now?" I asked.

He turned around, surprised to find me already in the water. He fitted his own mask over his face, and I couldn't help but laugh. I don't care who you are in this world; everyone looks goofy in a swim mask.

He shoved his clothes into the tote and then hid it in some tall plants. Nobody would find it unless they literally tripped over it. When he turned around, he had a large, waterproof flashlight in his hand. He waded into the water after me, sucking his breath in when it hit his chest.

How weird we must have looked to anyone who happened to see us: two kids up to their shoulders in a part of the ocean that wasn't exactly beach-like, matching masks on our faces and a suitcase-sized flashlight.

"Are you ready?"

"Ready for what? My swimming lesson?"

I wasn't trying to be rude. It just kept happening. Like Margo.

"Trust me," he reminded me. "Hold my hand, and keep swimming."

I looked away from the shore out to open water.

There was nothing.

Nothing to aim for.

Where was he taking me?

He held my hand. I pressed the mask over my face, making sure it was sealed around my nose. We swam, paddling out fifty feet or so from shore. Then he stopped, looked at me, and smiled.

"Just swim until you don't think you can anymore," he said, his words almost lost on the sea breeze.

"Until I don't think I—what?"

He took an exaggerated deep breath.

I did the same.

We dove.

Or he dove. Fairly gracefully too. I kind of belly flopped.

And we were under.

It was hard to keep hold of his hand.

The surface light only reached ten feet or so, and then he clicked on the flashlight.

I could tell the beam was strong, but even so it distilled in the water. I could only see a few feet in front of me.

The water chilled noticeably the farther down we

kicked. I followed Sam's lead, squeezing his hand hard, kicking harder.

Down and down and down.

I needed to breathe.

What if my aunt had been wrong about him? What if Sam was actually a sociopath (an eternal sociopath) who'd felt shunned by her all those years ago and had come back now to take his revenge on me? What if he was like one of those clam divers who could hold their breath for twenty minutes? What if he was going to drag me to the ocean floor only to hold me down until I drowned?

I didn't want to drown.

Drowning was on my list of deaths I most didn't want. It was up there with being burned alive. It was up there with being drawn and quartered. It was up there with being covered in honey and left for fire ants.

My list was very specific.

We kept swimming.

I needed air now. My head was getting fuzzy, and my lungs were burning. Without meaning to, I slowed down. Sam swung the flashlight at his face so I could see him. He pointed frantically: *almost there.*

Then he swung the flashlight back down, and I followed its beam to see probably the scariest thing I've ever seen in my life.

The mouth of an underwater cave.

But I didn't have a choice.

I needed air, and at this point I didn't think I'd be able to make it to the surface. I'd either drown down here or find air in that cave.

Letting go of his hand, I pushed again, propelling myself through the water with a speed and urgency I didn't know I had.

I wondered how long it would take them to find my body.

I wondered if Sam would cover my tracks, make it look like I'd never even been to Enders Island.

I wondered if my family would miss me or if they were maybe all mourned out.

And then I was through the cave.

And the short tunnel led up, up . . .

And air.

I pulled myself up on a rocky ledge, gasping like crazy, filling my lungs again and again with musty air that tasted sour and still and thin.

Sam followed just after me, breathing heavily but nowhere near as short on air as I was. He set the flashlight on the ledge next to me and pulled himself up to a sitting position.

"Made it," he said.

"Yeah, I'm just not sure about the return trip."

"It's much easier going back up. You have buoyancy on your side."

"What about the bends?"

"The what? Oh, you mean decompression sickness? Don't worry, we're not deep enough for that."

My brain ticked off the symptoms, just in case. Joint pain. Severe headache. Disorientation. Back pain. Chest pain. Lots of pain.

Nitrogen bubbles in your tissue and blood.

Stroke. Death.

Okay. Relax.

"Where are we?" I asked.

I looked around and answered my own question: a cave.

We were in an underground cave.

We were in a cave underneath the ocean.

Okay.

Okay.

"Breathe," Sam said, putting his hands on my knees. I didn't even have the strength to push him away indignantly.

"What is this place?"

"You'll see. Can you walk?"

He hopped to his feet and bent to help me up, but I didn't take his outstretched hand. I got to my feet shakily, feeling every muscle in my body protest. I put a hand against the cave wall to steady myself, breathing slowly and deeply, seeing spots of light dance across my vision.

Sam put his hand on my elbow. "I'm fine," I said.

"It's not far."

"What's not far?" But of course I already knew.

We started walking, Sam in front with the flashlight and me so close behind him that I kept stepping on his heels.

The cave was small, the ceiling just a few inches above our heads. In some places we had to squeeze through a tunnel that narrowed without warning. But he was right; it wasn't far. In under a minute, we emerged into a slightly larger cavern. It was the size of a small living room, and there was a deep indentation running through the middle. Like a scale replica of the Grand Canyon. There had been a river here once, running through this room and disappearing into countless rooms beyond.

"No shit," I said, stepping forward.

"Yes shit," he whispered.

"This is where . . ."

"Yes."

"How did you . . . ?"

"I found it," he whispered. "When I was your age. *Missi-tuk.*"

"A river with unsettled water," I said, remembering. "This is the river?"

"This was the river," he corrected. "It's been dry for a very long time."

"It's real?"

"Real," he said. He bent down, searching on the ground for something. When he stood up, I saw he was holding a jagged piece of rock. Before I could guess what he was doing, he'd dragged the rock across his forearm, leaving a nasty trail of blood in its wake.

I watched, my stomach sick and churning, as the cut knit itself up before my eyes.

"No shit," I said.

"Yes shit."

"Did you show that to my aunt?"

"Yes. She told me I have an accelerated rate of coagulation."

"That sounds like her."

I sat down on the floor. I breathed as deeply and as slowly as I could. I thought I felt Sam's fingers in my hair, but I might have been imagining it; when I looked up, he was ten feet away from me.

"How old are you?" I asked him.

"Three hundred. Give or take."

Three hundred years.

"And my aunt?"

"My best friend."

"But you only knew her for a year. A year out of three hundred."

"I'd been traveling for a long time. I hadn't let myself settle down anywhere for more than a few months, a year, and I certainly never made friends. Invisibility—that's always been the key for me. But with your aunt . . . She didn't let up, didn't take no for an answer. Three hundred years, yeah, but she was the first person who ever really took the time to get to know me. Even when I was doing my best to push her away."

I tried to picture Sam and my aunt—Sam the same as he was now and my aunt only a teenager, almost my age. I had seen the pictures of them together, but it wasn't the same as trying to imagine it, as trying to really believe it. Twenty-five years ago. But to Sam's elongated timeline, that would feel like just a few minutes. Just like how humans feel like they own the universe, but really, we're nothing more than the tiniest of blips on the evolutionary scale.

"Lottie?"

"Three hundred years," I said. Had I already said that? Had I just thought it? "What do you even do for three hundred years?"

Sam laughed. "You just found out I'm immortal, and you want to know what I've been doing?"

"It seems relevant."

"Well, mostly I just travel around. You can't stay in one place for too long—maybe six or seven years, depending on where you are, what you're doing. I try to keep a low profile. I work small jobs, easy to get. A bookstore clerk or a local tour guide. Basically every tourist city has those ghost tours, you know? I've done thousands of ghost tours. Something that won't ask for a lot of qualifications or references. And I don't really own that much. Just one suitcase holds everything. A few changes of clothes. A toothbrush. I get a library card wherever I go, that's important."

"And you make enough money that way?"

"Usually," he said.

"Are there others?"

"I don't know. I don't think so."

"Did you know, when you drank it?"

"There were rumors. It was a different time back then; people thought an eternal spring could really exist. When I found it . . . I think a part of me just knew. But I was young and stupid. And who doesn't want to live forever? If you give that choice to the majority of people . . ."

"What about now? Do you regret it?"

The air around Sam's head turned blue, then black, then back to normal.

"Almost every day," he said.

"And she wouldn't drink it."

"I shouldn't have asked her. I just wanted a friend. Someone to share the world with. It had been so long already, and I was so lonely. Just running from one place to the next."

He was crying, silent tears running down a face already wet with salt water. They were friends, my aunt and Sam. He must have read about her wherever he went; he must have read the Hatter books and known he was her inspiration. He must have known how successful she was, how she had done just fine without him. Without the water.

"Do you come back here often?" I asked.

"Every once in a while," he said. "Just to see it. I was born here. I miss it."

"How did you meet my aunt?"

Sam smiled, suddenly a million years away from me. I wished I could step into his brain and remember what he was remembering. I wished it was twenty-five years ago and I was hiding behind a tree watching Sam and my aunt as teenagers.

"She was walking home from school, cutting through a graveyard. She saw me reading with my back against a tombstone and stopped to ask me what kind of person was creepy enough to read in a graveyard."

I wasn't surprised. Aunt Helen was exactly the type of person who would interrogate a total stranger to deduce how creepy he was.

"Friends immediately," Sam continued.

"And me?" I asked.

"What about you?"

"You asked her if she'd drink the water. What about me?"

"I'd never ask you."

"Would you want to?"

He faltered, and I tried to imagine what it must be like to grow older than anyone you ever met. To watch everyone around you age and change and die. Nobody escaped death. You came to peace with it, maybe, but you didn't sneak past it.

"It's different with you," he said finally.

"How come?"

"With your aunt, I was selfish. It's easy to be selfish with our friends. We just want them to do what we want, be what we need. You're different."

"Are you saying we're not friends?"

"That's exactly what I'm saying," he said.

Of all the places I'd imagined this moment happening, an under-the-sea cave was not one of them.

His lips tasted like salt.

From tears or ocean water or both, I didn't know.

We came back to earth.

I put my clothes back on over my still-wet skin, and placed the wooden box in Sam's hands, making sure he kept it while half-wanting to snatch it back, run away with it, find somewhere quiet and faraway to drink it. I made my feet back away and my hands stay put by their sides. I made him promise that he wouldn't disappear.

My parents were both home when I walked in the front door, sitting in the living room watching a movie. Dad paused it when he saw me, his eyes widening, and I realized my clothes were still damp, my hair was half dried and frizzed to all hell around my face. My shoes squeaked and tracked small puddles across the hardwood floor.

"Lottie?" he said cautiously.

I got a towel from the guest bathroom and spread it on

the ottoman, then I sat down and faced them both.

"I have something I need to talk to you about," I said.

I watched them age a hundred years in front of me as all the possibilities that followed a statement like that ran through their minds. (Pregnant? Arrested? Addicted to drugs? Murdered someone?)

"You can tell us anything," my mom said, leaning forward, putting her hand on my father's knee to either give him strength or borrow strength from him or some combination of both.

"It's about me. I think I need help."

An eternity had passed between now and when Alvin Hatter had pushed open the door to the house in the middle of the woods, to when Margo had drunk the potion, to when the Overcoat Man had pushed her off a cliff, to when Alvin, in solidarity, had drunk the Everlife Formula so she wouldn't have to be immortal alone.

An eternity, and yet, for Alvin and Margo, what was an eternity?

Time was endless, still, and meaningless.

Margo was still eleven and Alvin would be thirteen forever, until he was the last thirteen-year-old on the entire planet, until it was only him and Margo and whatever future-world was left to them.

They would not find their parents here, on this faraway island, just like they hadn't found their parents in the countless other places they had looked.

Their parents were gone forever. Alvin wanted to give up. He was tired. For a forever boy, he could really do with some sleep.

But Margo was with him, and Margo showed no signs of slowing down.

Margo took his hand and led him off the ferry.

"Funny little place," she said brightly.

And that was all it took to wake him up.

They kept looking.

—from *Margo Hatter Lives Forever*

24

I had one letter left from Aunt Helen.

It was Sunday, graduation was tomorrow, and I felt adrift, lost, with no direction and no way to manage the grief that was bubbling up inside me. Like she had just died. Like I was only now figuring it out.

Once I read this letter, she would be gone completely.

No, not gone. She would never really be gone; in her own way, she would live on forever.

But I still couldn't bring myself to read it right away.

There was something else I could do, though, something I'd been avoiding, putting off, stepping carefully around whenever I walked into my room.

My aunt's things.

They were still there, waiting for me, still covered up with the blanket I'd thrown on them when I couldn't bear to see them so brazenly holding my aunt's possessions, both the things she'd left for me and the things I had taken from her house.

I removed the blanket now, folding it and setting it in its proper place at the foot of my bed. I sat on the floor and pulled the smallest box toward me. It was her jewelry, packed carefully in tissue and surrounded by thin bubble wrap. I freed piece after piece. A small handwritten note was attached to every single piece. I picked up a slightly misshapen silver bangle and read its description: *sterling silver, England, 1973.*

I removed the note carefully and set it aside where I wouldn't lose it, and then I slipped the bangle on my wrist.

Did I want to be immortal? I asked the bangle and Aunt Helen and myself.

Every old fear, every old anxiety seemed to rear up in my brain at once. Death! Illness! Loss! Pain!

It was like one of those marquees, recycling the same information in bright LED letters.

The answer seemed obvious: *yes, I want to be immortal.*

But an obvious answer wasn't necessarily the right answer.

Sometimes you had to be even more careful of the obvious answers; they snuck up on you while you weren't looking. They were effortless.

And they were so tempting. It could be so tiring, feeling scared of everything. It could be so nice not having to carry that weight around anymore. Like a journal filled with anxiety-ridden thoughts, an exercise from a past therapist ("Write out the demons every night before you go to bed, and that way they'll have a harder time following you into your dreams.").

The talk last night with my parents had gone better than expected. Maybe they were just happy it wasn't anything as serious as they'd knee-jerkingly been expecting.

They talked among themselves, listing doctors they knew, therapists they knew. We would call someone on Tuesday.

"There is never, ever a reason to be ashamed to ask for help," Mom said later, sneaking into my bedroom after everyone had gone to sleep. "You could have come to us sooner. I'm happy you came to us now, of course. But in the future, okay? There's no shame between us."

Did I feel shame? I don't know. I guess I must have, a little, or else I wouldn't have waited so long to tell them.

My mother sat on the edge of my bed and rested her hand on my forehead (always cool, her hands).

"What was your one big cry?" I asked her.

"Oh my," she said. "I'll tell you sometime soon, okay? It's not a story for just before bed."

She kissed my cheek, and I fell asleep without thinking of anything scary, without thinking of any of the ways I could die before morning.

I had only one dream, but it wasn't so much a dream as a sort of prophecy. Sometimes our subconscious figured things out before us. Sometimes we had to just wait to catch up.

I texted Sam in the morning, holding the letter from Aunt Helen that I wasn't quite ready to read.

Can you meet me today? Are you busy? Noon?

I sent him a pin with an address.

I'll be there.

I didn't tell him to bring the box, because now that he had it back, I didn't think he'd be letting it out of his sight anytime soon.

I was worried my parents would look at me differently in the morning, having had time to really think about it and get used to the idea that their daughter was so out of control of her own emotions that she was having panic attacks.

But they were completely normal.

Dad made eggs and pancakes, and we ate at the table on the deck, Mom already dressed for gardening with her big floppy hat taking up its own chair, Abe carrying his plate around with him while he played a one-person game of croquet.

"I think we should take a vacation," she said. "We haven't had a nice vacation in a long time."

"I've been doing research on Scandinavia!" Dad said hopefully.

She gave him a long, funny look. "A beach, Sal. I want

to go to a beach. I want to sit in the sand and drink piña coladas out of coconuts."

"Oh, that kind of vacation," Dad said, slightly crestfallen but still on board.

"Next year we can go to Scandinavia," she promised. "This year: Hawaii."

"I'd go to Hawaii," I offered.

"Well, if Lottie will tag along, then it's settled," Dad said, smiling, winking, collecting our dirty plates and bringing them inside.

"I'm coming too!" Abe shouted from the yard.

"Do you have plans today? Do you want to help me pick beans? So many beans. I thought I'd make a casserole," Mom said.

"I have a thing, yeah. I'm meeting someone."

"The forever boy?" she asked.

"Yeah. I mean, obviously he isn't really immortal," I said. Covering my tracks. Aunt Helen would have been proud.

"Well, no. I didn't think so," Mom said.

Before I left to meet Sam, I took a photo from her journal: him and Aunt Helen, laughing, arms slung around each other's shoulders.

He was there when I got there, already parked in the lot, leaning against the hood of his car and staring out at the ocean. The wooden box was on the passenger's seat.

I handed him the picture, and he took it, hands shaking,

face lighting up in a smile.

"Wow," he said. "This feels like so long ago."

"Eternalism," I said.

"What?"

"Eternalism. It's a philosophical theory of time. It means . . . We have these limited brains, right? We can only understand so much at one time. So we experience life in a very specific way, in a linear, chronological way. Each moment leads to the next, and once one moment has passed, it's gone forever. Right?"

"Yeah . . ."

"But what if time doesn't actually work like that? What if that's only the way our brains process it? What if time really exists, like—everything all at once, all at the same moment, every single moment happening at the same time, over and over, for all eternity. Simultaneously."

"That would mean . . ."

I pointed at the picture. "That you and my aunt are still in this moment. Forever. She's still alive. No one ever dies. You're not that special after all," I said, bumping my hand against his knee. He caught it and kissed my knuckles. I didn't think I'd ever been kissed there before. I liked to think that there was a version of me that would be kissed like that forever, for always, eternally.

"I like that," he said.

"It's just a theory. But I like it too. It helps me."

"Where are we?" he asked.

"I'll show you. Grab the box."

I'd hiked this trail once already in the past month and a half. I went before Sam, leading him, checking every once in a while that he was still behind me. He held the box like it was the most fragile thing in the world. I guess it was. It was all that was left.

When we reached the top, we sat down in the dirt. Sam put the box on the ground in front of us.

"This is where we'll spread her ashes," I said. "The funeral parlor called, and the urn will be ready this week."

Sam didn't answer right away. He looked out over the water, and I noticed that his eyes were red and wet.

He still held the photograph in his hand. My aunt and him: best friends. I wondered how many other people he'd lost. A real-life Alvin Hatter. A real-life forever boy with no Margo to share it with.

Sam opened the wooden box. He removed the glass vial and then placed the photograph carefully in its place. In the sunlight the liquid looked completely unremarkable. Nothing out of the ordinary.

"The Everlife Formula," he said, laughing suddenly. "That was clever."

"She wrote all those books for you," I said. "Like a secret message. I think she was sorry."

"For what?"

"That she couldn't drink it. And that she couldn't help you."

He held it up to eye level, looked at it for a minute. "I want to get rid of it," he said, stretching his hand back and over his shoulder, ready to throw.

"Wait!" I scrambled to my feet, put my hand on his arm. "So dramatic," I said, panting. "Just hold on a second."

"Okay," he said, pulling his hand away from me, keeping the bottle as far from me as he could.

"I already told you I didn't want it." I rolled my eyes and sighed. "I want you to drink it."

"Me? Why?"

"Think about this scenario, right: you throw it out to sea in this grand, poetic gesture. But the bottle doesn't break; it floats on the waves until it gets to some faraway, uncharted island. There's been a plane crash, and someone who looks a lot like Tom Hanks is stranded on the island. He finds the bottle. He's really, really thirsty. So he's basically the only person on earth who would pull a strange glass bottle of water out of the ocean and actually drink it. And he does drink it, so now he has to spend eternity on that island, alone."

"That is . . . very specific," Sam said. "But I see your point. I guess I could just dump the water out?"

"I think you need to drink it."

"I already drank it, remember?"

"Has anyone ever drunk the water twice, though?"

"No, there's not really a point, is there?"

"Well, what's the harm? You can't get doubly immortal.

Oh, or maybe you'd become a god? Like Zeus? That would be cool."

"I don't think it would make me a god."

"So just drink it. I dare you."

"You dare me to drink the water that I have already drunk again?"

"Yes."

He thought about it for just a minute, lowering the glass to eye level, studying the liquid within. Then he relaxed, shrugged, unstopped the cork, and raised it to his lips. He drank deeply, and when he was finished, he replaced the cork and let the bottle fall to the ground.

And I watched the air around him change, just so, so subtly, nothing anyone would see unless they knew exactly what they were looking for. A slight shift, the most gentle of breezes. Something crooked tilting into place. A crack in the laws of the universe filled up with putty and made whole again.

I smiled.

"Come on, let's get out of here. I'm hungry."

That night Em came over with Jackie, and together with Abe and Amy and Sam, we set up Monopoly on the coffee table.

"Can I play?" Dad asked hopefully, sticking his head into the room.

"No!" Abe and I shouted at the same time.

Defeated, he retreated to the kitchen.

We put an Alvin movie on in the background but muted the TV. I glanced at it every now and then but tried not to get caught up; the Alvin movies always made me cry.

Sam had never played Monopoly. In three hundred years, he'd just never gotten around to it.

After an hour or so, I went into the kitchen to refill our supply of snacks. Abe followed me. When I turned around from the fridge, he was leaning against the counter, arms crossed, expectant.

"Well?" he said.

"Well what?"

"Was Ponce de León right?"

"No, of course not," I said. "There was a perfectly reasonable explanation."

"Are you okay?" he said.

"I don't know. I think so. Are you?"

"I don't know either."

"Maybe we could talk about it sometime? So, you know, I don't have to get the insight to your feelings via an essay in a literary magazine?"

"I'll think about it," he said, winking, grabbing a bag of pretzels from the counter.

I hung back a minute. I went upstairs to my room and took the last of Aunt Helen's letters from my desk. I thought I was finally ready to read what she had to say, what she'd chosen to leave me with. The last letter. But not the last of Aunt Helen.

Lottie,

You're on your own.

Thank you for tying up my loose ends, putting the final pieces of my puzzle together. I wish I could thank you in person, but alas, one thing life has taught me: you rarely get what you want.

(Something here about getting what you need, naturally.)

I have no grand last bit of wisdom to impart. I write this with a hand shaking and weak from chemotherapy and lack of sleep.

The other night I started reading the red journal over again, and I thought: My goodness. My little Lottie is this age now.

Write as much of it down as you can. It's sometimes nice to remember.

We are so alike in some ways. I know you have the same voice that follows you around, that you can't seem to get away from. The edge-of-sleep voice. The dark-and-quiet voice.

But you will learn to silence it, Lottie.

You will learn to push it to the side.

Even this, me being gone, will get easier.

And besides, now it's time to let a little bit of me go.

Throw my ashes, Lottie. Into the ocean—from the cliff we used to go to together. Have a picnic, have some fun, try not to let it be so heavy. (I've written some foods down on the back; living vicariously through this image while I can't stomach anything much stronger than bread.)

I hope I was an okay aunt. I hope you knew that from the very first time I held your little baby body in my arms, I was hooked.

A whole lifetime of loving you feels like more than a fair exchange for immortality. Don't you think?

—H.

I put the letter down on my desk.

My aunt could be a million things.

A little selfish.

A little bossy.

A little presumptuous.

But she was also right; it was about time I started figuring things out for myself.

I went back downstairs to the living room. Sam was winning by a mile in what Amy kept referring to as beginner's luck.

I imagined this night stretching on for all infinity, lasting forever.

I imagined that somewhere, in another universe, it did.

Next to me, Sam bought his fourth railroad.

On the TV, Alvin and Margo sat in the dusty foyer of the house in the middle of the woods and wondered if they would ever see their parents again.

Don't worry, you two. I've read the last book. You do.

Acknowledgments

To everyone who has supported me on this journey of writing my third book, to everyone who has emailed me or tweeted me or snail mailed me or texted me or called me or smoke signaled me to lend their encouragement and remind me that I had done this before and could, conceivably, do it again: thank you. Writing a book is ninety-nine percent lonely; thank you for being there for me when I poked my head out of my cave to take a peek around and see what I was missing.

Here are some of you:

My two unreal cool nieces, Harper and Alma, who made me an aunt and who made me want to write a book about an aunt. I hope I'm the best aunt ever—let's check in on this in a few years and you can let me know how I'm doing.

The rest of my lovely family, including my brothers and sisters-in-law and my parents, all of whom have never stopped supporting the visions I've had (visions both literally and figuratively, as it were).

My agent, Wendy Schmalz, who is also unreal cool, and to whom I owe a lot. Thank you for being my rock for this and every book I've written so far.

The lovely team at HarperCollins who continue to be some of the greatest people I've had the privilege of knowing. You've made this journey so easy and fun (especially you, Jocelyn, my editor-to-the-stars, who sees things I don't and graciously points them out to me).

As always, S: I do not know how you always have the exact right words, but I hope you never run out of them.